"A GOOD coming-of-age story . . . The author evokes the turbulent era of the latter Twentieth Century, during which a generation struggled to become adults. The story rings with a truth many readers of a certain age can relate to, and provides an emotional road map for younger generations."

– SUZANNA MYATT HARVILL, author of the *Shadow Bayou* series and the *Maybelline Mysteries*

* * *

A heart-capturing story of a young man's search for recognition and acceptance from an absent and distant father . . . A good read.

– DOTTIE REXFORD, author of Cora Pooler

* * *

LIKE *THE Catcher in the Rye*, this debut novel is a literary-historical smashup, a child-in-jeopardy story narrated by a voice readers can't stop thinking about.

* * *

IF ALL this sounds dark and edgy, it's also seriously funny.

* * *

TO DADDY, Who I Never Loved won a Royal Palms Literary Award for historical novels from Florida Writers Association.

TO DADDY, WHO I NEVER LOVED

Gary Robert Pinnell

A NOVEL BY

GARY ROBERT PINNELL

Copyright 2020 by Gary Robert Pinnell

Print ISBN: 978-1-09830-173-6

eBook ISBN: 978- 1-09830-174-3

To Mom
You insisted that I return to high school, earn a master's degree,
and remain in journalism.
You gave this gift of writing, so this novel is for you.

CONTENTS

BOOK 1

"The only thing new in this world is the history you don't know."
Harry S. Truman

CHAPTER 1

SOMETHING STUPID

As a boy, I believed in good. A mother's love was unconditional. Fatherhood was an undying pledge. Brother and sisters were ultimate protectors. Schoolmates were a gift. Life was a promise of success.

I did good things. I made friends with a black girl and a Down's boy. I worked hard in school and earned good grades. I delivered four paper routes. I bought my own bicycle and motorcycle. I did not fight.

I confess, I wasn't always good. I stole from Mother's purse. I detested my stepfather, but he wasn't really my stepfather. I loathed my brother, but Biggy picked on me all my life. I hated the Andersen boys, but they ganged up on me behind the high school. The meanest thing one human can do is to take away his self-respect, and that's what Biggy and the Andersens did. That's why I tried to commit suicide. That's why I sneaked away from home.

My story is mostly true. I've changed the names to protect the most despicable bastards, so I guess that makes me an unreliable narrator. I've made up a few details and I've hid ugly secrets, the way people do over fifty years. That's how long it's been since I came out second in two fights, got scared, screwed up suicide, stuck out my thumb, and hitched to California.

So here I go. Once upon a time in Oklahoma . . .

* * *

It was six A.M. when I stepped onto U.S. 81. Hell Creek was a mile behind me, and Palo Alto was seventeen hundred miles down the road.

Uh oh. I don't know how to hitchhike. Which way? California is west, same as Lawton? I need a better sense of direction. A car passed. Of course. The driver won't stop if he can't see my face.

I had to figure out how to walk backwards and face traffic at the same time. I turned sideways, but that felt ungainly. I backed down the highway and glanced behind every few feet so I wouldn't fall into a storm drain.

Still no sign of the sun. Good. Mother wouldn't be up for a couple of hours. By the time the cops caught up with me, I'd be with Daddy. He'd teach me how to fight. He'd train me like a Marine. My body would harden. I'd come back looking like a warrior, surprise Scooter and Spit and Pickle behind the high school, karate chop their necks, and leave them wiggling on the sidewalk. Biggy too. His eyes would X like a cartoon. Everyone would respect me. Then I'd take Murph with me to California.

A Mustang passed and a Neil Diamond song leaked from the passenger window. Was that the '64 and a half? It looked a little different from Big Guy's '65.

Bingo. A car stopped, a fire-engine red, 1967 Plymouth Barracuda fastback playing the same radio station. *Thank the Lord for my very first ride.* I could make out the driver's haircut from the yellowish highway lamps. Flat top. Whitewalls on the sides. Starched olive drab uniform. My defenses lowered. Dogface. A lot older than me, maybe twenty-five. But at fifteen, everyone seemed older.

The soldier leaned toward the passenger window. "Where you headin'?"

Oh shi– *Stop cussing. You've started a new life. Don't sound coarse. Use euphemisms. Feces sounds funnier.*

What if Mother woke up early, read my note, and had the cops put out an APB for me? This doggie was probably stationed at Fort Sill. Lawton was just forty miles away, so dogfaces hung around Hell Creek in packs. What if the cops tracked him down and the doggie told them where I was going? "Uhh. West."

"West? You'll have to let loose of a little more info if you're hitchhiking, Joe."

"California." *Joe.* I slid into the Naugahyde bucket seat.

"I can get you as far as Fort Sill. So, dude, how you doing?"

I don't think people actually want to hear about my problems. "Ginger peachy."

He smiled. "That's original."

And that was easy. I might be out of Oklahoma in a few hours. I was glad he was only taking me to Lawton, though. It was only May, but the weather had already turned hot and sticky, and this brand-spanking new 'Cuda didn't have an air conditioner. I cracked the window.

He hung a left at the Lawton-Hell Creek Y. "Don't see many hitchhikers around here."

I jumped.

"Sorry. Were you a thousand miles away?"

About six, according to the road sign. My vision adjusted to the green gloom from the 'Cuda's dashboard.

"You go to Hell Creek High? Wife teaches there." His face turned. It'd been pounded like cheap steak. Three stripes on the doggie's collar insignia.

Oh feces. I think I know who you are, Sarge.

"Gotta song for you. See that box of eight-tracks in the back seat?" Sarge asked. "Grab the third one. They're in alphabetical order."

I reached behind the slick plastic seat and grabbed a green rectangle. A square of broken window glass dropped into my hand. *That settles it. You're O'Murphy's doggie.*

His eyes shifted to me. "Stick it in the tape player."

"Nice ride."

"Thanks. I've only had it a few weeks."

"Yeah? Already had an accident?"

"Something like that."

His car passed a corner streetlamp. I could make out his nose and cheek; both roared yellow and purple and blue. *I guess we both came out second in a fight with a high-school thug.* "I like the sound of the engine."

The doggie smiled. "That's not the 273. It's the 383-cube four-barrel."

I love muscle cars too. The tape interrupted KOMA and played "I'm a Rambler, I'm a Gambler."

"So. You like Joan?"

"Baez?" The sergeant crunched a smile. "Mythic voice. Wife and I saw her two years ago when I was stationed near London. She toured with Bob Dylan, but he wasn't with her. They had broken up. We also watched the concert later on the BBC. This was her first hit, 'There but for Fortune . . . '"

Go you or I.

Three songs played before the eight-track skipped to the middle of "She's a Troublemaker." The tape fluttered, fluttered, fluttered, then jammed.

"Eject! Eject!" he ordered.

I was startled, but I pushed the button and the cassette popped out. The tape snagged.

"Halt!" Sarge barked, then softened. He pulled down his sunvisor and withdrew a ballpoint pen. "Slip this inside that little door and–real careful–lift up the heads."

I unspooled a yard of Hershey-brown film.

"Good. The tape isn't broke. Got a knife?" he asked.

I pulled Grand's Barlow from my left pocket.

"Pry off the cover. It's a Möbius strip–a continuous O. That's how an eight-track works." He talked me through respooling and threading the tape through the cassette guides.

I slipped it back into the deck. *". . . a hundred miles, a hundred . . ."*

"'500 Miles,'" the doggie mused. "That'll be your song now."

Right you are, Sgt. Dogface.

"Whatever possessed Dylan to give her up?"

Whatever possessed you to cheat on your wife? Why would you take a chance on losing Mrs. Lane? Okay, her bod is crammed into a short waist, but she isn't overweight. And she isn't half-gorgeous like O'Murphy, but she enlarged my world. Sarge, your wife may be the grooviest chick on this planet.

Sarge stopped the 'Cuda at Gore Boulevard. "Got a map?"

I shook my head.

"Then I wonder where you're gonna wind up, because it may not be where you want." The doggie introduced himself with a departing handshake. "Pepper Lane."

My hand felt limp, even to me. *If you want to be treated like a man, shake hands like a man.* "Curtis. Pye." I said it like "Bond. James Bond."

"Yeah. I thought it was you. My wife talks about Cutie Pye all the time."

Oh, feces. Does everyone know my stupid nickname?

"Says you're 'hyperliterate.' Is that the term? Read every book in the high school library? Brighter than the teachers? But you're not going back to school?"

I shook my head. *Got kicked out. She hasn't told you?*

"Don't worry. I won't have a chance to say anything till I get home tonight."

"Thanks." *And it's more like a quarter of the books, but I want to read every one.*

He pointed west. "Cache Road is U.S. 62, Curtis. Stay on it as far as it goes. And first chance you get, buy a map. Know how to read one?"

* * *

Thumb out, I backed down Cache Road. I should've written to Daddy before I left. My plan—I didn't really have one—was to sit by his post office box in Palo Alto until he found me.

I wondered who Daddy really was. Maybe some of what people had told me was true, and some was a protective blanket of lies that grandfathers and mothers and sisters spread over kids who didn't know their parents. I had few memories of Daddy, and those were from the last times I'd seen him.

Is it possible to forget a father? I'd been nine the last time he'd seen me. Would he know the fifteen-year-old me? I wouldn't know Daddy if he passed me on the street.

Before I left Oklahoma, I'd wanted to take Murph to a movie, hold her hand, and trace those long, delicate fingers. I'd wanted her to snuggle against me and fall asleep. I'd wanted to stroke that hollow spot at the base of her throat.

But I'd given up; now my life would be a highway. No matter how much I'd wanted life, life hadn't wanted me. I'd been the most invisible kid in high school. And when you're the most invisible kid, it's hard to believe you matter. In the past two days, I had realized that life had been better when I was invisible, that mistakes had the greatest consequences, and that sometimes we risked everything on bad choices because the other choices were worse. I had desperately wanted to leave Hell Creek. What I hadn't understood was that Hell Creek would never leave me. *Maybe it would've been easier to die.*

CHAPTER 2

NINE MONTHS AGO

In the fall semester of 1966, Scooter Andersen had been the first sophomore at Hell Creek High to own a motor. He made that clear the first day of school, blasting around campus on that junker without a muffler. He rounded the traffic circle, skidded his Yamaha sideways, and booted down the kickstand in one smooth move.

I watched O'Murphy watch Scooter.

He unfolded like a switchblade, gazed insolently into her eyes, and smirked in a way that invited her to . . .

She was seduced already. It was like *The Wild One*, where the good girl asks, "What are you rebelling against, Johnny?" And Brando sneers, "Whaddya you got?"

That'd been precisely what the good girl had wanted to hear. Maybe O'Murphy Scott went so Pavlovian because of Scooter's antisocial cockiness. Or maybe she was attracted to the leader of the pack. Or maybe it was secondary-school Darwinism: girls got curves; Scooter Andersen got arms veined with licorice ropes.

Hell Creek had been my tale of two schools: in the summer 1966–the best of times–we departed junior high on bicycles. Then high school rocked our sophomore year and led to the winter of our discontent.

* * *

"Your name, Miss?" Mrs. Macintosh asked.

The second time I saw her, I fell hopelessly, despairingly, hormonally infatuated with the wrong girl. She strolled into homeroom five minutes late. The new girl was five feet nothing–a little short for a goddess. She wore white go-go boots and a powder-blue Twiggy shirt skirt. She smelled like lilacs in bloom.

"O'Murphy Scott?" Her answer sounded unsure, but I was certain she had been born to be adored. Her toe-in-front-of-toe sashay jiggled her left hip, then her right. O'Murphy had the number-one, blue-ribbon, girl walk ever.

But you knew that, didn't you, O'Murphy? Because anything that sexy must be put on, at least a little. Even if they're also smart or good, Pretty Girls know they're not seen as Smart Girls or Good Girls, because every head–male and female–turns when they walk into a room.

I confess, I watch girl butts. Do girls watch guy butts? Because I don't have one. Daddy called me No Butt, so mine must have fallen off when I was a little kid. Everyone else has a butt, so if I ever win the Irish sweepstakes, I'm going to a plastic surgeon. I'm going to buy a butt.

The desk beside me was vacant. *Please. Please. Please, please, please.* But O'Murphy scatted by me and curled her legs onto the seat between Pickle Andersen and Marybeth Cannellini. And then she smiled at That Bastard. Scooter Andersen.

"If a car is traveling fifty-three miles per hour, how far will it go in fifteen minutes?"

My chance to impress. "Twenty-six something . . ."

"Who agrees with Mr. Pye?" Mrs. Macintosh didn't humiliate me; she wasn't that kind of teacher. She just clued everyone that my answer to her story problem was wrong.

She's right. My hand jumped: twenty-six *times* four is wrong. That's 104 miles an hour. I should've . . . "I multiplied. I should've divided fifty-two in half, then divided it again, so . . . thirteen-and-a-quarter miles?"

Our sophomore Algebra I teacher was as flexible as a thumbtack. Like Sidney Poitier in *To Sir with Love*, she called everyone mister or miss, something most teachers had quit doing in the informal Sixties. "You have the right answer this time, Mr. Pye, but why didn't you set it up as an algebra problem?"

Because I can't. I don't get new math.

O'Murphy's No. 2 pencil rolled from her slanted desktop and onto the linoleum.

I dove at the same moment she slid off her seat, so that put her shirt-skirt hem at my eye level. That morning-sky chambray–which I will always call O'Murphy Blue–had come into fashion that year. The tails stopped a fraction above her knees, barely legal by high school rules. She knelt, and I discovered white scars about six inches higher: tiny, jagged, but regularly spaced.

What caused those cuts? Book pages? That doesn't seem right.

She grinned with tiny Tinker Bell teeth when she saw my hand going for her pencil.

And there I was: dumb as a bump on a pickle. Fourteen years old, and I'd never spoken to a chick.

She smiled up at Scooter as if to say, "Is this guy for real? He's petrified."

Scoot didn't look at her, though; he stared right into my eyes.

* * *

Third period. Mrs. Lane wrote her name on the blackboard, then guided a hi-fi needle onto the LP. O'Murphy wafted past like a blossom on the wind and sat behind me again, between MBe and Pickle Andersen. My nose caught another whiff of lilacs.

She must've gone to pep-squad tryouts during second period. She had an all-conference chest, so she looked how every girl wanted to look in a letter sweater. A pleated scarlet-and-cream Hell Creek Demonette skirt made her legs seem long for such a petite girl. Now I understood the word voluptuous: her ankles and calves were elegant, upturned bottles; her curves were ripe, tart cherries.

"Nowhere Man" played.

"John Lemon," said the girl beside me.

"Lennon," I corrected, but a smile let me in on her joke.

"Oh, Lordy. I've sat beside a Negro," I whispered hugely.

"Afro-American." Her smile widened.

Holy feces! She gets my humor.

"I'm Sammie Davis."

Even at fourteen, I was already a little hard of hearing, so I cupped my ear.

She pointed to herself, repeated the words, and smiled a third time. "Sammie. Davis. He don't own the name, you know. What's yours, man?"

I'd never spoken to a Negro before. Before Sammie, the only student in school darker than me had a Coppertone tan, and she'd moved back to Corpus Christi. "Curtis. Pye." Mother said Frederick Douglass High had closed last summer, that Negroes would be bused to the white high school, but I'd never thought desegregation would affect me.

Mrs. Lane handed sheaves of papers to Sammie and me. "Pass these back, please."

I love the scent of mimeograph paper–lanolin and solvent with a hint of castor oil. I gave my pile to O'Murphy, who smiled. At me. I'd swim Red River for a girl who looks at me that way.

"Today, we'll study the lyrics of the Beatles. Anyone, what's 'Nowhere Man' all about?" In that moment, Mrs. Lane became our most far-out teacher. Most of us were sixteen, and Mrs. Lane wasn't much older–maybe twenty-two or twenty-three.

A light snapped on in Sammie's eyes. She knew the answer.

But it was Marybeth who raised her hand. "It's a folk song."

Mrs. Lane nodded. "And that is significant because?"

"Because the Beatles ain't folk singers?" O'Murphy put in. Her last word finished on an upbeat, turning her answer into a question.

"Aren't," Mrs. Lane corrected. "This is sophomore English, so I know all of you can speak it correctly by now. But yes. They were bubble-gummers. Switched to folk and rock. Why else is this song significant?"

"It's the first Beatles tune that ain . . . isn't about love?" O'Murphy ventured again.

"What's your name?"

"O'Murphy Scott? Murph?"

"Good. And what's your name?"

"Marybeth Cannellini. MBe."

"O'Murphy, how does this song make you feel?"

"It's sad?"

"It is melancholy," Mrs. Lane affirmed. "Anything else?"

"It's existential," MBe offered.

Mrs. Lane hadn't expected that. "How is it existential?"

"It says life is meaningless and absurd. Nothing is worthwhile."

Hmm. Is MBe is the female version of me? I hadn't met either O'Murphy or MBe before high school. We'd all come from different elementary schools.

Mrs. Lane beamed. "Where does the song say that?"

"The last refrain," MBe said. "Making nowhere plans. For nobody."

O'Murphy whistled through the diastema between her two front teeth. "MBe is smaaart!"

A thought struck me. "Why are we learning what songs mean?"

"My, aren't y'all insightful!" Mrs. Lane pointed a wry smile at me. "Name?"

"Curtis Pye."

"Cortez, in Español. Your name also appears on my Spanish roll."

I nodded. *Bueno. Mucho better than Cutie.* I glanced back at O'Murphy.

She winked. At me.

"You're right, Cortez, it is my little trick. After this, we'll study Bob Dylan. By analyzing 'Just Like a Woman' and 'Rainy Day Women,' all y'all will learn to dig Dylan Thomas."

I thought for a moment about pronoun usage, but Mrs. Lane had said it correctly. In Okie speak, "y'all" is singular; "all y'all" is plural.

"By the way, Bob Dylan is a pen name. What's his real name?" Mrs. Lane asked.

"Robert Zimmerman." Heads turned toward me and whispered.

O'Murphy punched her congratulations on my shoulder. "How did you knooow?"

It was my second chance to speak to her, but I half smiled instead.

"He always knows the answers," MBe muttered.

"And from which poet did Dylan borrow his *nom de plume*?" Mrs. Lane looked at me through round granny glasses.

Not this time.

"Come on," Mrs. Lane encouraged. "I've already given you the answer."

"Dylan Thomas?" O'Murphy ventured.

Art Fleming, O'Murphy would be a natural for *Jeopardy*. All her answers were in the form of a question. And thank you, *Tiger Beat*. It's a chick mag, but I'd read the article on Bob Dylan, then I'd gone to the record store and spun Bob's six-minute single, "Like a Rolling Stone." I hadn't understood the lyrics, so I'd returned the next day and written down the free-verse poem about a poor little rich girl who'd been misled.

Dylan and I had something more in common than liking Joan Baez. He'd dropped out of college to visit Woody Guthrie in a mental hospital. Woody–my music idol–was a good ol' Okemah boy.

"What did Dylan Thomas write?"

Do not go gentle.

No hand went up.

"Dylan Thomas," Mrs. Lane said, "was a Welsh poet who famously wrote, 'Do not go gentle into that good night.' We'll find out about him in a couple of weeks."

When I'd bought Bob's *Freewheelin* LP, I'd realized he didn't just write songs, he had established rock music's age of reason. "Blowin' in the Wind" was about our impending doom.

The bell rang, and the best half of our school day ended. Mrs. Lane shut off the record player and poked a green, sandwich-sized tape into a deck. Biggy had installed an eight-track under the dash of his Mustang, but I had no idea they'd made a tape deck for a cabinet.

"My husband's fave," Mrs. Lane raised her voice against the commotion of students switching classrooms. "He's a sergeant. We bought it when the army stationed him near London."

O'Murphy was beside me for a moment. "Joan Baez," she informed.

The woman who had reintroduced folk music to the 1960s sounded haunted as she sang "500 Miles." The character in the song had hopped a train. Her family would know she had gone because they could hear the whistle blow for a hundred miles.

I was determined to speak to O'Murphy this time, but she no longer saw me. Richie Richards grinned and rolled a secret finger wave. A senior couldn't be seen talking to a sophomore, particularly not a girl from the poor side of town.

I followed her eyes. Scooter and Spit glared and whispered to each other, but I sensed they were talking about me. O'Murphy honeyed up to calm Scooter. He shoved her shoulder.

Mrs. Lane shouted to us, "Tomorrow, Joan Baez."

"Stunning voice." Sammie walked alongside me now and watched.

"Your name is really Sammie Davis? Like *The Sammy Davis Junior Show*?"

She looked at me with a mischievous glint. "My daddy-o, Sam Davis, named me after himself, so I'm a junior too. He called me 'Sambo' until Sammy Davis Junior became the 'Magical Negro.' Now he calls me Sammie Davis Junior."

How should I deal with racial humor from a Negro? I grinned conspiratorially. "This class is going to be sooo much fun."

MBe faced her locker as Sammie and I walked by. "He likes you," she whispered.

"Cutie? Yeah." O'Murphy said.

"You like him?"

"Too nice. Not my type. Yours."

CHAPTER 3

IF DUMB WAS MANURE

I couldn't stop looking at the freckles dusting her nose.

"Hi." *That's it? Probably shouldn't write a book on how to talk to girls.*

"Hello." O'Murphy stood on the cafeteria steps. Those Siamese-cat eyes dazzled me: jewel blue, blinking slowly and vacantly at a far-away horizon.

For fourteen years, I've yearned to connect with anyone: my brother, a boy, a girl I could be friends with. This is the prototype chick. Third chance. Speak. "I, uh, oh . . ."

"I, uh, oh . . ." She tiptoed forward and teased with magnetic charisma.

I caught a third whiff of lavender perfume. Sammie had said it was Yardley. My new fave. "You're in my math class and my . . . "

She waved a tiny purple scroll from a five-cent vending machine. "Horoscope. What's your sign?"

"September twenty-fifth. I think it's a liver."

"Libra! Me too. Far oooout." She pirouetted on one toe and pointed an index finger at herself. "September twenty-seventh. We're very dip-lomatic and very nonconfrontational. Libras are the very, very best."

No need for all the verys. "Best" is a superlative. Cannot be exceeded. Like your hands. You have the most elegant fingers in the history of most elegant fingers. Long. Golden. They looked as if they'd been formed to spin silk. "Not even the rain hath such hands," I quoted–I don't know–somebody worth quoting.

She looked at her hands and then away, as if she were–not insulted–perturbed.

Pig Binson walked up. I invited him with a head motion.

"Cutie, how'd you get your paper route?" Pig spoke to me but stared at O'Murphy.

"You need money?"

"I don't know. Well, yeah. I could use the dough."

"Your wheels will hold up?"

Pig's hand-me-down bike had been white originally, but that had been spray painted green, then gold. All three colors were flaking, the sprockets were rusty, and the front wheel wobbled ambiguously from generations of collisions. "I think so."

"Meet you this afternoon. At *The Oklahoman* office. Know where it is?"

He nodded. "Oak Avenue, by the railroad tracks."

"I'll introduce you to the district manager."

"Thanks." Pig exhaled at O'Murphy, as if he'd been holding his breath.

Has O'Murphy been waiting for me to say something else? I just stood there, heat rising in my face. *Dumb, dumb. If dumb was manure, my brain would fertilize an entire greenhouse. Invite her into the cafeteria.* "Are you . . . "

" . . . waiting for my boyfriend." Her Scarlett O'Hara simper assumed we all knew her greasy boyfriend.

"Really? Who?" It was the best putdown I could think of.

"Tommy Annnderson."

She obviously thought he was hot feces. We thought he was a cold turd.

"He's in our home room. He rides a blue Yaaamaha–the fastest one in town."

"Yeah? My brother, Biggy, has a Honda Super 90. He races it. I've got paper routes, so I'm buying one, too." *Curtis, are you blurting? And fudging? Big Guy's motorcycle cost $350, and you've only saved $250. You're a year away from that much moola.*

A tiny light snapped on in those Doris Day eyes. "Right *ooon*. I love 'cycles. Are you gonna to take me for a ride?"

And every breath we drew was Hallelujah! Hallelujah! Hal-le-lu-lah! "I could teach you to drive. I'm gonna race mine, too. Dirt bike." *Stop trying so hard. I've driven Biggy's twice.*

"Neatooo. I've never been to a dirt-bike race . . . I forgot your name."

"Cuti–uh, uh, Curtis." I pointed to myself. I'm a big blusher, and I turned so red that I tasted copper. It's maddening, being unable to control the blood flow to your own face. "My mother called me Curtie, and Big Guy, my brother, tried to say Curtie, but Biggy–he was still learning to talk–and it came out 'Cutie.' And it stuck. My mother called me Cutie after that."

"O–uh, uh, O'Murphy." She pointed to herself and mocked me again. "I guess your brother would call me 'O'Murie.'" Her reckless smirk sanctioned her own cuteness, but it was a friendly-girl grin, one that included me as a confederate.

Her eyes darted over my shoulder. "Oops! Gotta trot. Tommy gets mad if I talk to aaanyone. I just said hello to Richie Richards this morning, and Tommy got sooo possessive. Then he told me we're going steady." She spun on her left toe and spread her arms to Scooter.

He commanded you to date him exclusively? And you just–did? I turned to leave, but I heard a voice behind me.

"Stick Boy." Scooter's head was cocked.

Oh, feces.

"I'm riding with Tommy to the Freeze." O'Murphy's eyes blinked quickly. Her nervousness clued Scooter that she'd said more than just a few words in passing.

Ridged brow, sloped forehead, meager brainpan. Can't you see he's Paleolithic? He's got two brothers who don't even walk upright.

"So, whadda you doin'?" Scooter's arm possessed O'Murphy's waist.

"Headed to the cafeteria. It's not the Freeze, but my dietary needs are simple."

"Funny little kid."

Then I realized Sammie had moved beside Pig.

"What are you two looking at?" Scooter stomped a foot in their direction.

Pig jumped, but Sammie posted herself uncompromisingly between Scooter and me. She stared at me and lowered her voice: "You try to steal his chick? And then you give him shit? Do you know where he lives? The junkyard. I wouldn't walk by there without a gun *and* a knife."

I looked at O'Murphy.

Sammie whispered more urgently. "You're not receiving my message. Stay away from her, or Scooter Boy is gonna perform impromptu dental surgery."

Unwisely, I stared at him. *So, Greasy Boy, did you use an entire can of STP in your hair?*

"S'go." Scooter towed O'Murphy's left hand. She half staggered away.

And then Scooter gave me that look for a second time. That's when I should have realized I couldn't stay in Hell Creek.

CHAPTER 4

SPRING SEMESTER

My bedroom door opened. Startled awake, I rolled onto my flashlight. *Oh. No.* I reached under my side and set it on the Remington typewriter between Biggy's bed and mine. My eyes closed in resignation.

"You still read under the covers?" Mother came in each school-day morning to make certain Biggy and I had awakened to our morning alarm.

I hadn't been able to sleep after this morning's paper route, so I'd reverted to a fourth-grade habit. Mrs. Bailey's class had been the Hardy Boys repository. I'd brought home a book every other day and read under the covers to avoid disturbing Biggy in the next bed. *The Hidden Harbor Mystery* had seemed so real I'd gotten hooked. I'd finally broken the practice fifty volumes later when Robert E. Lee Elementary and the Hell Creek Municipal Library ran out of Franklin W. Dixon novels, but I'd wasted a lot of paper-route money on C cells.

When I was eleven, Mother had said she couldn't give me money for the sixth-grade carnival, so I'd swiped twenty cents from her purse. She'd caught me because they were the last two dimes she had. I'd gotten an afternoon paper route and repaid her the next week.

Since I didn't sleep much anyway, I'd asked Mr. Presley for a morning route too, then a second morning route a few months later to make getting up really worth it. I could usually deliver both morning routes, be back in bed by six A.M., and read for an hour before school.

"Why don't you wake me up the next time it's cold and rainy?" Mother was in the kitchen by the time I finished showering. "I'll drive you." She had boiled a pot of rice, melted butter over the top, added sugar, then poured enough milk in my bowl to make breakfast soup. She could have just served Rice Krispies, but she insisted a hot meal was better for growing boys.

"At four A.M.? You don't close until ten o'clock. When would you sleep?"

"When else do I get to see you?"

I had finished *Waiting for Godot* this morning, and so I'd put the book in my newspaper bag. I was working my way through the high school library.

"Let us do something while we have the chance," Estragon had said.

That's when I'd gotten the idea to leave home. *But go where?*

＊ ＊ ＊

I hadn't seen O'Murphy since before the Christmas break, and there they went on his Yamaha. Scooter glared at me in triumph.

Hey, I'm not your competition. I've spoken to her a half-dozen times since school started.

O'Murphy lay contentedly against Scooter's back, arms wrapped around his waist, the top of her head barely reaching the bottom of his. Her eyes opened for a moment and saw me.

When I biked into the parking lot a few minutes later, she bounced up like I was her besty. "Tommy didn't want the teachers to see him cutting, so he dropped me off a block away. He's riding to Richie Richards's lake house on Clear Creek. They're going ice biking."

Banker Boy is buds with Thug Boy now? That's an unholy combination.

"And Richie's ditching his paper route this afternoon so they can ride his Indian."

That's why it's such a darn good idea to be born into a filthy-rich family: Richie had inherited a preposterously handsome 1946 Indian Chief from his grandfather, who'd been president of Boomer National Bank. Yellow-and-black, skirted fenders, black-fringe saddle, genuine silver-conch saddlebags. The first time I'd seen it, I'd moved closer just to inhale the testosterone.

"If I had a 'cycle, I wouldn't dump you a block from school."

She faced me. "I thought you were getting one."

Stanley Jones staggered toward us.

"Hey, Stan."

"Hi-uuuh." His mouth gaped when he talked, and spit ran down his chin because the bottom of his left lip drooped lower than the right. Stanley didn't notice the drool.

O'Murphy turned her head and muttered, *sotto voce*, "Eww! That boy. Why do they let him in school with us? Obviously, he's a mental. Don't you think he's a little creepy?"

I reached for the white linen handkerchief his mother always tucked into Stanley's back pocket and whispered, "He's sweet. He's funny, if you get to know him. Besides, what are Special Ed kids supposed to do? Stay home? For the rest of their lives?"

"I'm in two classes with him. He takes a lot of the teacher's time," O'Murphy grouched.

"But think about what you learn."

"From him?"

Don't get upset. Teach. "You're more used to people like Stan. Were you afraid of him before?" Parents told girls to stay away when mainstreaming had begun last year. Stanley Jones might assault them and get them pregnant with a retarded baby. I wiped Stanley's chin and stuffed his handkerchief back into his pocket. "Got your gym bag? Good. See you fifth period?"

"Yea-uh. Futh peeer-i-od," Stanley squealed. His head wagged, and he took off.

I saw something in her eyes. Was she impressed? Just a tiny bit? I sensed that O'Murphy hungered for human contact, just like Stanley, just like me. *Now. Make contact with her now.* I reached for her left arm, slid my hand down to hers, and paused for a second.

"Well, when you get a motorcycle, come by my house and give me a ride to school."

* * *

"That's all she asked me," Sammie said. "Do you sit next to Cutie?"

"But MBe already knows that."

"You are so adroit at missing the obvious, White Boy."

Why was I white and Sammie not? She was just a few shades darker. "What did you say?"

"I said yeah."

"And then?"

"She said, 'He's your friend?'"

"I said, 'Sorta.'"

"You're too, too gracious. What'd she say?"

"Does Cutie go out with anybody?"

"That's what it was about?"

"No," Sammie said. "It wadn't."

"Well then, what?"

"She wanted to find out if I like you."

"And what did you say?"

Sammie stared. "You're my friend. But I couldn't even say that."

"Why?"

"Because you're white!"

"Barely." I'm swarthy. Part American Indian, part Black Dutch. "And you are my friend."

Sammie's expressions changed from pleased to a little proud to frustrated. "It ain't about talking to each other. The day my moms enrolled me in this school, she tole me, 'Don't you never let nobody see you smilin' at no white boy. You'll ruin him, and they will visit a terrible destruction upon your head.'"

"Sorry. Now, do you have anything for me at all?"

"She called you Nice Eyes. And then she said, 'But he doesn't realize it.'"

"And then you said?"

"Nothing. But I remember thinking, 'Green. I wish I had green eyes.'" Sammie stared directly into my eyes for just a second, then dropped hers.

"So what do you think was her point?"

"She was sendin' you a message."

"What's the message?"

"I just tole you."

CHAPTER 5

PLASTIC FATHER

We'd never really known how Vin Trainer felt about us. I'd tried to like him, but he'd kept repeating his bad-man patterns. Nan and Grand were teetotalers, and so was Mother. She'd carp about his drinking and Vin would storm away. Then he'd get drunk or sorry or lonesome and want return to the fold, and slowly and creepily drive by our house. He knew Mother wasn't here this evening; he just wanted us to spot his Chevy. He could've stayed more often if he wasn't perpetually embalmed.

"He must be drunk. He's driving about twelve miles an hour." Vin had bought the pickup new, but he'd never waxed it, so ten years of weather had worn green paint to brown primer on the fenders and the roof.

"Horny bastard. Hard to miss," Big Guy muttered through the curtains.

My frown admonished him. "That's not a nice thing to say about your own mother."

"It's true. He's going to whine and apologize, and then she's going to invite the bastard over for a late-night snack."

"He tries to be our dad, a little. Remember when I told him about the rodeo parade and the clowns on stilts?" Using two-by-fours, Vin had supervised while I'd sawn four-inch blocks from each eight-foot board. Then we'd halved those square blocks at forty-five-degree angles and nailed them to the planks, and my old leather belt became two stirrup straps. Vin couldn't walk on stilts because he had a stiff right knee–one of two World War II wounds he showed off as he sat in his white boxers and undershirt on what he'd adopted as his living room rocker. But he'd shown me how to swing my shoe into the left stirrup, then step onto the right block. *Voila*. I was nine feet tall.

Vin parked in the driveway.

"He's coming in," Biggy said. "Stay out of his way, Cutie."

Vin opened the kitchen door without knocking, groaned as he sat in "his" rocker, and watched TV without a word to us. I could smell his breath; he'd had more than a passing acquaintance with Adolph Coors tonight. Five minutes later, he went back to his truck.

"Good," Biggy said. "Call Casa la Bello."

Although he was already bleary-eyed, Vin returned with a six-pack, sat it beside his rocker, and guzzled two cans in two minutes flat. From the thousands of empty tins at his four-room shack, we knew alcohol and loneliness were Vin's steadfast companions.

Mother arrived in ten minutes. "Vin, do you want to talk to me?"

He didn't look up.

"In the bedroom."

"I don't need no bedroom to talk. I don't got no secrets. But you do. What th' hell you doing, signin' my name?" So, he had gotten liquored up to pick a fight with Mother. And he wanted Biggy and me to hear. We already knew: she'd never divorced Daddy, so the loose talk about Mother and Vin had become family legend. And we knew that Jonathan Robert Pye had busted their credit, so Virginia Pye had told Montgomery Ward that she was Ginny Trainer in order to buy a new divan. We'd seen her sign checks with Vin's name. She could almost argue it was to make a better home for us all, but she was the one who wanted new furniture, not the corner-worn couch Biggy and I had pushed out of a dumpster six years ago while she'd pulled from the outside.

"I'm signing my name."

"Ginny Trainer? Ginny Trainer's your name?" A forked vein lit his forehead like a lightning-blue wishbone.

Someone had to get between Vin and Mother. It was brave of Biggy, but what he said was stupid: "You son of a bitch. You're just a missed opportunity for an abortion."

Mother knew what would happen next, so she grabbed Vin's hand. "Com'on."

Vin pulled away, but his eyes followed her to the bedroom.

* * *

They argued loudly, and he finally left in the middle of the night. He must've hit her hard; the next morning her shiner was already a prism of red and orange and yellow.

I wished he'd hung around; I wanted to call the cops. I didn't blame Mother for getting hit, but I was exasperated at what she said.

"I'm going to invite him back tonight. To live here. We can't make it without Vin's money." Mother appealed for Biggy's approval. "We don't have Daddy's allotment checks anymore, and Casa la Bello only pays me twenty-five a week. The mortgage is twenty-seven. It's thirty more to feed all three of us. After that, I don't have enough left to pay the water and the gas and the electric and the phone. And keep the Rambling Wreck running."

All true, but she also left Monkey Ward every few weeks with a throw rug here or a knickknack there. These days, we had the best turned-out house in our family.

"He's dangerous. 'Goddamned old sonofabitch,'" Biggy imitated Vin's guttural voice.

Mother sighed, but she had made her decision. "Call Nan."

I'll say this: when one of us needs help, our family responds post-haste. Nan and Grand's house was twenty miles away, but they arrived at Mother's house in seventeen minutes. Big Guy and I—and our big sister Sandy before us—had spent many of our growing-up days at their farm, where we couldn't walk a mile without crossing a cousin's path.

Aunt Alexandria, trained by the Red Cross in World War II, examined her sister's discolored skin for ruptured blood vessels. Her thumb pressed the eye socket. "Does this hurt?"

Mother winced. "Not so much, Zandy."

Zandy sighed. "Why do men always go for the face?"

"Whose fault is this?" Grand interjected.

"Oh, mine. He just lost his temper. I said something I probably shouldn't have."

Actually, Biggy said it.

"What could you say that would make a man punch a woman? I'll tell you this right in front of your daddy." Nan took every opportunity to refer to Grand in the third person. "If my husband ever woulda hit me, I'da told Papa, and Papa woulda went and got my brothers, and then my husband never woulda hit me again."

Grand's sheepish look said he wasn't allowed to defend himself, so he condemned Mother instead. "You keep choosing the same worthless drunk: Xavier Charles Thurman and Jonathan Robert Pye. Not one worth two shakes of a mule's ass. Just in case you wonder, that's why—of a million men in Oklahoma—you picked Vincent Elvin Trainer."

"I thought I could change him." Mother looked for confirmation from Nan and Zandy, but felt cold comfort instead. "He's a good Christian man when he's not drinking."

"Good Christian," Grand scoffed. "Vin Trainer couldn't name the four Gospels if you spotted him Matthew and Mark."

"Where is he now?" Nan asked.

"He's coming over tonight. I'm going to tell him not to come back." Mother looked mortified at her own lie. "That's why I want you to take the kids till tomorrow."

Grand huffed and puffed about blowing down big bad Vin's unelectrified shack. Nan's expression told us her husband would do nothing. "Well then," he said, "guess we'll get to know our grandsons a little better."

Aunt Zandy gave us the poor-relations stinkeye.

"Sandy," Mother said, "take your little brothers outside."

"Come here!" Our sister opened the kitchen door.

Uh oh. The feces is just about to strike the oscillator.

Biggy looked at me, deciding whether to obey, but walked toward the kitchen. "Sonofabitch's too cheap to go down to Hell Creek Hotel and pay a prostitute," Biggy whispered quietly enough for Mother not to hear.

"Don't never talk that way about your mother." Sandy laid a firm, disapproving hand on Biggy's shoulder.

Biggy never considered disobeying Sandy. Sandy was everything Biggy wanted to be, but he could never live up to her cool persona: competent, responsible, high achieving. Mother always said she loved her children equally, but Sandy Thurman had always been first among equals. Biggy demanded most of Sandy's attention, so I knew what it meant to be last among equals. She was the oldest, and she was Biggy's and my favorite sibling.

We sat at the picnic table under the carport. "What do y'all want for Christmas?" Sandy, who had never wanted to be a girl, stuck her boycut between us. Her face was identical to Biggy's, but her hair was cropped closer on the sides.

I took up the conversation. "Our favorite Christmas gift came from you."

"Oh? Yeah?"

"After Mother left Daddy," Biggy nodded. "Our first Christmas in Oklahoma."

"What'd I give you?"

A year after Mother had married Xavier Thurman, Zandy had taken her second husband, but he'd only lasted a few years. Probably died in self defense, knowing Zandy. The first of our generation, Sandy and Marsha been each other's only cousins for twelve years, when Biggy came along.

In 1961, the navy had given holiday liberty to Sandy. Our holidays were always at Nan's. We'd arrange ourselves around the tree on Christmas mornings with Aunt Alexandria and Ethan and Seth and Marsha and Marsha's four daughters. They piled so many gifts under the tree, it was hard to find ours. Mother was usually broke; she could only give us one box–always shirts or jeans. Or worse, underwear.

"Did you hear that, Marsha?" Sandy had cupped a hand to one ear.

"Bells." Marsha had made big eyes at her brothers and daughters on the floor. "Is someone coming?"

Sandy went outside and came back a minute later with two Woolworth sacks. Wrapping paper was not the important feature of her gifts. "Saw an old fat man in a red suit at the end of the driveway. He said to give these to you."

I'd never gotten such a heavy Christmas present before, so I was ridiculously thrilled. This one must have weighed five pounds. It was a genuine leather gunbelt with Fanner .50s–two cast-iron popguns, each in its own holster, each with enough gunpowder caps to smoke the living room with the acrid smell of carbon and a dirty hint of charcoal. Which was exactly what Biggy and I had done. Sandy grinned every time we squealed.

Nan had been annoyed. "Take those things outside." Her voice never allowed argument.

Biggy rarely touched anyone, but today he threw an arm around Sandy. "You gave me my best birthday present too. Two years ago, after I bought my motorcycle, you gave me tools."

Exactly Biggy's opposite, Sandy turned on the tears for every occasion. "Oh, that was just a little chest of used screwdrivers and wrenches."

We shared the same mother but we all had hollow fathers, unworthy of the honor, so Sandy had become our protector-at-large whenever hearts needed guarding. Grand and Nan had been surrogates too, but all were substitutes for the real thing.

"I know I'm just your half-sister, but I try."

"You're our only-ist sister," Biggy said. I nodded.

Sandy studied our faces and tried to changed the subject, but her eyes overflowed. "Y'all look more alike every day."

So people say. Same brown hair, but Biggy was inches taller and bigger boned. I was built like a skeleton from a doctor's office. Sandy was the only true white person among us three: ginger hair like her father, Irish freckles, milk-bottle forearms.

Mother hadn't been able to support three kids, so Sandy had joined the navy as soon as we'd moved back to Hell Creek. We hadn't seen much of her in the last six years. "Y'all don't like Vin, I know."

Biggy shot me a knowing look.

As a twenty-seven-year-old woman of the world, Sandy explained that even at forty-seven, Mother was still a young woman. "She has needs. Y'all aren't gonna understand this now, but someday you will."

"Yeah, well, we get it that Vin is horny," Biggy said. "But that old goat is a good ten years older than Mother."

Grand had been right: our mother was an eternal misjudger of men. She'd known all three mates were flawed and that she couldn't change them, but she'd engaged in magical thinking about whether they'd be good family men. Somewhere in the back of the hall closet, a green duffel stamped U.S.M.C. was filled with Daddy's civvies and shoes. Why had she brought that bag when she left him in California? Had she really expected her husband to put aside his loose women, stroll through her front door one day, and beg her pardon? Forgiveness, as some insightful philosopher had once said, is love practiced poorly.

"Sandy," Biggy asked, "what was Daddy like? Was he better than Vin?"

Sandy had sat facing Biggy, but she scooted down the bench a few inches and curled an arm around me. I could see his eyes burn. I've never gotten along with my brother. Or, to be more accurate, he's never been close to me. His envy had always goaded him to harass me, and his sibling jealousy incinerated whatever sibling affection had existed.

"I was born after Pearl Harbor, so I never met my daddy until World War II was over. Then Mama divorced Xavier Charles Thurman a year later–1946–so I knew your daddy sixteen years longer than mine." My family had a funny way of referring to our fathers in third person, and by all three names. Something far away appeared in Sandy's eyes, in her voice, and in her avoidance to answer Biggy's exact question. "Jonathan Robert Pye, well, he was good to me."

"What happened?" I prodded for details. We'd gotten fractions of Daddy's story third-hand from a dozen family sources, but Mother and Nan and Grand and Zandy had always dropped their conversations about Daddy whenever we walked into the room. "Why did we leave him in California?"

"The day before mama lit out for Oklahoma, Jonathan Robert Pye made his mortal error. Mother had to go to work, so she asked him to pick me up from school. He had to work that night too, but he was supposed to bring me home to babysit y'all. Now don't never mention this to Mama . . . "

"Why?" Biggy challenged.

"She'd be hurt."

Biggy and I looked at each other. We didn't understand.

"He told me he had to manage the NCO Club. Instead of taking me home, he put me in the back seat, went inside, and it was sunrise when I woke up. We were parked at a house. I went up to the porch. Some strangey woman came to the door, put her arm around me, and marched me back to the car."

"Where was Daddy?"

"He came out a few minutes later and finally took me home." Sandy turned to me. "Mama still hadn't gone to work. She'd waited up all night, and let me tell you something: when we walked in the next morning, she threw a double-geared, walleyed hissy. She demanded to know where we'd been all night. That was Jonathan Robert's great fault: the truth weren't in him. Ever' word that came out of his mouth was a lie, including 'pass the black-eyed peas.' So as soon as he left for the base that morning, mama started in on me. All day. You know your mama; she's a snapping turtle. And she didn't let go till I told her where we'd been."

"Then what?" Biggy ate family gossip with a spoon.

"When he came home that night, Mama marched your daddy into their bedroom. She tore into him like she was God's own wrath." Sandy sniffed. "Your daddy came out of that room so mad, he only spoke to me once after that."

"Why?" Biggy didn't get it.

"Daddy wouldn't take the blame?" I asked, but it was a comment.

"He told me once, a long time ago, 'Don't put your faith in me. I'll disappoint you.' Guess he never spoke truer words." Sandy's nod was miserable. "Mama told him that she'd forced me to tell the truth, but Jonathan Robert, he never forgave. Now let's drop that right here."

CHAPTER 6

NO RESPECT WITHOUT A MOTOR

"Cutie, can you ride with me today?" Mr. Presley asked. "I need to throw Richie's route."

So, Richie quit? "I'll deliver it."

"His route and yours? This afternoon? On a bicycle? Can you finish both by six?"

Presley's Rule: every *Daily Oklahoman* on its doorstep by six A.M.; six P.M. for *The Oklahoma City Times*. "Sure."

"You already have two morning routes. Why do you want four?"

"I want to buy a motorcycle. Can I make an extra five a week with Richie Rich's route?"

He chuckled at the nickname. "Seven. How much more do you need?"

"To buy a motorcycle? A hundred dollars."

"Want a loan?"

I waste chances to make friends. Whether it's an acquired fear or something deep inside, I resisted asking for help, even from people I like. And no one–except Sammie Davis Jr. and maybe O'Murphy–ever tried to make friends with me. Especially not Big Guy. But then, Biggy wouldn't have been civil even if I'd been whiter. I was odd looking, gangling, uncool, uncoordinated. Every time his eyes rested on me, I sensed trouble in his unrestrained disappointment. You haven't felt invisible until your brother doesn't want you.

I would've picked Mr. Presley for a father. My boss even had the same steel-colored hair and perma-tan I'd seen in Daddy's color photos. He pulled a hundred dollars from his zippered bank bag. "Don't want things, Cutie, do things. You're my best carrier. No one else types their monthly reports. I'll take twenty-five dollars a month out of your collections?"

"Sure." After I bought gas, I'd still be broke, but I'd be broke on a motorcycle. People don't respect anyone–not even a kid–who doesn't have money and a motor. And O'Murphy would be mine. Actually, it wouldn't be quite that easy. I was too young to sign a legal document, so how could I buy a vehicle? And apply for a title and tag?

* * *

Mother was waiting in the driveway. "Let's go to Fort Sill. I'm off tonight, and we're out of groceries. We can't get as much. No more allotments, so no more thirty dollars a month."

Because of Vin. "The Marines didn't cancel our ID cards?"

"Your ex-daddy tried. I called them and told them that if they took our cards, I couldn't take care of y'all. How would we see the doctor and buy groceries?"

With military ID cards, soldiers and their dependents could buy clothes and groceries at the PX and the commissary for cost plus 10 percent. Since we lived fifty miles from the base, we stocked up: ten loaves of Wonder Bread. We'd eat fresh sandwiches and burgers for a week. The rest went in the freezer, so nothing but toast for the rest of the month. We drank fresh milk for a week; seven gallons were frozen into butterfat flakes and blue water. We shook the cartons to re-ho-mogenize the milk enough to pour over cereal. We filled our cabinets with dried beans and pasta, canned soup and corn, fruit cocktail and peaches. Mother fried many a stinky Spamburger.

"And Mother, I'm going to buy a motorcycle."

"I just told you. No money."

"I have it."

"You have $250 in your passbook."

"Mr. Presley is doing me a favor."

"Favor?" Mother had always been suspicious of the kindness of strangers.

"He loaned me a hundred dollars." I injected a few words before she could object. "He'll give me a fourth route if I have a motorcy-cle. I'll make more money." My paper routes–and jerking sodas on the occasional weekend at the Freeze–had made me self sufficient. I'd saved three bucks a week, paid for my comic books, and bought school lunch tickets since I was eleven.

Mother saw me rub a cheek and grimace. "Toothache? Get an aspirin out of my purse. Hold it on the gum above the cavity until it dissolves. Then drink this." She handed me the rest of her Dietetic Dr. Pepper. "And drive that new motorcycle to the dentist next week."

Make your own money, and you decide a few things for yourself. Even if you're a kid.

* * *

The Honda dealership was on our way back. I paid the $350; Mother lent fourteen dollars for the tax. I'd have thirty days to buy a tag. The two dollars left in her billfold would have last until Friday, when the pizza parlor paid her twenty-five dollar weekly wage.

Mother co-signed the title, but she seemed reluctant. "Let's get back to Peaceable River."

I returned on my white Honda, shiny with chrome. Mom followed until we got to Hell Creek. I arm-signaled on Fourteenth Street to go my own way.

Her driver's window was down. She wiped her tears.

I shook my head. *What's the big deal? I bought a motorcycle.* But that's what my mother did. She'd get frustrated, or overwhelmed, or just need attention, and she'd cry. I'd rather open a vein than show my feelings to anyone. I cruised across Peaceable River bridge to O'Murphy's house. No cars in her driveway.

MBe stepped into Eleventh Street. She had wide, intelligent eyes, but her face wore a stoic hint of Dust Bowl, a rawboned, pre-matronly expression like a black-and-white photo. Boys my age demanded the sexiest, the most sociable, the most extroverted girls; MBe wasn't pretty, so even teenage boys with spoiled faces like mine hadn't chosen her.

"Cool 'cycle."

"Thanks. I just bought it. Where's O'Murphy?"

"You won't believe it."

"What's wrong?"

"She's in the hospital. They think she's got kissing disease."

"Mono? That blows my mind. How'd she get mono?"

She grabbed my sleeve. I have to think before I touch anyone; MBe does it instinctively.

"It gets better. She two-timed Scooter; he just doesn't know who with."

With whom. I'm just glad it's not me. Not until Scoot gets a new chick.

MBe smiled with tight lips. "And Mrs. L said she can't go with Scooter anymore."

I couldn't help but grin. "They split the sheet?"

She laid her hand on my arm and tossed one more meaty piece of gossip. "Now O'Murphy has to tell Richie. He might have mono too."

O'Murphy Scott. Making Hell Creek smile, one dude at a time.

CHAPTER 7

BITTERSWEET CHOCOLATE LOVE

I skimmed *16 Magazine* for Valentine's Day gift suggestions while the dentist Novocained my jaw for the drill. The choices, it seemed, were an armload of flowers or a box of candy. I cruised into the Rexall on Main Street.

The druggist walked as if he were under water. "Young man?"

"Ka'dy." My jaw was still puffed from the anesthetic.

"You have a lisp?"

I drew out the syllables. "A booth of choth-ah . . . "

"Cleft palate?"

I pointed to boxes of chocolate on the shelf.

"Oh." He indulged me with a smile. "Who's it for? Girl?"

Oh, eat my diaper gravy. Old bastards think they're so funny when they tease boys about liking girls.

He reached past the Whitman Samplers and the Russell Stover's to a top-shelf, heart-shaped box: Bittersweet Chocolate Love, wrapped in crinkled red tissue.

Probably a Valentine's Day leftover, but I borrowed his fountain pen and wrote, "Your Secret Admirer" on the linen cardstock.

Now, where to give it to her? Not school, too public. I threw my evening routes with a scarlet heart peeking from my canvas saddlebag.

The next morning, in the twilight before dawn overtook darkness, I drove to O'Murphy's house, killed the engine three houses away, and coasted to her front door. I propped the box on the stoop. She'd know who it was from. *Whom. Who is for the subject of a sentence; whom is for the object.*

* * *

On Friday nights, girls steered their boyfriends to The Freeze. They didn't have to; boys wanted to be seen just as much. The self-chosen in-crowd dragged Main from six P.M. to midnight: A&W was a mile south, Sonic was five blocks north, the Pig Stand was the eastern leg of Main Street. The Freeze was our pivot, the point where every high schooler sojourned if they owned a motor or could snag a ride. It would've been unthinkable to walk; I'd been mortified to pedal my bicycle there on work weekends, even if it was a Schwinn Deluxe Typhoon.

The Freeze was full at eight o'clock, so I parked my Honda at the cafe next door, El No Deseado, the Unwanted. The sign suggested how contentiously migrant workers were received here in our little town. I occupied the back booth and started reading *The Catcher in the Rye*.

Spit walked in a minute later. Scooter followed: "Hey, Bookworm, where's O'Murphy?"

Growing up with Biggy had taught me not to respond to taunts.

"Hey goddammit! I'm talking to you!"

"Not in that tone, you're not." Mr. Marion stepped out of the kitchen with a steel spatula in his right hand. He'd spelled out three rules when he hired me: no fighting, neither boy nor man was allowed to take the Lord's name in vain, and he'd personally remove anyone who disrespected his wife, his son, his daughter, or his staff.

"If I find her you was with her," Scoot shook a finger as if he were teaching me a lesson, "I'll cream your ass."

"OUT!" Mr. Marion shouted without raising his voice. "Don't come back without two apologies." After a two-week probation, transgressors were required to say they were sorry, then express regret to prove sincerity.

Scoot's Yamaha revved, and he squealed a half-donut out of the parking lot. It shrieked as the two-cycle engine wound to the top of first gear, but cut off completely a second later.

MBe and O'Murphy walked in two minutes later. O'Murphy cut mirthful eyes at me and raised her hands over to cheeks in *faux* innocence. "Did we just miss Tommy?"

Out of the hospital? Already? Must not have been mono. I'd looked it up in the *Family Medical Encyclopedia*. Mono would've laid her up for a month with a fever and swollen tonsils.

They ordered three cherry limeades, giggled something into each other's ears, and kept glancing at me. Her purple scent remained after O'Murphy sashayed out with two drinks. It had taken three hundred thousand years of evolution for women to walk like that.

Feces. You've known O'Murphy for what–five months now–and your relationship has regressed to a few words and glances.

MBe took her cherry limeade, dropped a nickel in the Wurlitzer, matched my blues with Ray Charles, and plopped at my table. "Banker Daddy bought Richie Rich a Shelby GT 500."

A few of my sophomore class had turned sixteen, and we were finding out who among us were the most privileged. "Yeah, I saw it last week at school. Mustang Super Snake. I heard Richie tell Scooter it cost $7,500." *Three times the price of Biggy's '66 coupe.*

"Wimbledon white with Guardsman-blue rocker stripes," MBe repeated verbatim what Richie must've bragged to her. "Police Interceptor engine; 650 horses, 427 cubes."

I pointed two fingers inside my mouth. "Gag me with a salad fork. Better than Scooter, but why Richie?"

"You know, O'Murphy's been my best friend since second grade, but she's always set her mouth for the wrong kind of boy. However," she paused, "if you don't like her boyfriends, you should ask her out."

"I can't compete with Richie Rich."

MBe rolled her eyes.

Sammie Davis Jr. walked in. As Sammie waved hello, MBe lowered her voice to an exasperated tone. "Have you got even one romantic bone in your body? You know she likes you!"

"No, I don't know. Am I her type?"

MBe searched my eyes for seconds, deciding what to say in front of Sammie. "That was first day of school. You'd be good for her. If I tell all y'all about her, what are you going to do?"

"Do?"

"Are you going to drop a dime on me?" MBe turned to Sammie.

"Lips." Sammie closed an imaginary zipper across her mouth with a finger. "Sealed."

"Because she would cordially detest me," MBe emphasized.

"I keep secrets," I said. "Besides, who would I ever tell?"

"Richie dropped us off here, but she left with a doggie. A lot older than she is."

Sammie's eyes turned to me. We were both stunned.

MBe bit her lip. "He's married. You both just met her first semester, right? She was a lot different in elementary school. Smart. She actually loved every class, every teacher."

"I thought she just moved here," Sammie said.

"Nope, born here. She was in my first-grade class when her dad got sent to Norman."

"Norman. Norman the mental hospital Norman?" Sammie coaxed.

"It was such a bad scene," MBe slurped the last of her cherry limeade. "Don't ever go nuts. It sucks. Her daddy didn't die until last year. Her mom remarried within a few months, and then they moved back last summer. Now O'Murphy's sick too."

I caught MBe's insinuation, that O'Murphy was mentally ill. But because I've always been stupid to know when I'm being stupid, I joked about it. "Maybe she's just got the girl flu."

MBe shot me an exasperated eye.

"You know. The Scarlet Pimpernel. The Period Fairy."

MBe and Sammie girlcotted me until I shut up. "Sorry. Inappropriately funny?"

"You're half right," MBe stated flatly. Then she continued, "When they came back from Norman last summer, she was wearing makeup and dressing sexy."

"Was that when Scooter became her boyfriend?"

"They didn't go out until the first day of the tenth grade. She got moody after her mom met her stepdad-to-be in Norman. Chewed her nails. Stayed on the telephone with me. She'd want to talk all night. And baby, did that make her stepdad go ape. We'd go to a dance, and the next night Murph would reconstruct the entire event. We'd be on the phone for two hours."

"But you talk at school," Sammie pointed out.

"Of course. But it's different on the phone."

"Like how?" Sammie asked.

"Sealed?"

"Vault."

"We can talk about 'it' on the phone."

"Why do you need a phone for that?" I asked.

"I guess because we can't see each other's faces. We have privacy, even from each other."

I nodded, but I didn't understand. "What's with the scars on her legs?"

MBe opened her mouth, then ignored my question. "Did you ever read *The Glass Menagerie*? She's like Laura. She can't see through people."

"And you see through everybody."

MBe smiled as if I'd offered a huge compliment.

I hate it when someone starts to tell me something and then doesn't. I played along because I desperately wanted to know more about O'Murphy. "And so, the scars?"

"After they moved back here last year, her grades dropped. She'd be a chatterbox, high as a kite. The next minute, she'd cry in her pillow, hate the world, and everything was stupid. And then O'Murphy started closing the drapes on me."

"Because of Scooter?"

"Not everything's about him." MBe shook her head. "Except tonight. She didn't tell him where she went, so he's out looking for her, even though she broke up."

"But why does she cut?" Sammie pressed for me.

"How do you know she cuts?"

"Her gym locker's next to mine. And I see her in the showers sometimes," Sammie said.

"I saw scars on her knees when she wore a short skirt," I added.

"At first she hid it," MBe said. "Now I think she wants people to know."

"But isn't that self mutilation?" I asked.

"Something about how her dad went out. Did you know about that?"

We shook our heads.

"He was a lifer Marine: Korea, Viet Nam. He had brought this hari-kari sword home from World War II. One day, he ditched the mental hospital and disemboweled himself. O'Murphy came home and she . . . "

"She found him?" Sammie asked incredulously.

"At first she dropped ten pounds, and she was already a skinny-mini. Then she started eating. It was so weird. You're a boy, so you don't know this," MBe glanced at her own chest, "but some girls gain weight here. O'Murphy's step called her a milk cow, so she stopped eating. Then all she did was sleep. She'd scream at her mother and Mr. Larsson to leave her alone. When she was thirteen, Murph told me she hated the way she looked. When her stepdad—or anyone, for that matter—told her she was pretty, she'd glare at them. She told me that her step 'Looks at me in a way I don't want to be looked at.' So she changed everything about herself. When her mom made roast beef for dinner, Mr. Larsson loved it, but O'Murphy was suddenly a vegetarian. She was always Miss Homebody—she didn't even like staying overnight at my house, she'd get homesick and call her mother—but after Mr. Scott died and Mr. Larsson moved in, she was Miss Independence. Nobody knew what she'd be next.

"But here's the clincher," MBe said. "Fall semester—that's when y'all met her—she got to know this married guy. She started dressing sexy: she'd put on a scoop neck over her bra, and then a pep squad shirt. And as soon as school was over, she'd hike up her skirt, take off her shirt, and unhook her bra so her boobs would swing while she walked home."

That's who she was with when Scooter thought she was me. "Why? What was the point?"

"When I look back, I think she wanted to get pregnant," MBe confided.

All three of us were stunned into silence. "And this has nothing to do with Scooter?"

"No!" MBe sounded frustrated with me. "But you–you've gotta be careful. Every time she two-times him, Tommy gets the idea she's with you. He ain't the shiny toy in the box."

"So why are you telling us all of this?"

Another bombshell. "Because she thinks Richie left a box of candy on her porch."

My mouth opened in dismay. "I probably need to move while the spirit's on me. Four A.M. comes early these days."

I walked across the parking lot, sat on my Honda, and thought about what MBe had said. Just before I kicked the starter, I heard voices a couple of cars away. And I knew who they were.

" . . . how to calm her assss down," Spit's tone was a lecture. "Get her PG."

I made out Spit's profile–more like a monkey than a man–in the driver's seat through the window of the dark hot rod. That dwarf mountain beside him must be Pickle.

"Now why in hell would I do that?" asked a third shape in the back seat.

"So she'll drop out of school."

"But then . . . " Scoot said. A car whooshed by. " . . . have to marry her."

"That's the point, smarty. She's home. She can't flirt with every turd who's got a motor."

The back door opened and seconds later, Scooter's distinctive two-cycle engine vroomed to life. He revved the handle throttle two, three, four times and popped a wheelie.

" . . . still haven't gotten any, have you?" Spit asked.

Pickle's head toggled from side to side.

"You want a piece of O'Murphy Scott?"

Your brother's girlfriend? Spit, you're one nasty piece of work.

A green light released five cars. Now their voices were audible in waves.

" . . . nose stuck up in the air like she's somebody. She ain't no better than us," Spit said.

" . . . if she calls the cops?" Pick's face turned away.

"She won't say shit."

"You've got a girl. Sort of. Why would you force someone?" Pickle asked Spit.

"I don't ask," Spit said. "I take what I . . . *whoosh* . . . like a man likes to feel. It's a rush, believe you me . . . *whoosh* . . . no one ever called the cops . . . *whoosh* . . . Same with MBe."

You did this to MBe? You bastard. I'm going to make it my job to pay you back if I ever get the chance.

"Why didn't MBe call the cops?"

"I told 'er, soon as I bail out of jail, I'll do her again. But I'm gonna do O'Murphy next time. It'll be her best birthday present ever."

CHAPTER   8

ESCAPE FROM
BIZARRO WORLD

I'd always treated myself to the Saturday show at the Ritz Theater after I finished my afternoon paper routes. *Thunderball* was the matinee. Just as SPECTRE captured James Bond, Pickle Andersen walked up beside me.

I was so focused on Largo and 007, I flinched when Pickle fake-punched at my nose with his right fist and loudly thumped his chest with his left. Of course I flinched. Why on hell did he do that? It was a prank a friend might pull on a friend, but we didn't know each other.

Dillon Andersen–Pickle–should've been two grades above me, but he'd been sent back after the third grade. Then he'd flunked sophomore year, so now Pickle, Scooter and I were in the same class. Pickle punched three more times. Bam, bam, bam. I flinched again. For a guy built like Winnie the Pooh, Pickle was as fast as a blink. "You know what that means?"

I think it means you've escaped from Bizarro World.

"You're a chickenshit," he said in the voice of a petulant five-year-old, "so I have to kick your ass."

Someone ordered you to do this? Of course, I made my usual mistake and smart mouthed. "Yeah? My bladder has loosened in fear."

He didn't react.

Good. I would've regretted that.

Fickle Fate had made Pickle Andersen the most feared bully in high school. He looked at the back rows for a few seconds, then fake-punched again. Bam! He slammed his left fist violently into his chest to sound like his right had broken the sound barrier. "Hulk. Smash!"

"Well, now I know what's on your summer reading list."

He didn't get that either.

"Your name is Cutie."

"What do you want?"

"You're messin' with O'Murphy."

"Not really, but thanks for telling me what this is about."

Bam. Bam. Bam. "I'm waiting for you outside," Pickle said. Three rows from the back of the theater, someone tall stood and left with him.

Yeah, and Scooter too. So, they'd followed me. Marlin Perkins had said this was the way cheetahs hunted stray gazelles in *Wild Kingdom*. If I went outside now, the Andersens would be on the dark side of the building, where I'd parked my Super 90.

Maybe I'll hang around for the evening show.

CHAPTER 9

THAT DOUBLEMINT SMILE

I didn't see him for a month, and then, holy feces, there he was in third-period English. "Why did Pickle come back to school?"

"Truant officer," Sammie Davis Jr. said.

"How do you know?"

Sammie watched my face. "My moms was the school secretary when they closed Fredrick Douglass. Two weeks ago, she caught a gig with Mr. Boone. She said Pick's one strike away from spending the rest of the semester at Lost Boys Ranch."

Reform school. And now there's a Negro in the school office? Bob Dylan, the times they are a changing.

Mrs. Lane commanded our attention by moving between Sammie Davis and me. "Cutie, MBe has just told us that Fitzgerald doesn't take women seriously. Do you agree?"

I shook my head, an admission that I hadn't been listening.

"Please, read this line." She pointed to a page in my *Gatsby* novel.

"Dishonesty in a woman is a thing you never blame deeply," I read. "I was casually sorry, and then I forgot."

"Did Nick blow off Jordan Baker's dishonesty?"

I shrugged at MBe. "I guess so. Nick saw Jordan cheat at golf. But she was a foxy chick, and mysterious, and a heck of an athlete. So yeah, the dude probably slid her a pass."

"Because she was desirable." Mrs. Lane drilled deeper. "And is that ironic?"

"Sure, because Nick says he's the only honest man he knows." And then, for a reason I couldn't explain, I felt compelled to cover for Nick. "But beautiful people always get passes."

Probably five people in the entire classroom were really, actually interested in Gatsby and Daisy. The rest were window gazing, waiting, of course, for the lunch bell. We shared an un-air conditioned room with thirty-one warm bodies on a late-spring morning, and Sophomore Lit was apparently just too uninspiring for Pickle Andersen. His eyelids flew at half-mast for two minutes before he gave up interest in remaining conscious.

"Don't you dare lay your head on that desk," Mrs. Lane aimed a low voice at his ear.

And that's when six trivial events flowed into a nexus that changed my life. One: Pickle's head propelled upwards like the bobblehead Precious Jesus on the dash of Nan's Chevy. Two: he blearily eyeballed Mrs. Lane. The third: cheerleaders and pep squad girls were permitted to show up late on football Fridays, so O'Murphy Scott sauntered in wearing a virgin-white letter sweater, scarlet D centered on her chest. In a moment of translucence, sunlight struck those morning-glory blue eyes. And so that sizzle was number four: every school has a babe that sizzles, and for Hell Creek High that was O'Murphy Scott.

It all just struck me as hilarious. I suppressed a giggle–actually, it was more of an involuntary snort. That was number five, and after that my numbering gets a little fuzzy, because then O'Murphy snickered at my snort, and then she flashed that Doublemint smile to everyone, and then all thirty-one of us cracked up. So maybe it was seven or eight.

O'Murphy turned and grinned as if she really admired me.

Gee, I wish you wouldn't look at me like that. Don't you know I'm stuck on you?

And that's when Pickle shot me a look, and I realized my giggle had been *l'erreur fatale*.

Mrs. Lane–probably the smallest teacher any of us had ever seen–stepped into Pickle's line of sight and intercepted his warning shot.

"Is Teach an actual midget?" Sammie Davis Jr. murmured from one side of her mouth.

"Hey! I love Mrs. Lane. She's my fave." I wanted a girlfriend just like her. Anyway, she was more like a teammate than a teacher. She was energetic, she valued us, and she assumed we could do whatever she challenged. "Anyway, there's no height requirement for teachers."

Sammie grinned.

"Seriously." I always say "seriously" when I'm not serious. "Legally, she's not midget anyway. She'd have to be four-foot six or under. Look it up. It's in the dictionary."

"What's Gatsby really about?" Mrs. Lane demanded of Pickle.

Pick said nothing. He turned so red I could've lit a Lucky Strike off his nose.

"Best guess?" Sammie whispered. "Pickle hasn't touched a book since *The Little Engine that Could*."

But instead of answering in that preposterously strangled school-girl voice, Pickle turned to me. And in that moment, I felt a little sorry for him.

Mrs. Lane intercepted again. "Anyone want to let Dillon off the hook? What's one theme of *The Great Gatsby*?"

That put me between a rock and a rigid spot. Three years ago, our seventh-grade teacher had passed out his own list of the one hundred greatest books in the English language. I'd spent that summer on *1984, Animal Farm, Catcher in the Rye, East of Eden, Gatsby, Grapes of Wrath, Lord of the Flies* and *The Maltese Falcon.* Everyone knows I'm hyperliterate, so Pick glared red when I didn't answer the question for him. I should've, but my two worst qualities picked that very moment to stir up a doodie pile. I admit, I get a little Rosa Parks when someone tries to intimidate me. My second-worst quality is that I gloat when a teacher the size of Shirley Temple hands Dill Pickle his head. Which is sorta the point of gloating: some testicles-for-brains thinks he won–but whoa, sorry, Dillon Andersen just lost.

"It's a love story?" O'Murphy answered without really knowing.

Sammie leaned into me. "This is the chick who put the choo in your coo-coo-ca-choo?"

I blushed like a virgin bride. Sammie and I also shared a spring semester French class. "*Respect, s'il vous plaît.* One day, I intend to make O'Murphy Scott an honest woman."

"Anybody? Anybody? What's the one overarching theme of *The Great Gatsby?*" Mrs. Lane stared at Pickle but addressed me: "I'll give you a hint: Cortez, is Daisy Buchanan for sale?"

"For sale? That's such an unmusical way to put it . . . "

She and Sammie Davis chuckled, and the rest of the class laughed on my cue.

Mrs. Lane smirked affectionately. "Avoid being the class clown for another four minutes."

"Yeah, I guess 'Money is the root of all evil' is the big theme. The whole book is about how people act differently because they have money."

"So how does wealth affect all the rich people?"

"Well, Daisy ditched Gatsby because he was as poor as a red-dirt Okie. And she married Tom because he . . . "

"So she sold herself into marriage slavery?" Mrs. Lane interrupted.

"Her parents have cash registers for hearts, so no ma'am, I think they sold her into marriage. And her cousin, Nick, is a moneychanger. And freeloaders come to Gatsby's parties just to mooch his food and liquor; most of them don't even know what he looks like. Gatsby's bud fixed the World Series so they could bet on it. Myrtle Wilson is a cheap version of Daisy; she prostituted herself to Tom because he's rich. So, didn't everybody sell themselves?"

"Including Gatsby?"

"Yeah. Sure. Tom Buchanan was right. Gatsby became a criminal."

"So he could . . ." Mrs. Lane prompted.

" . . . so he could get rich and take his best shot at Daisy."

"And so . . . "

"I think Gatsby sold his soul to the devil," I concluded. "That's what people do; that's how they get what they want."

"Yeah," O'Murphy and Sammie chorused. O'Murphy cut her eyes at me, something she did more and more these days.

Pickle watched O'Murphy and turned to me. I saw his suspicion. So did O'Murphy. "And . . . " she started.

"Murph?" Mrs. Lane asked.

" . . . well, devil sounds like evil? When you deal with the devil, you're choosing evil?"

"MBe, do you agree with O'Murphy?"

I thought for a second. "Is what O'Murphy said a moral truth?"

"A profound moral truth," Mrs. Lane said. "Yes. I think that is a *mot juste*–just the right word. Does that make Gatsby a moral monster?"

My classmates looked surprised by Mrs. Lane's question. Like me, they'd probably just assumed Gatsby couldn't be the villain if the story were named for him.

"Yeah, hmm, themes," Mrs. Lane asked. "Let's recall, what is a theme?"

O'Murphy answered Mrs. Lane with a question: "It's the central idea?"

"Yes, thanks, that is the textbook definition. MBe, can you tell me in your own words what Murph means?" Mrs. Lane paused. "How can you tell–just by reading–what is a theme?"

"It's something that keeps coming up," I said. "The slick cars, the food, the parties, the rich peo . . . "

"You see, Curtis and O'Murphy recognize the themes of *The Great Gatsby*. And how do they do that, Dillon?"

Pickle glared at me again.

"Look at me," Mrs. Lane stepped into Pickle's line of sight a third time.

The bell rang.

Saved. Wow, eleven-twenty-five A.M. already.

"Before you leave, take one of these books," Mrs. Lane handed a thin hardback to Pickle. "I think you may like this. A Tulsa girl your age set *The Outsiders* right here in Oklahoma, and the publisher sent us a box of advance copies."

As much as Pickle detested school, I loved learning. I was always disappointed when my school day was done. Mother worked split shifts, so she watched afternoon soap operas–*The Edge of Night* was her fave. School was my daytime soap: gossip, sports, pep rallies, library, Romeo-and-Juliet romances . . . When classes were over, I had to deliver papers and go home. I stuffed *The Outsiders* and *Gatsby* into my canvas newspaper bag.

"Cortez!" Mrs. Lane began. "You're one of my best students. But you underestimate yourself, don't you? You ought to get to know yourself better. You're creative with words. You've got a sardonic literary wit. When you talk, other people grin, but I don't think you'd smile if you had a coat hanger in your mouth. How can people know you're a loveable person if you never smile? Devote five minutes a day to smiling–smiling–and it will come naturally."

"Is that the sound of B.S.?"

"Maybe. But, of course, you've never tried it, have you?

Good point. Maybe that's why I'm such a loner.

"Do you think other students see you as a nerd?"

"Maybe. Or maybe it's because I am a nerd."

"Okay, well, maybe I'm too intellectual too. That's what my husband says, anyway. You know where that word came from? Dr. Seuss had a creature in . . . "

" . . . *If I Ran the Zoo*," I finished her sentence.

"A nerkle, a nerd, and a seersucker too. You're fortunate to have a brilliant mind," Mrs. Lane said. "One-thirty-five IQ. That's a great enabler."

So they say. Lucky to have a genius IQ. But being smart separates me from the herd. It's why the other kids don't like me. It's why I can't communicate with girls. I think it must be why I have nothing in common with anti-intellectual dunderheads like the Andersens, why they bully me out of their sight. Maybe it's just human to be hostile to outsiders. I need to find a tribe of smart, educated people. But where do such people live?

"See you Monday," Mrs. Lane called out.

CHAPTER 10

EPIC FIGHT

Pickle stood outside Mrs. Lane's classroom. "Parking lot, Cutie. After school."

I didn't see his lips move. I'd been watching his eyes.

Sammie Davis Jr. looked solemn. "You gonna fight Pickle?"

I shook my head. "Why should I?"

"Because you can't back down."

"That's written in the student handbook?"

Sammie's hand clasped my shoulder. "Because everyone will know. The good news is, it's Pickle, not Spit or Scoot."

"Right on. Write that on my tombstone: 'He had the great good fortune of being pummeled by the golem Dillon, not the demon Spit, nor the banshee Scooter.'"

"Pick's a bully, but he's not mean."

"What a consolation!"

"It is. When he wins, he'll stop. He won't maim you. I haven't had a chance to tell you what Tommy did. I watched him fight the doggie."

"What? When?"

"Friday night."

"At the Freeze? The night we talked to MBe?"

"At the Sinclair station. You left before I did. I was waiting for Daddy-o in the parking lot when Spit saw the soldier pull up in a cherry-red Barracuda. After they drag Main, doggie and O'Murphy come back to the Freeze and stop a few inches from me. O'Murphy's not even sitting on her side–she's sittin' all the way on the doggie's console. Spit just jumps in the doggie's 'Cuda. Doggie says, 'To what do we owe this faint pleasure?'"

"Mockery in the face of fear," I said. "Gotta admire that."

"Spit points at the station. Tells O'Murphy, 'Bring your new boyfriend. Ten o'clock.'"

Ma Andersen's Sinclair was directly across Highway 81 from the Freeze parking lot. That's why they'd been sitting in Spit's jalopy. They were lying in wait for the dogface.

"Spit says, 'Tommy's gonna kick the shit out of you.'"

"The doggie's not scared of a high-school janitor, but he sees O'Murphy's scared shitless, so he raps, 'Should I bring a few girlfriends, just to make sure it's a fair fight?'

"Spit says, 'Bring every doghead at Fort Sill. We don't give a rat's ass.' And then he says, 'You bring Murph too, so she can watch.'

"Doggie says, 'What if I don't?'"

"And Spit says, 'Tommy'll probably beat the ssshit of out her.'"

Pig Binson approached from the opposite direction.

"Hey, Pig." Sammie smiled.

He tried to backhand her.

"Hey," I chided him. "What's that about?"

"She called me Pig."

"Sammie's half your size. And she's a girl. And we all call you Pig."

"That's not my name."

"Cutie's not mine, but everybody pins it on me."

Pig made the you-don't-understand face.

"I offended you," Sammie said. "Okay. I'm sorry. What do you want to be called?"

"My name."

"No sweat then. Siggy."

"Seymour," he insisted.

"You're right." I withdrew a No. 2 pencil from my pocket protector. "Bend a knee, mighty Seymour."

He looked at me askance.

With an exaggerated gesture, I arched the yellow pencil over his left shoulder. "First of His Name, Principal Acolyte of Higher Education . . . "

Seymour grinned self-consciously as the pencil swung to his right shoulder.

" . . . defender of Hell Creek High School." I suspended the pencil over his eyes. "I knight thee! Arise, noble sir."

He beamed goofily.

"Now look. Sir Seymour. Do me a favor."

His eyes turned down. "Yeah."

"Be a friend to Lady Sammie. She's what, five-three? Buck ten?"

Sammie nodded. Seymour didn't move.

"You know, defenders live by a code. We help each other. We respect each other. We fight only to protect others. Be her gallant friend?"

That sank in. With a half-grimace, Seymour acknowledged his responsibility, plopped a hand on Sammie's shoulder, and silently walked away. Sammie smiled her reply at Seymour.

"So, you were saying, the Andersens belong in trees," I said.

"Darwin had it backwards," she agreed.

"Absolute proof that apes evolved from Andersens," I said.

"Yep," Sammie said. "Stone Age Boy says his piece in front of O'Murphy, so the doggie's gotta show up for the showdown. Long story short: Daddy-o was working OT, so I was still there for a legendary beat-down, just across the parking lot of their mama's service station."

"O'Murphy too?"

"Splitsville. Scooter's between the gas pumps when the doggie drives up. Lights are off; everybody's gone. Doggie opens his car door and Scooter kicks it so hard, the window cracks on the doggie's skull. Only thing holds it together is the new-car window sticker. Door bounces, and this time Scoot slams the doggie's noggin' on the frame. Kicks it over and over. Just whales on Soldier Boy till the doggie's as near to dead meat as he's gonna be without bein' evacuated from a war zone. Scooter really, actually grinds this doggie into an Oscar Meyer. No way the doggie gets to lift a hand. Daddy-o works at Hell Creek ER. Said next morning, an ambulance transferred the doggie to Fort Sill Army Hospital."

Sammie's tight lips showed her contempt. "Dirtiest fight I ever seen or heard of. And dumbass doggie didn't bring nobody to watch his back. Hell, even if he had, there's movie mean and there's Andersen mean. They're that scary."

My eyes must have bugged like a toad on blacktop, but I pretended. "So the Andersens scramble a soldier's head like Humpty Dumpty. What's scary about that? Well, next week."

"You really ain't comin' to your own fight?"

"Sure. When 7-Eleven serves Slurpees in Hell."

"You don't have to beat him; you just have to show."

"And his brothers? What if they gang up on me?"

Sammie grabbed my arm. "Dude, fight him here. On the school grounds. In front of people. That's your protection. I'll watch your back."

"Yeah. Right. You're a girl."

CHAPTER 11

OUT OF THE BLUE

After I finished my Saturday routes, I drove by O'Murphy's house and learned how the slightest act could have the greatest consequences.

She called an hour later, out of the blue. "Cutie? This is Murph."

"I. Uhh." *That used up just about every word I could think of.*

"Did you ride by on your motorcycle?"

"How would you know?" *And why are you calling me? And why now?*

"It wasn't Richie. I know what his Indian sounds like. It was yours. And then I heard Tommy's Yamaha. But nobody stopped."

Scooter followed me? "O'Murphy, would you . . . " I almost asked if she wanted to ride with me on Sunday morning's routes. I'd formed this image of her arms wrapped around my chest, of me pointing out Jupiter and Venus and our shared constellation, Libra. "No."

"No, that wasn't you riding by?"

"Uhh."

"Cutie, do you like me? I mean, really, really like me?"

"Like you?" *Scooter Andersen will beat me a lot worse than that doggie.* "You don't mean, like a friend? I—I've never really liked anybody before. I don't know what it feels like."

"Well then, okay." Her voice wasn't hurt, it sounded–what–vacant? "Bye!"

You are such a coward. She called. All you had to do was say something.

* * *

I delivered my Monday morning route and crawled back into bed. *Who do you want to avoid more, O'Murphy or the Andersens?*

Mother woke me two hours later. "Aren't you going to school?"

"Mother, I don't feel good."

She touched my forehead. "It's not hot."

She knows I was faking, but she let me stay home.

On Tuesday, I skipped first hour to avoid O'Murphy, then ditched third hour so I wouldn't run into her or Pickle. I went to every class on Wednesday, but neither were there.

On Thursday, she walked into Mrs. Macintosh's class with Scooter. His blood-red hair looked like a fox had died on his head. He caught me looking and returned a stare full of menace.

On Friday evening, I resolved to find my courage. Mrs. Larsson answered the phone.

Speak. "Mrs. Larsson, my name is Curtis. Is O'Murphy there?"

"Yes, Cutie, she's outside with Marybeth. She'll be with you in a minute."

Feces. I was so scared, my mouth had gone dry.

"Hi, Cutie," O'Murphy came on the phone, no trace of Sunday in her voice.

While I fumbled with what to say, she took a breath and then schmoozed for two minutes straight. "So, Cutie. You called me, and I've been a Chatty O'Murphy."

This must be what girl talk sounds like. Scared I'd hang up, I blurted. "There's a new movie. Tomorrow night. *Dr. Zhivago.*"

"Oh, I've heard it's sooo romantic. Are you gonna take me?"

OhmysweetbabyJesus! She actually asked me? "Sure. If you want."

"On your motorcycle?" she verified.

"Uh. Sure."

"Okay. Gotta trot. I have another guest. Seven o'clock show?"

CHAPTER 12

STOOD UP

I worked Saturday's two-hour lunch rush at the Freeze, then read a quarter of *The Outsiders*. I couldn't decide whom to root for: the socs were rich; the greasers were poor like me. But the Andersens were greasers, and I hated them.

Just before I started my routes, MBe plopped at my table. "Has O'Murphy called you?"

I shook my head.

"I can't believe her," the messenger grimaced. "Richie came over right after you called last night. He asked her to the Senior Banquet."

"Tonight?" My mouth popped open. "She can't go with him. We're seeing *Dr. Zhivago*!"

* * *

Mother was in the kitchen, about to leave for work when I got home.

"Splitting shifts this weekend?"

She grimaced. Great for Casa la Bello Pizza, but merciless on her because work took up morning, noon and night: ten A.M. to two P.M., then six to ten P.M. "Some flit-tail girl called."

"What's a flit-tail?"

She fixed motherly disapproval upon the first girl who'd ever called me on the telephone. "Said her name was O'Murphy. And she's a flit tail because girls don't call boys."

Poop. We only had one phone; it was in the kitchen. I dialed, turned my back, and stretched the four-foot cord into the living room for every inch of privacy.

Mr. Larsson's voice sounded peeved. "O'Murphy's at the formal shop with her mother. May she call you tomorrow?"

Must be picking out a gown. I kept my voice barely above a whisper. "Could you tell her I'll call back at six-fifteen?"

"Surely."

I threw both routes as fast as I could, not porching papers even at houses that had tipped me. My Honda was cruising for home when something rattled and struck my right boot.

I braked to a stop and rocked the bike onto its kickstand. Grease snaked across my jeans leg. I walked back ten yards to retrieve the chain on the shoulder. The master link had broken. And something else: bright aluminum shavings and rubber rubble around the wheel hub. Mr. Presley had taken final payment from my check three weeks ago. And now my motorbike–four months old and therefore a month outside its ninety-day warranty–was DRT: dead right there.

Feces on a stick. I coasted to the bottom of the hill and started pushing. My watch said five forty-five. *You have to call O'Murphy. And say what? That she can share my Schwinn's banana seat?*

I got home at six-seventeen P.M., dialed the phone, and hung up when Mr. Larsson's Electronic Secretary answered. I showered in two minutes flat, brushed my teeth, and changed into a white Ban-Lon shirt and O'Murphy-blue hip-hugger jeans. I phoned again and taped a message this time: "O'Murphy, this is Curtis. The chain is off my motorcycle. Please, just meet me at the movie."

Even better. If she can't reach me, she'll feel compelled to come. Nothing left to do except pedal thirty blocks to the Ritz Theater on my Schwinn. I could be there in fifteen minutes.

Sweating and puffing, I took my place in the ticket line. A newsreel, two previews and a cartoon always came first, so the feature wouldn't start for fifteen minutes anyway. I inched closer to the cashier's booth. Seven people in front of me, then five. *She'll come. This is a test. If she's the girl for me, she'll choose the smart kid over the rich boy.*

Three people were ahead of me, and I let another man go first. A girl got out of a car down the block. From the back, she could have passed for a tall O'Murphy. A boy joined her. Now I was first in line. I hesitated and looked behind me.

"Girl stand you up?" the cashier asked intuitively.

Eat me. "Two." Defiantly, I handed over two dollars and pocketed both tickets.

Twenty-five minutes passed, and I still stood there. The cartoon and the previews were over. Zhivago was probably in medical school by now.

"You want a refund on those tickets?" the cashier asked.

My stomach slid into freefall. I didn't know what to say. Finally, I handed back one ticket. "Her name is O'Murphy. Please tell her I'll be on the back row."

The cashier nodded.

And at that moment, Scooter rode by and glared.

Yeah? Thought O'Murphy was with me, didn't you?

* * *

She called the next day. "Cutie, I am so sorry for the mixup. Maybe next Saturday?"

"Mixup?" *That's it. I finally know what to do. The scalpel will be my weapon.*

"Won't *Dr. Zhivago* still be playing?" Her voice sounded uncomfortable.

Insert the knife: "O'Murphy, I like you better than any girl I know . . ."

"Oh, thank you. You're such a nice guy. Is your motorcycle fixed yet? I could use a ride to school Monday. My step goes to work early, and Mother will be in Oklahoma Cit . . . "

Bury the steel: " . . . but I know you went with Richie to the banquet . . . "

"Ohhh! I will never speak to him again. Some varsity type invited him to an after-party, and he ditched me! He asked if I wouldn't mind bumming a ride home. I wanted to find a pay phone and call you for a ride, but I haven't memorized your number yet."

Twist the blade: "I waited for you. I left a ticket at the booth. Maybe it's still there, if you want to see *Dr. Zhivago*."

"Cutie, I am sooo sorry. I . . . Please understand. It was the Senior Banquet. I was the only sophomore invited."

Good. Plead for understanding.

"You'd have done the same thing. Wouldn't you? If someone–if a soc–if a really, really pretty and popular soc, who you liked sooo much, had invited you . . . "

"You weren't my first choice, O'Murphy Scott. You were my onl . . . Look, I don't think I would be a very good boyfriend."

"That's not tru . . . "

"You don't need Richie Rich. You have options. But not Scooter. You can't trust . . . "

"Don't tell me what to do." O'Murphy seemed steamed by advice.

She was the bad guy, but I remained convinced that our almost-relationship would always be the sweetest, the rawest, the most magical year of high school.

CHAPTER 13

CARELESS PEOPLE

Sixth-hour study hall was a gift: an entire hour in our high school library. I finished *The Outsiders,* a tiny masterpiece written by a girl my age about life in her city. Not New York, not Los Angeles, not Dallas. Tulsa, not even two hundred miles away.

Can it be that simple? Can I write about the teenagers in Hell Creek, about how high school endows the jocks and the cheerleaders with exceptional looks and groovy personalities, but afflicts the nerds and the losers with ruddy faces and funky personas?

I'd started with Alcott in the literature aisle and, midway through sophomore second semester, read through Graham Greene. I had even read a magazine article on the Q Document, about how Satan had tempted Jesus in the desert. Tomorrow, I'd move onto Hemingway's short stories and consume "Big Two-Hearted River." After the final bell rang, I'd passed the hall leading to the back door when Spidey sense raked my spine. I turned around.

Like the Grim Reaper, Pickle Andersen had stalked me to the west exit, where my Schwinn was parked. "It was funny last week. Is it funny now?"

"Hey, Pickle, sorry. I didn't mean to laugh. It probably sounded mean. I apologize."

"PPPickle!" Spit sputtered from the janitor's closet and fell into step beside his brother.

Two Andersens. Jesus, I might need your need help.

Spit's gray uniform shirt hung from arms that were so short, his fingers probably couldn't reach the bottoms of his own pockets. "Are you ssshitting me! You gonna let him get away with that?" His Cyrano de Bergerac nose flushed into cheeks so red they appeared well slapped.

"My name is Dillon." Pickle's snarl was as crimson as his Hell Creek Demons T-shirt. "Not Dill. Not Pick. Not Dill Pickle."

"This is the guy who laughed at you?" Spit habitually pulled up his Dickies; the hems behind his heels dragged in tatters.

"Okay. Dillon, I promise . . . " I reached for the back door. *Maybe I can outrun them.*

Scooter jerked open the door.

Hell, hell, the gang's all here.

"What's a matter? Can't ssstand up?" Spit sputtered.

"You're as funny as a ssscreen door on a ssspace ssship." I instantly regretted that. Mockery is an underappreciated form of humor, especially when avoiding a confrontation.

Spit turned even redder and said to Scooter, "Cutie called Dillon 'Pickle.'"

Scoot faked concern. "Oh. You shouldn't. He hates that. We're the only ones who call him Dill Pickle. Ain't that right, Dill Pickle!"

Pickle inflated like an agitated pufferfish. "You're afraid of me."

Five students saw the scared in me and stopped to watch the Friday Afternoon Fight.

"Okay, Dillon, A: big deal, everybody's afraid of you. And B:" I dropped my voice, "don't let your brothers do this. Don't let them humiliate you."

Spit's face darkened like a beet. "What are you saying about my brothers?"

I was going to die anyway, so I did to Spit what I'd done to Biggy. Both wore their jeans too long. I lowered my pants past my hips and hunched my shoulders. "Amos Andersen," I announced, arms above my head. The crowd tittered.

Bullies don't care, do they, Gatsby? They smash, they retreat back into their vast carelessness, and they leave other people to clean up their messes. Scoot and Spit pretend to protect their brother but, of course, they torment him. Time to expose the Andersens for what they are. "Dillon, don't let your brothers push us into a fight. I've never done anything to you."

"He's talkin' shit about us," Scooter sneered to Pickle.

I focused on Pickle. "Dillon, we can be friends."

Spit pulled a custard doughnut out of a bag. "Who's calling the ssshots, Pick? You gonna let Egghead talk you out of this?"

I took the oval pastry from Spit's hand and stuck it on my head. I grinned and mugged the crowd: "I'm an egghead."

Now the crowd smirked knowingly at each other.

Spit's face turned apoplectic. With a thumb and index finger, he flicked the doughnut. Yellow jelly flew onto the tip of my nose.

I tasted it. "Mumm. Custard's my fave too. Okay, Spit, I know you don't come from a warm, loving family, so someone needs to tell you: you're overcompensating like crazy. The girls already know you have a Ken-doll penis."

Could you say anything stupider?

Spit leaned in. "Why don't you go hang yoursssself?" His sibilant droplets hit my ear.

Well, I keep thinking about killing myself. Maybe, after this is over . . .

Time slowed. I knew everyone in the crowd. They were mostly socials: Poodle Brown could've been a drum major if she'd been born with a Y chromosome. Twitch Baker lived on Country Club Drive; both of her sisters were cheerleaders. Twitch should have been, but she lost her sense of balance back in the fourth grade when her right ear got infected. It quivered so much, we called her Twitch. Minute Mann, her boyfriend since U.S. Grant Elementary, was where he always was, beside Twitch.

O'Murphy stood beside Sammie Davis Jr. Both looked concerned. I opened my mouth to say something, but Murph disappeared.

"Knock him down!" Spit shouted to Pickle. He held up both hands like a circus barker. "Destroy this skinny queerbait!"

Twenty students formed their own coliseum to watch the lions eat–well, me, actually. I was the apostate in this arena. My turn. I raised my voice. "Some people–let's call them heartless bullies–use the term 'queerbait' to taunt smaller boys into fights they can't possibly win."

"He's too ssscared to fight," Spit interpreted for the crowd, "and he's too ssscared to run."

Perceptive, my dear Sssnidely Whiplash. But how do Pickle and Spit and Scooter and Biggy know that? I'm not afraid of blood, roller coasters or leftover chicken. How do bullies know which guy won't fight?

"Kick him." Spit, who was twenty now, had wrestled in high school. He leaned into his brother's face like a coach. "Then sssweep. Take hisss legs out."

Pickle kicked my thigh with his pin-box boot.

"Pickle, don't." It was like reasoning with a terrible two-year-old. But I didn't feel much pain. *I had never realized that before. Is pain easier to ignore during a fight?*

"He's ssstill ssstanding, you pussss!" Spit slurred. "Sssweep!"

"Anyone got a hanky?" I touched my chin. "Amos, you've got a little drool right here."

Spit took the bait and touched his chin.

"No," I moved my hand across my cheek, "a little to the right."

Spit's jaw dropped when people in the crowd grinned.

"Joke. Sorry. That hurt your feelings?" *Every time I zing, you stop to figure it out. Because your IQ is the caloric equivalent of Melba toast. Nineteen calories a slice.*

Frustrated, Pickle looked at Spit but swept at my knees.

A half-dozen football players could've stopped the fight, but they just watched and smiled. Scooter leaned against the door frame with that dangerous James Dean grin.

This jerk has been given so many advantages, but he uses them to seduce a nice girl. "Why do you hurt your own brother, Spit?"

"Wha'd you say?" Spit's soul darkened his eyes.

That's when I was most afraid. But it was also when I felt my face flush. When I get mad, my brain blocks my vision and I lose control. *Careful, anger resteth in the bosom of fools.* My right hand clasped Spit's left shoulder like I was imparting wisdom. "Sorry, I'll speak more slowly. I said a low IQ is nothing to be ashamed of."

Scoot knocked my hand off Spit's shoulder without even moving his jackal eyes, and then punched both my jaws. Whap, whap.

"You like that, Stick Boy?" Scoot smiled cunningly.

"Kick the shit out of him," Spit boiled. It was an order.

Pickle kicked me. Wham.

My left knee buckled.

Sammie Davis Jr. moved in front of me and mouthed, "Cross your arms."

Pickle kicked. I X-ed. His boot heel snagged between my fore-arms. Off balance, he couldn't pull back, and he couldn't lift his foot higher without falling. His shoulders hunched round like Boo-Boo Bear, and he pitched forward to keep his balance. His panic sounded childlike, especially from such a badass. "Let go!"

If you show mercy, maybe he will too. I dropped my hands.

He kicked again.

I crossed my arms, and his heel fell into my right hand again.

"Leggo!" he screamed, terrified as a wiener over a campfire.

A movie played in my mind. *If I lift his boot over my head, will he fall and crack his brain like an egg on the sidewalk? Can I then leap onto his chest, pin both his arms with my knees, and beat his nose bloody? No. Don't. Respect the code. Fight only to protect others.*

"If you don't let me go, I'm gonna kick the shit out of you!" Pickle's voice rose an octave.

"If you promise to leave me alone."

"All right. Let go."

Now I felt a different vibe from the crowd: from first grade to high school, the Andersens had picked on dozens of us. The twenty or so who surrounded us sighed a crescendo, relieved that the Andersens' reign of terror might end. I saw admiration on their faces. For me. I released Pickle's foot. "Are you neo-Neanderthals done?"

Spit and Pickle looked at each other, dumbfounded.

Oh feces. If you had just kept your self-righteous mouth shut, this humiliation would be over. There was O'Murphy again. Out of breath.

Spit turned to his brother. "Kick his assss," he commanded.

Given permission to break his word, Pickle kicked for my stomach.

I X-ed once more, and this time, I looked him in the eyes and lifted an inch.

For a moment, his free knee wobbled. Nothing was within reach, not even his brothers. His fear was uncontrollable. His eyes shrieked his horror.

"Break this up!" We all knew Mr. Boone's voice.

I held fast to Pickle's foot.

Scooter gave me the death stare. But where had Spit–our high-school janitor–gone?

I wanted to tell Mr. Boone that they'd started it, but that would break the Ninth Commandment: Thou shalt not bear witness against thy fellow student. Even if they're kicking thy butt across the parking lot.

Mrs. Lane moved between us. "Cutie, let go of Dillon's foot."

I let go.

"Shake hands," the principal commanded.

I held out my hand, feeling more adult than I ever had. "Dillon, I never wanted to fight. I have no reason to hate you. Forget your brothers. Let's be friends." In that moment, something changed in Dillon's eyes. I saw no anger.

O'Murphy looked directly at me and then, a guilty look on her face, took Scooter's arm.

Now what did that mean?

"Both of you. Take off," Mr. Boone commanded.

"But," I started.

"Don't come back next week," Boone didn't want conversation.

"It wasn't my fault."

"Suspensions are automatic for fighting on the school grounds," Mrs. Lane interpreted. "You'll have to appeal to the school board to get back in class."

CHAPTER 14

WHAT IF A MARINE TRAINED YOU?

Something hit my back and I started shaking.

"Dude! Epic fight!"

"Sammie Davis! Don't do that!" I shot her a nasty look. "You scared the poop out of me."

"Sorry," she smiled. "Didn't mean to startle you."

I wish I could smile like Sammie Davis Jr. She smiled winningly. She smiled jokingly. She was always either smiling or getting ready to smile.

"But you told them off. And you *had* Pickle!" Sammie smiled her jubilation.

"That wasn't a fight; that was a train wreck."

Sammie smiled triumphantly. "No, Cutie! I'm proud. You're everybody's hero. You stood up to all three Andersens. All three! And you're even faster than Pickle. You could've fractured his skull. Which is what you do next time. You get someone down, you make sure they don't get up."

"Next time? What about his brothers? What if Spit catches me outside the Freeze? You don't get arms that short unless your family's been crossbreeding since the Age of Reptiles."

"No, man," Sammie deflated. "Don't let them scare you. They'll just keep doing it."

"What am I supposed to do?"

"Just what you did. Fight."

"Great advice. And get humiliated?"

"Man, they didn't put you down. They tried. But even if they kill you, they can't eat you."

"So my mother often says. But she doesn't have to fight Pickle. Neither do you."

"No one bothers me because they know I'm not afraid. And even if some chick does kick my ass, I'll kick hers too, and then she'll respect me."

Is that really all it takes to gain respect? Act tough? "I don't know how to fight."

Sammie's eyes widen with shock. "You ain't never been in no fight?"

"Yeah. My brother. About a thousand times."

"You hate him?"

"No, he hates me. I regret him. He's an economy-sized rectum about a third of the time. And I'm disappointed I didn't get a best friend like you for a brother."

"You can't beat him?"

"In a fair fight? He's got fifty pounds on me."

"Dude, everybody's got fifty pounds on us. You can't not fight them all."

Truer words. And Sammie Davis is a head shorter than me. But why is she unafraid? "How'd you learn to fight?"

"My brothers. I boxed their ears to make 'em leave me alone." Sammie changed the topic. "What do you want to be? I wanna be an astronaut. If I could close my eyes and imagine what I want to do, I'd be on the next Apollo mission. Dorothy Dandridge, dancin' on the moon."

"I want to be Fitzgerald. Or even better–Capone. I want to storm the Andersens' house and vigilante Pickle and Scooter. Then I want to Tommy Gun their mother for raising these three apes. Spit will be the last one. I want that fascist to suck the end of my barrel and beg. I'll write my autobiography while I'm on Death Row."

"Jeez, that's actually kinda funny," Sammie's eyes widened. "I'd pay to watch."

"Dying's easy. Irony is hard."

"I thought it was just something you needed in your blood," Sammie smiled at the old joke. "You know what would be sooo groovy? Your dad was a Marine?"

"Yeah. Island fighter. World War II."

"What if your dad trained you how to fight? Marines know judo."
What an excellent idea.

We sat quietly for a moment, and then Sammie Davis spontaneously brought up O'Murphy. "We sit next to each other in Chem. She wanted to know if I like Scooter."

"What did you say?"

"I asked why she liked him. She said, 'You'd never know it. He's really sweet. One day, he left me this huge heart-shaped box of candy at my door.'"

My jaw dropped. *O'Murphy thought of everyone but me.*

Sammie Davis caught my unspoken look. "Don't worry, I'll never tell. But one more time–why don't you fight?"

"Don't you believe that if we all stopped fighting . . . "

"A'course. No war. Better planet. My biggest bro is already in the navy. Vietnam. And you know the black man, who are all my brothers, they unjustly carryin' more than they share of the burden. I'm gonna join the air force–they treat women better. But you get drafted, you have to fight."

"If I'm a grunt. But if I test high, I'll probably be radioman. Or a code breaker."

"So what're you going to do now?"

"Go back to school and grab my bike. I still have to deliver my paper routes."

Sammie Davis smiled. "When are you going to fix your motorcycle?"

"Can't. I bought a master link to fix the chain. But it turns out, when the chain broke, the hub kept spinning and stripped the aluminum baffles in the back wheel."

"Baffles?"

"Drive sections. The rear wheel won't go without them."

"How much does that cost?"

"Hundred for a new rear hub. Another twenty for the rubber baffles inside."

"Maybe your moms or your bro would spot you the green?"

I shook my head. "We're so poor, even the cockroaches have better housing."

Sammie smiled. "Maybe you could just fill the whole hub with rubber cement? If the glue breaks up, just squirt in some more."

"What if it gums up the hub and it won't move? I might not ever be able sell it."

"Can't get much for it if it don't work. Where's your dad live?"

"I have his post office box. Pallo something. We used to live in California, but it's not like I know how to get back there."

"California is west."

"Which way is west?"

"You some kind of savant? You read a thousand books and still you don't know your directions? Okay, memo: Dallas is south. East is–I don't know–for-god-sakes Alabama. Go north on 81 to Oklahoma City. Thataway," she pointed toward the high school. "Turn left and you'll wind up in the Pacific. Why don't you go? You could hitchhike."

"Sure, like the movie."

Sammie Davis Jr. grinned. Just a month ago we'd watched *The Hitch-Hiker* at the Ritz, about two fishermen who'd picked up a psychopath. Negroes were required to sit in the balcony. We went upstairs before the lights dimmed. Every head in the theater turned to watch the dark-skinned white dude with the light-skinned Negro chick.

"You think anyone would give me a ride after that movie?"

"One way to find out."

So just me, standing there alone on a road, sticking out my thumb until a car stops? How far would I have to walk? What would I do if cars didn't stop? And what if the wrong guy in the wrong car stopped?

CHAPTER 15

TWO KINDS OF PEOPLE

Despite what Sammie had said, I realized that life had been better when I'd been the most invisible kid in high school. I felt too miserable to do anything but write. I'd journaled ever since Mother had bought the portable Remington a couple of years ago, and I just wanted to sit at the typewriter and pour out everything that had happened.

"Chickenshit." Biggy slapped the back of my head.

The machine made so much noise, I hadn't heard him come into our room. "I'm not going to fight you."

"Because you're a chickenshit." Biggy flicked off an imaginary chip off my shoulder. "You just stood there and let Pickle kick you."

So, you watched. And did nothing? There were three of them.

"You know, there are two kinds of people. People who won't fight, like you . . . "

"And assholes, like you, who divide the world into kinds of people. Fighting is wrong. Martin Luther King says we have to end the cycle of hatred and violence.'"

"Yeah, well, you know what Martin Luther King is, and I hear your girlfriend looks just like him." My brother was two years older, but he wasn't two years wiser. Mother had always wondered why I didn't like Biggy. Before he was born, the Nazis brainwashed him with Hitler Youth propaganda.

"Not a good move, Einstein. Everyone says you're never gonna get a white girlfriend." He swatted both my cheeks, as if he were slapping sense into me.

"I'm not going to fight you," I insisted.

"Then I'm gonna keep slapping you. LOOK! I'm the man of this house, and I'm telling you, you have to fight. Hell, since you're too queer to do it yourself, I'm gonna to screw your girlfriend. Will you fight me then?"

"Who?"

"That little blonde from the wrong side of Eleventh Street. She'll do it with anybody who's got a car."

"Shut up. She's not like that." *I hope.*

"I gave her a ride last Saturday. She was walking home from the Junior-Senior Banquet. She asked if I was Cutie's brother. She knew I had a red Honda. She loves my Mustang."

"Please. Leave her alone."

"Awww! Are you begging?"

"Wendy will find out."

"You threatening me? Besides, we broke up."

Yeah, she told me. "Nobody really gets away with anything. Everyone eventually finds out what you hide."

"You tell Wendy and I'll kick your ass."

"And Wendy'll kick yours. And Scooter Andersen will tear your face off."

"Phwt! He fights girls." He grabbed my hair.

"Let go, damn it."

"Com'on. I'll teach you how to fight. Fight me, puss."

I shook my head.

"Then I'll buttface you until you do." He tossed me onto the bed and splatted onto my mouth and nose.

It was as if a thousand-pound bull were riding my face. I couldn't lift him off. I twisted and kicked my legs in panic. "I can't breathe!"

"Then hit me!" He was an immovable object.

I pounded his thighs and back.

He shifted his weight and allowed me to wrench out from under him. "See what happens when you fight for yourself? Gotta go to work. See ya."

Now would be an excellent time to kill myself.

CHAPTER 16

BLUE CHUNKS

"What happened?" Zandy sat on the arm of my chair.

"Why did it happen?" Marsha asked from the couch. Her four daughters filled the other two cushions.

I looked at no one.

"It was an accident," Mother said.

"No it wadn't!" Biggy said from the kitchen door. "Don't lie for him."

"Shut it."

"Just keeping the situation honest."

"Cutie, you tell us." Zandy baited her sister. "Was it just an accident?"

"He tried to off himself, but he just blew chunks instead," Biggy said.

"Blue chunks?" Marsha was confused.

"He urped the pills," Biggy interpreted joyously, "and his lunch."

"He threw up the aspirin," Zandy whispered across the room to Marsha.

"But why?" her daughter insisted.

"Biggy, you're the man of the family. You should know this is not something to laugh about," Mother said. "So shut it!"

"We're just concerned," Marsha soothed. "After all, you were three days in the hospital."

"Sister, I can't imagine why a fifteen-year-old would want to kill himself," Zandy said. "I think it's better if we get the truth out."

Here's the truth. After this little family reunion is done, I'm blowing this Popsicle stand.

"It was an accident!" Mother screamed at the living room itself.

"He took three dozen pills by accident," Biggy assured with a satisfied smirk to everyone.

I should've known thirty-two aspirin wouldn't do the trick. They looked too small.

"Was it like Sister said?" Zandy kept up her living room psycho-analysis. "And why three dozen aspirin?"

"Because that's all that was in the bottle," Biggy smirked his amusement.

Mother swatted Biggy's flattop harder than she meant to.

Biggy cringed but retorted, "Don't let this embarrass you, Mom. Hold your chin up. In fact, hold all three of your chins up." He started a self-congratulatory grin.

Mother's face turned rigid. She was always mortified when any-one referred to her weight.

Nan grabbed him by the wrist. Biggy had the muscle to pull away, but Nan had the tenacity not to let go. "You stay right there, Big Guy. You need to hear me."

Biggy's chest deflated. "I was just joking."

"That is your mother. Cutie is your brother. Do not disrespect your family." Nan pinched Biggy's lips together with her thumb and a fore-finger. "You think it's funny to hurt Sister's feelings?" Nan had referred to her first daughter as "Sister" ever since Virginia and Alexandria were children, and the nickname had stuck.

"You hurt people's feelings all the time," Biggy defended himself. "So does Aunt Zan."

"So we do." Nan looked chagrined for a moment, then owned up. "But I do it with good intentions. To help people. We don't intend it to be mean."

If Mother hadn't rolled her eyes first, I would've. "Biggy wasn't joking." That shut them up. Their silence was a magnet; every face swung to me like a compass. "And I wasn't either. I just didn't know how many pills I needed. But if you ever want to know, thirty-two aspirin just gives your brain the drizzling shits."

Every mouth unmuted at the same time, and the living room sounded like nine people in a phone booth.

"Everyone. Shut it!" Confused, they looked at Nan because the shout had sounded like her. But it was Mother.

I didn't think about what suicide would do to Mother. I just wanted to kill myself to get back at you, Biggy, but you've figured that out, haven't you? And you don't regret it. I think you're thrilled.

"Marsha." Zandy nodded at Marsha's daughters, who were drinking in every word.

"Go play in the back yard," Marsha snapped her fingers. They scattered like yearling calves. "Sister, why is Cutie so unhappy?"

Finally, a sensible question. Shall we make a list? Vin's a drunk. Mother's never home. And then there's her unspoken fall from grace–I think everyone knows Vin sleeps here part time, even though he's not her husband. And the Andersens. And Hell Creek is just a wart on the Oklahoma prairie. And I may have gotten expelled from school. And I lost two fights in one day.

"What did it accomplish," Zandy asked, "trying to kill yourself?"

"Do you think you're helping?" Mother screamed at her sister.

"Girls!" Nan scolded.

"I don't give a damn," Mother said. "Don't correct me. Zan started this; tell my sister."

"I'm telling you both. You're over forty years old. When are you going to decide to get along?" Nan sounded wounded. "What did I do wrong to have raised such hateful daughters?"

Hah! You deserved that, Mother.

"Cutie, weren't you going to write history books?"

"Actually, Nan, not textbooks, more like novels about historical events. I want to write history that's like TV for smart people."

"Won't that be grand," Nan encouraged.

"I hope he can do all that." Mother sounded dubious.

"Aint Sister," Marsha prodded, "are you ready to give Cutie his home-from-the-hospital present?"

I opened the package from Mother. Three brass figurines.

Mother rushed to explain. "A month ago, we were in the PX. I saw you looking at these brass statues, so I bought a giraffe, an elephant and two seagulls. They're for your room right now, but when you go off to college, you can decorate your dorm."

"Thanks." I held them up. "They're so heavy. Are they solid brass?"

"God damn!" Biggy whispered at the top of his voice. "We should just tie a frilly apron around my little brother."

You know all my buttons, don't you? Because you put them there.

"Biggy!" Mother shook her head at him. "You are not helping."

"I think they're gorgeous, Aint Sister." Marsha soothingly disagreed with Biggy. "And they're something you can collect, Cutie. I think they're the perfect gift for a boy. They're decorations, but they're–handsome."

"Why must you always ruin our get-togethers?" Mother accused Biggy. "You always wait until everyone is in the room, and just when we're having a good time, you say something to hurt Cutie."

"Is not the wool of the black sheep not as warm as the white?" Biggy's face feigned a wound.

Every eye followed as I headed for the bathroom. I checked the medicine cabinet. Mother had removed the razor blades. I slipped from the kitchen to the picnic table in the carport.

"You're missing your own party." Mother crowded next to me. "What's wrong?"

"What do you think?"

"Billy does love you. And he protects you."

"Yeah. How many times have you said that? It never fails to piss . . . " I didn't finish because I detest the coarseness of public cursing. "Biggy has never loved me. And you should have his head examined. All those hateful things he says? Can you really not see how sadistic that is? You're my original source for that information. You're the one who keeps telling about how Biggy used to steal my baby bottle just to make me cry, and how he used to bite me. I've still got the scar on my cheek. Which makes me his lifelong victim."

My anger rose, but I stopped short of hurting her with what I really meant: *Why haven't you protected me?* "Maybe Biggy does have a heart the size of a pickup truck, but even if he treats me badly just five percent of the time, that means he hates me, and he makes me hate him."

"Billy doesn't hate you. He's the middle child. Middle children demand attention because they don't think they get enough. He's just a little jealous."

"You know, you keep telling me to let it go, but you've never forgiven Zandy. And you always excuse Biggy. She's a bully; he's a bully.

How can anyone defend bullies? It makes no sense. And what does he have to be jealous of? He has a car, he has friends, he had a girlfriend."

"He broke up with Wendy?"

"Other way around. He got mad last week. Punched her while she was driving."

"I don't believe that."

"She told me herself. Now she's scared of him."

"I don't believe it."

"He did the same thing to me. He picked an argument while he was riding behind me on my motorcycle. He clubbed me in the back of the head."

Mother looked shocked, but she didn't condemn him. She'd always told us: no matter what we did, no matter what we became, she was still our mother. Which was probably why she defended her bully son. "I wish you could see that he's got a good heart."

"Does Zandy have a good heart? They're just alike. She waits until the room is packed to rake you over the coals. Your exact words. Isn't a good-hearted bully still a bully?"

"She's just a loudmouth. Nan is the same way."

"Mother, you keep defending them. And instead of having confidence in me when I say I want to do something, you say, 'Well, I hope he can do all that.' That's some cold shi– feces."

"You know Billy brags on you all the time?"

"So? Who cares? He never says he's sorry after he hurts me."

"Billy never apologizes for anything. I guess he got that from Nan and Zan too." She looked at her watch and sighed. "I've got to get back to work." She'd opened Casa la Bello Pizza this morning, and she would close tonight so the manager could take a day off.

"TV Guide," she said from behind two waterlogged Kleenex, "says *Oklahoma!* will be on Sunday night. I can trade a pizza at Dairy Queen for hot dogs. Do you want to watch it together?"

Not really. "Sure. Chili and yellow mustard on mine. No relish. And no ketchup." Zan eats hers with sauerkraut. Nan relishes Tabasco and hot peppers. Mother desecrates hers with mayonnaise, for the love of Baby Jesus. No respect for the dog.

Mother started her car and waved goodbye.

I've always wanted a just-add-water kind of life, so maybe I should've found a bigger bottle of aspirin. Or run away to California. That would solve my Biggy problem, and I won't have to go back to school and face the Andersens. Maybe Sammie's right. If I have to fight for survival, I need Daddy to teach me how. I was inside the kitchen door when I heard Nan knock on glass. Mother leaned to roll down the passenger window.

"Are you going to let Big Guy continue to terrorize Curtis?" Nan was hard of hearing, so she spoke too loudly.

"What am I supposed to do, Mother? Take sides? Then Billy will hate me."

"I've learned: if you've never been hated by your child, then you haven't been much of a mother. So yes, get mad at Big Guy. Choose when he does something wrong. Choose. There will be some drama, but if you don't, you won't like the result. I didn't."

CHAPTER 17

FOR SALE

I watched TV after everyone left. For the thousandth time, Brutus grabbed Popeye by the top of his head. Popeye flailed away like a windmill, but his fists never touched Brutus. That was me, but I couldn't rely on a can of spinach to win my battle.

If I stayed in Oklahoma, Biggy would always be my focus. He'd goad me into fights until I screamed to be left alone. Then he'd provoke me again, and then I'd scream again. And Mother wouldn't–or couldn't–stop him from baiting me. Then I'd finally get tired of the insults, the put-downs and the slaps and I'd bow up to him again, and we'd clash again. The only way I could ever beat Biggy would be to walk up behind him and cave in his skull with a two-by-four.

Mother kept a Kerr jar with pencils and pens in the secretary in her bedroom. I folded down the writing leaf and wrote a for-sale ad: "1967 Honda Super 90. Needs repairs. $175."

I rode to the newspaper office, paid $1.95 with my last two dollar bills, then past O'Murphy's house on my way home. She sat on her porch with MBe. Both waved and O'Murphy smiled, and her smile wasn't just an, "Oh, hi, I know you from my class and I see you drive by occasionally." It said, "I like you."

CHAPTER 18

THE DEVIL AND
CURTIS PYE

One buyer showed up the next day. "Twenty. That's all it's worth to me."

"That's not fair. It cost me three hundred and fifty dollars."

The man had a Van Dyke goatee and a red complexion. "Fair to us. You said it'll cost a hundred dollars to fix the wheel. Maybe more. And maybe it will work, but does it make sense to pay $175 and risk $100 more on a broken $350 bike?"

"I need more money. A hundred."

He looked back at his son. "Aaron. Come." The kid–he looked twelve–started to whine.

My mouth opened. "That's not right. It's nearly brand new."

"Yeah, but it's a busted toy. It's smarter to buy a new one."

It's not right, but this shiny Honda is no good to me. I've lost two fights in two days, and I don't want to try suicide again. If I hitch, even twenty-five dollars could be my ticket out of Oklahoma. And I want to leave here worse than I want to see if anyone will offer more money. "Do me a favor. Make it twenty-five."

He scribbled a check and offered the oddest smile. "Smart boy like you should know. Never ask the devil for a favor."

CHAPTER 19

MY FACE IN HIS MIRROR

A month after he'd cut off our allotment checks, Mother had written to the Marines to ask where her husband lived. They'd sent the address where Daddy collected his checks. I saw her put the letter in a Buster Brown shoebox in the hall closet.

"I ditched him in California, so now he's getting back at all of us," she had said. "I don't know why it's such a wonder to me. He's zapped our allotments before. The Marines sent him to Hawaii the year you were born at Balboa Naval Hospital. After he got there, he decided he needed more money. Zap. Then, when you were seven, he got stationed in Japan. There went your ex-daddy, and he zapped our allotments."

"He's not my ex-daddy; he's your ex-husband."

"You're right," she had said. "Don't let me turn you against him. I called him two months ago. I wanted him to know his sons were okay. I told him twenty-five dollars a week at Casa la Bello was all I made. And I said Vin helped us get by."

So that's what happened. Vin gave us money, and instead of feeling obligated, Daddy had convinced the Marines that some other guy was supporting us. Swell dad.

"I know why he's that way." Mother said. "When he enlisted, he had to show the Marines his birth certificate. That's when Olivia told him he was a bastard. She never cared about him like a son. Rory was supposedly his stepfather, but he always thought Jonathan was in the way."

"How old was I when we left him in California?"

She had seemed pleased by the word "we."

"You were nine; Biggy was eleven when we came back to Oklahoma. Back then, Marines could go to the brig for not paying car payments. They made them support their wives and kids," she had said. "But that was the old Corps. They don't care about families these days."

Mother also stored pictures in the hall linen closet that separated our bedrooms. I went to the Buster Brown shoebox and laid it on my bed. Inside was the sepia-toned photo Mother had shown me of a boy about four years old, dressed in a short suit.

"You know who that is?" she had asked once.

I hadn't recognized the clothes. "It's not me?"

"No, but he looks just like you, doesn't he? That's how you looked when you were four."

"Who is it?"

"That's your daddy," she had said.

If we had looked that much alike then, maybe he still sees my face in his mirror. I knew so little about Daddy. My last memory of him was from 1959. He had been getting dressed for the base: a tersely ironed khaki shirt, khaki tie, forest green suit jacket, and worsted slacks with incisive creases. He'd been the non-com in charge of Camp Pendleton's rifle range. Daddy must have been a terrific rifleman, because he outshot the other Marines. I remembered a blue Tupperware bowl with forty-eight medals in it and seven trophies nearly as tall as me.

The Marine letter with Daddy's Palo Alto post office box number was in the shoebox, and another photo from when Mother had married Daddy in 1950, the year Biggy was born. Daddy had been in green fatigues and a khaki belt. Mother had probably weighed one-fifty then; overweight, but not the gross two hundred pounds she'd ballooned to after he started fooling around on her.

And there was a group shot from the battlefield. "Peleliu" was written on the back. *I'll bet he wants this.* He was born on Dec. 30, 1924, so he would have been was sixteen when the Japs had bombed Pearl Harbor. He had joined the Marines the day he turned seventeen. This black-and-white would've been shot in 1945; Daddy would have been twenty then. *Is that what I'll look like in five years?*

The four-by-four inch World War II photo felt heavy, like a crinkle-edged postcard. Daddy had stared frankly–perhaps arrogantly–into the lens. Seven of the rifle squad held M-1s. The private beside Daddy– tall, thin, rabbity face, Saturday-morning-cartoon teeth and a tuft of hair on the crown of his head–had flashed a Browning Automatic Rifle. At least, that was my guess from watching *Combat*. Biggy and I had marched with Vic Morrow and Rick Jason and Pierre Jalbert for five TV seasons, and we'd studied their armaments.

I packed two pairs of Levis, two long-sleeve shirts and a week's worth of socks and underwear in the wooden typewriter case Mother had given to Biggy and me. I hated leaving the Remington. I was the only one who ever used it. Biggy had taken typing in high school too, but that portable typewriter had been my confidante.

I put the photo in my typewriter case. Everything else went back in the shoebox. I went to bed at nine P.M. I hoped for sleep. I wanted to get up an hour early to deliver my two routes.

CHAPTER 20

SHOULD I STAY OR SHOULD I GO?

I grabbed the alarm to keep from waking Biggy. Three A.M.

Decision Day. Should I leave?

Biggy usually lapsed into a coma as soon as he swooned into bed. Once asleep, he was hard to wake up. This morning, though, he rolled over. "S'up?"

"Paper routes."

Maybe he heard something in my voice, even through the inertia between sleep and awakening. He turned his head. "Wha' time is it?"

"Four," I lied.

I twisted the winder once, twice, three times, and dialed the alarm hand ahead to seven A.M. so Biggy would wake for school. It would take two hours to bike to TG&Y, roll one hundred papers, and deliver two routes. I wanted to be out of town before the sun came up.

I saw Vin's shaving bag in the bathroom. *Mother, when will you learn?*

How long will it take to hitchhike to California? Days? Weeks? Hopefully not a month. After all, how long can twenty-five dollars last?

A floorboard creaked in our room; Biggy's eyes popped open again.

"Vin's back."

His look cursed the messenger; however, he closed his eyes and rolled away. I dressed quietly, but Biggy rolled over again. I couldn't see his eyes in our dark room. *If he's watching, he'll see me reach for the typewriter case. He'll know something's up. I'll have to take my chances.* I picked up the typewriter case, but no matter how softly I tried to tippy toe, I couldn't keep my Wellingtons from clomping down the hall.

I hated to just quit without notice. Mr. Presley would have to deliver my papers until he found a replacement. And I couldn't let everybody just wonder if I'd gotten kidnapped. They'd call the cops for sure. I'd have to write a note. "Mom, I've gone to California to find Daddy. Please call Mr. Presley." I laid it on the kitchen table.

That's when I spotted the chocolate chip cookies and blackberry cobbler. Our back door was always unlocked; Nan must have left them after we'd gone to bed. The cookies, still warm, were in her yellowed Tupperware bowl. I bit off a third of one. A chip threaded liquid chocolate across my lower lip. I wrapped two in last night's classifieds, which contained my motorcycle ad.

The cobbler was in her iron baking pan, which was dying the death of a thousand steel Chore Boy nicks. Melted butter congealed on the surface. We thought Nan was such a good cook because she overloaded everything: red earth cake with chocolate frosting, Christmas Jell-O with whipped cream and pecans, upside-down cake with crushed pineapple inside and pineapple rings outside. Her cookies contained so much sugar and butter and chocolate, they'd knock your socks off and your penny loafers too.

I would've felt like a thief in the night if I'd taken one of Mother's Tupperware set, so I reached under the countertop for a waxed cottage cheese carton. Cardboard was more reliable than Kaiser foil anyway. With a pie server, I chopped a six-inch serving from the side of the pan and scraped more indigo berry juice into the carton. I folded the lid, rubber banded it, and turned it upside down. No leaks. As an after-thought, I stuffed a can of Campbell's vegetable beef in my typewriter case. I chose a spoon with U.S.M.C. engraved on the handle, obviously to keep Marines from stealing them.

To buy more time, I moved Nan's Tupperware onto my note. Mother would put the cobbler in the fridge first thing in the morning, but the cookies would stay there until tonight.

It would kill Mother when she woke up and found I had left. It always killed me when she cried, especially when it was about me. I opened the back door, turned, and said goodbye to the house. *Mother, I'm not leaving you, I'm leaving my brother. Biggy will crush my soul if I stay, and it's up to me to save my own life. Besides, he'll finally have your attention all to himself. That's what he wants. He's the real mama's boy.*

* * *

O'Murphy's house was on the way. I waved, but I wanted to tell her that she was my North Star, that I'd need her to find my way back. Maybe I'd see her again when I deserved her.

I stashed my typewriter case behind the dumpsters at Nabours' Grocery and biked another two miles to the shopping center. My bundles of papers–one for each route–waited inside TG&Y's front-door alcove. Every morning. Every Thanksgiving. Every Christmas. Sundays were the biggest because of all the inserted flyers. I sat on the first route's bundle to fold my papers, then stuffed the canvas bag and sat on it while I rubber-banded the second route.

If it had rained, I would've ridden up the driveways of a hundred customers, tossed a dry paper onto each porch, then slogged across the lawn to the next driveway. But driveway delivery would do today, so I was done in fifty-five minutes. By the time Mother sent the cops after me, I'd be in Texas. Or wherever was beyond there.

I rode two miles back to Nabours for my typewriter case. The fence behind the store–where I had once gotten caught stealing beer– was unlocked. No way my bike would be here when I got back, but the other option was to ride it home, and then Mother or Biggy would know I hadn't gone to school. I rolled the bike inside the gate and pushed it over so anyone who saw it would assume it had been there awhile.

* * *

Nabours' night clerk was an old-timey beauty contestant, Miss Whomever 1941 or some way-back year. Mr. Nabours had introduced us when I'd stocked groceries there two years ago.

"Still throwing papers, Cutie?" Irma was tall, even for an Indian, maybe five feet eleven, and she had one of those high, funky hairdos that looked like a beehive had committed suicide on her head. Dyed hair looks dyed because it has no highlights; Irma's was Krylon black, which must have dripped an angry inch and inked her forehead purple.

Irma looked at me, then the check. She handed me a blue pen. "It's not made out to anybody, Cutie. Write 'Cash' on the 'Payee' line, then endorse it on the back."

And she cashed it, right there on the spot. I stuck five dollars in my jeans pocket and folded the twenty into my billfold. If I got robbed, they'd grab my wallet first, but hiding cash in my suitcase didn't sound wiser.

A plastic bucket of Double Bubble sat beside the cash register. Toe-sized chewing gum plugs cost a penny. *If I'm on the road for a week, they'll supplement my chocolate-chip diet.* I counted to twenty-five and stuffed twelve pieces into each shirt pocket.

"Twenty-five cents, and a penny for the governor," Irma said.

I untwisted the blue-and-yellow waxed paper on one side and popped in a chaw. If pink had a flavor, it would taste like Double Bubble: cloying, sweet and syrupy. Like beef jerky, a bubblegum cud is an impossible chew until it's softened with spit. Even wet and mashed, it's a mouthful. But it's sugar, so I wouldn't tremble when I couldn't afford food. I spotted a yellow pad. Maybe it was too late, maybe my life had already happened, but I wanted to journal this trip.

"Something else, Cutie?"

"Yeah, I'll take the legal pad. And a BIC Stick."

I started for California at five-thirty. Peaceable River cleaves Hell Creek, a long, narrow town. Of the fifteen thousand inmates, 14,998 were still asleep. I was two blocks west of Nabours' when headlights moved behind me. *Oh no. An unmarked unit?* I conjured a quick half-truth: I'm a paperboy. Something's wrong with my bike so I ditched it at Nabours', and now I'm walking to school. It was verifiable. But what if they ran me in for questioning? Sometimes on *Dragnet*, the cops would just stop a guy and quiz him. If he looked nervous, they'd run his fingerprints, and that's how they knew he was an ax murderer. The white Bel Air continued by.

I walked down five more blocks to U.S. 81 to cross Peaceable River bridge. I faced north, raised my thumb in front my eyes, and said aloud, "The world itself. The world itself is on the other side. Oklahoma is flat and dusty. Will the world be flat and dusty too?"

I thought about the Q Document, about how Satan had tempted Jesus in the desert. I might wander the desert for forty days and forty nights too. I wondered, what price would Satan ask to help me find Daddy? And to make O'Murphy my girlfriend? Just two minor favors.

BOOK 2

"Is a new world coming? We welcome it."
Lyndon Baines Johnson

CHAPTER 21

FROM THIS VALLEY

I spotted her after the doggie turned toward Fort Sill. She had stepped off the shoulder of U.S. 62 west, and the first driver had just missed her.

Little Miss Armadillo was a darn good judge of traffic. She moved into the slow lane, pulled in her head, and waited for an eighteen-wheeler to pass. Like a cross between a centipede and a hedgehog, she wasn't quite as long as my forefinger, and she probably weighed less than a quarter pounder with cheese. Other armadillos are scaled like reptiles, but a pink fairy looks like the mammal they actually are: yellow-white fur, pinpoint eyes, coral-pink banded shell. More quickly than I would've believed, she scurried into the center lane and then curled into her armor as faster traffic passed over her at thirty-five miles per hour.

The traffic signal was still green. I set my typewriter case on the shoulder and stepped into the center lane. The drivers of two cars swerved past me, unaware of the animal.

"Are you blind?" shouted a mother with two kids in a Corvair station wagon.

No. You are.

A Firebird driver spotted the furry yellow animal at the last moment and zigged into the fast lane. "Hey! Get a motor!" Her three passengers—probably on their way to Lawton High School—laughed uproariously, as if insulting an armadillo was hilarious.

Finally, the center lane was vacant. I straddled her. She withdrew her head.

Now a bright yellow taxi with black-and-white checks barreled down the fast lane.

I shook a finger at him. *Not so fast, Taxi Man.*

He swerved and his back tires squealed. His side-view mirror slapped my shirt sleeve, and he stopped in front of me. Taxi Man laid on the horn, but his cab roadblocked the center lane. I was glad for the time out, but apparently Miss Armadillo marched to a reckless urgency. She scuttled into the fast lane at the same moment as a lime-green muscle car.

I closed my eyes. "Oh, Jesus."

The Dodge Charger grazed her shoulder.

"¿Qué es *eso?*" a voice asked.

I jumped.

"*Amigo. Lo siento, no quise asustarte,*" he said.

Taxi Man thinks you're Mexican. "It's okay. I startle easily. She's an armadillo. I didn't want you to hit her."

"Her? Yeah. Sorry I yelled, *nino.* I thought you were doing something stupid. I didn't realize. Wow, she's tiny too, a *viejita.*"

We both squatted. The armadillo lay on her side. I pointed at the blood. "Shell's cracked across her rear."

"That leg is broke *tambien.*"

"How can you tell?"

"It ain't moving like de other ones. What is dis?"

"A pink fairy armadillo. They're from South America. We learned about them last week in biology class." Cars blew by. "Shouldn't we get her off the shoulder?"

"Don't look at me," Taxi Man said. "I ain't gonna touch her. Dis how you get leprosy."

Something else I'm not afraid of, but how should I pick up an injured, runty armadillo? I slid both hands under her shell. She curled into a golf ball and, faster than I could react, raked a toenail across my fingers.

I dropped her. *Sorry, madam, that must have hurt like crazy.* I looked at Taxi Man.

He shrugged. "Why move her? You going to take her to a vet? *Si,* a better question–you going to pay the bill?"

I picked her up, and she flexed in half again, but her eyes watched me.

You can't pay the bill and go to California, so it's your life or Miss Armadillo's. "What'll happen to her if I don't?"

"What eats *minusculo* armadillos?" Taxi Man shrugged.

"Without a vet to set her leg and board her until she's healed, she will be on the menu for vultures and ants, not to mention infections. We can't let her be eaten alive."

Taxi Man nodded.

"Then I'm going to set her under your front wheel." I stroked Miss Armadillo's front shoulder and chatted soothingly as I moved to the front of his cab. "What are you doing so far from home? You were probably just hungry."

Taxi Man looked at the yard across from us. Red-orange fruit ripened on the trees; a few already lay on the ground. "Maybe her sweet tooth got her killed. She was going toward that persimmon tree."

"Maybe I should carry her over there instead? She could live for days."

"No. You were right the first time. She's in pain. Better to give her peace. How you tink she got here?"

I placed her under the driver's front wheel. "Argentinian soldiers, they train here. I see them in Hell Creek–my hometown. Maybe she got away. Or maybe they set her free."

It was nearly seven A.M., so Mother could be awake by now. I needed to get across the Texas line. Taxi Man did the job, and I crossed three empty lanes back to my typewriter case.

His taxi backed toward me. USMC was tattooed on his left forearm, tanned and leathery, which stuck out of the driver's window. "Where ya headin'?"

"California. But I can't afford a cab."

"*Yo conozco*," he said understandingly. "Get in. You really hitchin' to California?" Five syllables came out, but divided the Hispanic way: Col-ie-for-ne-ya.

I opened the passenger front door.

He shook his head. "In the back seat."

"Palo Alto."

"What for?"

"To find my dad."

"*Por qué?*"

"I want to live with him."

"You play basketball?"

"No sir."

"Football?"

"No." Biggy had gone out for football in the seventh grade, and even though he always acted like such a tough guy to me, he'd quit after two practices. He'd fessed to Mother's teasing that he hadn't liked getting kicked in the butt by the coaches. I guess bullies don't like getting bullied by other bullies. Hell Creek coaches had berated us every day in P.E., threatened us, and set us upon each other. It would've been child abuse if they'd done it off the school grounds.

I hadn't gone out for sports, mostly because I had that "*Yuk!*" revulsion at touching other boys. Call me irrational, I have a fear of being forced to the ground and suffocated under a dogpile of twenty-one other football players. Biggy, on the other hand, was a boy grabber. Sometimes, when he wrestled me to the ground, I could feel his groin grind into my butt. His statement of dominance.

"You hitchhiking? Papa," the cabby accented the last syllable, so it came out pa-PA, "din't give you no money for no bus?"

I haven't checked the price of a ticket, but I'm pretty sure twenty-four dollars and change won't pay my way to Colieforneya. "No sir."

"Cripes, kid, your old man radder have you kick 'round the country?"

"He doesn't know I'm coming."

He was driving at forty-five mph, but Taxi Man's head spun. "What de hell?"

"I'm trying to find him."

"In Col-ie-for-ne-ya?"

"That's where he lived when he got out."

"Doggie? Squid?"

"Jarhead."

"*Semper fi.* How long since you see him?"

"Six years."

"*Ni hablar!*" The cabbie bit his tongue. It was another five minutes before he stopped the cab at the west edge of Lawton, where the speed limit increased. A black-and-white sign ahead read, "Altus 55 miles."

"Okay, kid. You get a ride easier here. Dis is federale highway 62. It keep going in Texas. When it meet with U.S. 83, go north for Shamrock. That put you on Route 66. Stay off Interstate 40. It ain't finished noways. The Mother Road, she run you aaall the way to Col-ie-forn-e-ya. Good luck finding your old man." He waved and U-ed across the highway. *"Vaya con Dios."*

I started walking – uphill, so this must still be Hell Creek Valley– and whistled the notes Mr. King had taught us in sixth-grade music. "From this valley they say you are going."

CHAPTER 22

GIL LEBEOUF

Cars and trucks whooshed by.

How far am I from Lawton? If I'd walked five miles in one hour, that would be five miles an hour. Jim Ryun had run the one-mile record: three minutes and fifty-one seconds–about fifteen miles an hour. I looked at the fence posts on my right. About ten feet apart. Divide by 5,280 feet, and that's 528 posts per mile. I counted posts for fifteen minutes. I was walking about 2.5 miles an hour.

* * *

"Anyone know you're out here?" Buick Guy asked.

"No sir."

"I wouldn't think. You know, my son's about your age. That's why I picked you up. Any chance you'd let me pull over at a pay phone and call your parents?"

"No sir. Anyway, I don't know my daddy's phone number."

His face twitched at my half-truth. "I'm a high-school counselor. I'm obligated to take truants to a police station."

"Then I'll jump out."

"Never mind. No one can stop a runaway for long." He pointed to a distance sign that said Indiahoma was three miles away. "That's as far as I'm going. Do you know where you are?"

"Yes sir." *If I keep walking west, I'll wind up in California, won't I Sammie?*

"Open the glove box. Take that Oklahoma map. It shows the Texas Panhandle," his finger marked an X, "here. North is always at the top. See that sliver on the left side? New Mexico. When you get there, you'll need a new map. Don't throw away this one, though. You may need it to get back home. You're young, and you're going to realize, very soon, that this business of living on the road isn't easy."

* * *

My second chocolate chip cookie was brunch. Berry cobbler would be supper.

I stepped sideways a couple of miles, getting into the rhythm and watching approaching cars. Air brakes locked ahead and eighteen wheels smoked blue clouds. I ran half a city block and learned my first lesson of the road: semis take a long time to stop.

On the radio inside the cab, Joan Baez mournfully advised that her mother could hear the train whistle blow five hundred miles.

"Jump in, *boo! Allons!*"

I reached up for the door handle, past "LeBeouf Trucking," printed in purple letters above "Ville Platte, LA," on the gold door.

"What the hell, *boo*? What choo doing out here alone?"

Enjoying the solitude. "I'm going to California."

"Christ on a crutch. What fo'?"

"To find my daddy."

"Mudda o' God. Well, get in, *cher*. The day you meet Gil LeBeouf goan be lucky."

I practiced his name silently. It started with a G that sounded like a JH. He pronounced his last name "LaBuff." I study faces to determine what makes people handsome or humorous or dopey. I have zipper lips, transparent eyebrows and heavy-lidded eyes. Gil had pudgy cheeks, a Roman nose, and puffy lips that formed a cherub's grin. "What's the town painted on your door?"

"Ville Platte."

"Does that mean Flat Town?"

"*Presque.*" He tipped his cowboy hat to me. "Flat City. It be in South Louisiana. Dat make me a coon ass. Where at you from?"

"Here, so I guess I'm a Dust Bowl Okie. How far are you going?"

"Headin' for Amarillo. Be dere in tree hours. When we hit a truck stop, I find you a ride with somebody I trust. You know a little French."

"I'm taking French and Spanish in high school."

A sprinkle started, and the windshield wipers slapped rhythm with the fence posts. I cracked my window to let out his cigarette fog, but the vacuum sucked more smoke my way.

"How long it be since choo seen your daddy?" Talk propped open Gil's overused eyes.

"About six years."

"Where at he be in California?" His accent was nothing I'd heard before: a white man who spoke what sounded like a Negro dialect.

"San Diego, when we moved back to Oklahoma, but I think he's in Palo Alto now."

"Tink?"

"I have his post office box."

"Dat's it?" Gil shuddered. His "th" sound was a "d," so "that" came out "dat." "You don't got de telephone number, de street?"

"I'll call Information when I get there."

"*Boo!*" Gil removed his black Stetson and tossed it on the dash.

I defended my decision. "It'll only cost a dime then."

"*Cher*, you be saving a long-distance call, but you's taking a torrible chance. Why you doin' dis?"

"I just want to live with my daddy."

Gil lit another Viceroy. "You been wid maman?"

Mother. "Yes sir."

"Yeah, I get that, *boo*. You growing up. You needed *mère* den, but now you need *père*."

I practiced the sounds in my head. They rhymed with pear and mare.

"Me and my ex . . . she be so mad at me, she rip me a doublewide butthole when I leave her. I regret dat. Regrets is pathetic, ain't they? You know, we regret 'cause we cain't forgive ourselves for what we do. But when Son 'bout yo' age, he want to live with me too. Tank Jesus I convinced *Mamam*," he said ma-MOOH, "to let Son come to my trailer."

Exactly what I needed to hear. "He lives with you?"

"Naw, *boo*. He be twenty-four now. Got his own wife. Tree kids already."

Three, I interpreted. "How come he wanted to live with you?"

"He grew up without me from grade school to high school. I saw him ever week, but only for an hour or two, so I never teach him 'bout fighting for hisself. Fact, Mamam teach him not to. She say if some boy try to fight, walk away. But it don't work like dat for boys, do it?"

Not for me.

"Dese two big boys–one way bigger–just wouldn't leave him alone. So I take Son for my whole vacation. In tree weeks, I teach him how to box. And I tell him, 'Son, next time dose punks mess wid you, fight the big 'un. Make de others promise to stay out. Make de bully promise too, den just start whalin' on him. Hit his nose as fast as you can, as many times as you can. He cover up dat nose, you hit de eyes. And dat's what he did. He hit dat bully so many times, Son give him a bloody nose and a black eye. Son lose, but they lay off."

That's it, teach me how to box, Daddy. "Why did they stop picking on him?"

"Fightin' about respect. De brave boy may lose, but he lose once. Den dey respect him for standin' up. You know, nothin' tears up a woman more dan having to raise boys by herself. Mamans, dey diplomats; dey try deir best, but dey don't know what to do. Cain't nobody 'cept a man teach a boy how to be a man." He lit a third Viceroy and crowned his head with the cowboy hat. "You gonna see de sights while you in California?"

I hadn't thought about it. "I would like to see Disneyland. And Hollywood."

"Don't go to no Hollywood." It sounded like a fatherly order. "It be all queers and porn."

We hit a bad patch of road. I was tired from all that walking, so despite the pitching and shaking, I steadied my head in my corner of the cab. *Now I know what a milkshake feels like.*

His hand was short, his fingers stubby, and they constantly ground the gears higher and lower. "De road get better when we cross into Texas, *boo.*"

"What does *boo* mean? And *share?*"

"*Boo* and *cher* be like kid and dear. Bout de same ting. I call my kids and my wife and my brudder all de same."

"You studied French?"

"Cajuns grow up wid French."

A bilingual truck driver? Who woulda thunk it?

But Gil was right about the road: fifteen minutes later, the Texas blacktop was darker and smoother. Tired from walking, I closed my eyes and rested my head in the nook between the back window and the side window.

"What yo' daddy do in California?"

"He's in the Marines. Or he was." My whole family was lousy with Marines. Daddy's brother had been a chaplain; his nephew was a Navy corpsman who served with the Marines. The G.I. Bill would pay for his college, so Biggy would probably join as soon as he graduated from high school.

* * *

It must have been two hours later when I felt Gil's hand on my knee. I jumped.

"Sorry, kid. You ain't used to bein' touched, are you?"

Feels creepy.

"Son, he be de same way. Anudder reason why boys shouldn't grow up without daddies. When I was a *gamin*, most every boy had a daddy, even though so many daddies be in World War II and Korea. But lotsa homes, in de bayous where I come from, dey be broke. Dese days, lotsa daddies be in prison. And some just give up on bein' daddy."

Give up on being Daddy? That's what Biggy had kept asking: exactly why had Daddy disappeared like a ghost? Had his pride been wounded because we'd left him? Or maybe he'd rather run around with trashy women? That's what Sandy had implied. I looked at my watch. If Mother hadn't read my note at breakfast, she'd find it now, when she went home for lunch. And then she'd call the cops.

"Anyway, we here. Didn't mean to scare you. You ain't been running into no queers?"

My expression said I didn't understand.

"Forget I mention it." Gil was silent for a moment. "Come to think, don't forget. They ain't just queers, I could forgive dat. Dey child molesters. Dey keep the roads hot, prowling for *enfants* like you. You just tell 'em, '*Au contraire, mon frère,* dat ain't my bag.' And then you tell 'em to let yo' ass outa dey car. Right den. Tell 'em to stop dis shittin' auto-mo-bile, and say it like you commandin' de devil."

He downshifted nine times to slow the truck, and turned the front wheels across U.S. 66 into the Armadillo Truck Park. "Let's get out. I'm gonna buy you de best cheeseburger in Texas, den we walk around de yard and see who got California tags."

CHAPTER 23

DOWN TO THE SEAS AGAIN

Gil was right again. The meat tasted so fresh, it was as if they'd butchered a heifer and fried it right in front of us. The buns had been toasted beside the burgers, which had popped little grease slicks on the crowns. When Mr. Marion had trained me at the Freeze, he'd said grilling buns caramelized the flour and sweetened the bread. And never mash the meat with the spatula, greasy burgers tasted better.

Mr. Marion had been right. The juice trickled down my arms. Besides cookies and chaws of Double Bubble, this was the first solid food since lunch two days ago. I could save the berry cobbler for when I got good and hungry.

"Hey, Jill." A trucker walked by and offered to shake Gil's hand. "Drive all the way up from Louisiana just for a hamburger?"

"Man's gotta eat, Edward." Gil deadpanned with a face as leathery as jerky. "Sit with us."

"Bring yore grandson with you?" Edward spun a chair backwards and sat.

"Naw, Edward," Gil said. "Dis *petit garcon* hitchin' for California. We lookin' for somebody to take him–where?"

"Palo Alto. But I have friends in Ontario. I could stop there first."

"I couldn't get you very far. I'll one-eighty at Glenrio, and then I'm deadheading back to Corpus Christi." Edward had a bass voice and an educated Southwestern accent. He pronounced every careful sylla-ble and didn't drop his final Gs.

"How many kids you got?" Gil deadpanned, then stage-whis-pered to me. "Dese Texans, they bear children in biblical proportions."

"Five," Edward countered with a grin. "You'd think we were a flock of French Catholics."

"How much longer you gonna stay on de road?" Gil asked.

"Oh, I think I'll just keep rolling down these byways until my wife quits kissing me goodbye. What about you, Jill?" Edward pro-nounced Gil's name like an American girl's.

"Oh, I love de truckin'. Cain't imagine nutin' else. Maybe I was a sailor in my old life, and dis my square rigger. You know, 'Gimme a tall ship and a star to steer her by.'"

"Hawthorne," Edward nodded.

"John Masefield." I was immediately sorry. It's not nice to cor-rect anyone. And besides, old people get sensitive if young ones know more than they do.

"Still a schoolboy," Gil explained. "What, you just read dis or somethin'?"

"I recited it in the seventh grade. But John Masefield died a few days ago and . . . "

"De poem writer?"

"Yes. Yes sir. It's called *Sea-Fever.* I've been trying to remember the lines."

"How much you still know?"

I couldn't forget the first two famous lines, but I stumbled through the rest:

"I must go down to the seas again, to the lonely sea and the sky,

"And all I ask is a tall ship, and a star to steer her by,

"And the wheel's kick and the wind's song, and the... something,

"I must down to the seas again, to the vagrant gypsy life . . .

"Something something . . .

"And quiet sleep and a sweet dream, when the long trick's over."

"See? It be about truckin'," Gil smiled facetiously. "Any California tags on the lot?"

"Nope," Edward searched his memory. "'Grand Canyon State' though, on a pair of reefer units over in the west yard."

"'At'll have to do," Gil said.

As it turned out, both truckers had been doubling their hours. Gil guessed they'd convoyed California lettuce and spinach eighteen hundred miles to Little Rock, and they doubled back to Tucumcari with chicken fryers. Small like midget Indians, they'd driven eight hours on a return trip, and the lead driver needed help staying awake the last 120 miles.

"Okay. Pull you suitcase outta my cab. He gonna be back in," Gil paused, "five minutes?"

The refrigerator unit driver nodded.

Gil looked like he wanted to kiss both my cheeks, but instead planted his cowboy hat on my head. "Protect yo' face in de desert. And 'member my CB handle. 'Coon Ass.' That mean I be from South Louisiana."

"You help me stay awake?" the lead driver confirmed.

"Dat's yo' job. *Oui*?" Gil said.

I nodded, although it was close to bedtime hours for guy with a morning newspaper route.

Gil mussed my hair. "You stay safe, *boo*. I get to California, lots. You get in wid another trucker, you ask if 'Coon Ass' be on the CB. *Oui?*"

* * *

The next cab was less smoky and the seat more comfortable, but this dark, hairy rat of a man was the sweatiest trucker in the history of sweatiest truckers. I considered leaving behind my Right Guard as a silent, if not-so-polite reminder that others could smell his lack of hygiene, even if he couldn't. I yawned, shut my eyes and practiced shallow breathing.

"*Amigo*. You stay awake. Or we both go in de ditch."

"Okay." But that burger and fries had sedated my brain. I placed Gil's hat on the console.

"Dis is your first time? To Col-ie-for-ne-ya?"

Am I the only guy on Route 66 who knows how to pronounce California? "No sir. We used to live there with my daddy."

"Where do he leeve now?"

"Palo Alto, I think."

"Fifty-tousand people." He said "thousand" like Gil.

Interesting: Gil's Cajun; Aztec Man is Mexican; neither can pronounce the th sound.

"I leeved in Santa Clara County. Dat's six hundred tousand people. Which post office?"

"I don't know." *And how am I going to find out?*

* * *

"*... gumption? I don't want...*" I jolted from a dream when the air brakes whooshed.

"You here. We dropping dese reefer units at Moon Ranch." He pointed to a spot on a map. The trucker's words dripped with accusation. "It six-turdy in Tucumcari."

In the morning? In New Mexico? I had been so wiped out from walking and riding during my first long day on the road, I'd slept from the middle of the Texas Panhandle into New Mexico. But we should've been here in two hours, so the truckers must have pulled over and dozed too.

"Reset your watch to Mountain Time," the driver reminded.

"Oh, yeah, thanks. Can I borrow that for a moment?" I pointed to the dome light.

He clicked it on – a grudging favor, since I hadn't served him well.

I picked up his map for a moment and overlaid a memory onto the back of my left hand. My palm stood in for Arizona and New Mexico. New Mexico ended at my palm's center–the fate line. My first three fingers were Nevada and Utah and Colorado. I tripled the length of my thumb to replace northern California; from L.A., Palo Alto would still be another three hundred or four hundred miles north–as far as my whole journey so far. From Mother's house to Palo Alto had to be more than fifteen hundred miles.

I'd been nine the last time I was in Tucumcari, when us four had left Daddy in California. Sandy had driven her own '51 Chevy. Since I was the smallest, I'd ridden the entire way on an ironing board near the back-seat ceiling front in Mother's Rambler. Biggy, of course, had called shotgun before I'd even thought about it.

I opened the truck door.

"*Precaution, amigo.* It's dangerous out here," my Aztec driver advised. "Stand in de light. Dey see how young you are, dey may stop."

"Thanks." People had been a lot nicer than I'd expected. So many had been so kind in the past twenty-four hours.

He had dropped me at the east end of the city, so I'd have to walk miles down Tucumcari Boulevard to get back to Interstate 40. That took me past the Blue Swallow, a flashing azure bird over the crimson word "MOTEL." And under that, "TV" flickered as the neon shorted.

Twenty blocks later, a green highway sign stated, "Now leaving Tucumcari, N.M." For a city with a famous name, it was even smaller than my lowly little burg of Hell Creek.

I looked at my watch. Eight A.M. Passing motorists paid no attention.

CHAPTER 24

BALDY'S GAME

The first time I saw Glenn Garibaldi, I wondered what the Gods of Easter Island had done to his head: elongated face, outstretched nose, ears that provide lift on the Santa Ana winds.

It had taken three days of walking and a series of rides to cross New Mexico. Nothing but sand, Roadrunner, and the cacti that Wile E. Coyote kept slamming into.

Then Baldi had picked me up in a '58 Studebaker Champ, and for three days we'd worked our way across Arizona. His game was cleaning typewriters and small-office machines. He removed the label from a Miracle Whip jar, bought a nickel's worth of gasoline, and walked behind me from office to office. He trained me as a front man because a fifteen-year-old boy gave him legitimacy. And maybe sympathy.

"Call me Baldi. And smile," he whispered, *sotto voce.* "That's your job." After we stepped inside an office, his persona became so cool, a Hershey bar wouldn't melt in his mouth. "Top o' the morning." He charmed clerks and got them to let us out their back door with their typewriter or adding machine. He flirted mercilessly with a pathetic fiftysomething office manager dressed a generation too young. Wrinkles cut deeply into her skin; her breasts conjoined in a topography of folds and freckles and age spots. But to my amazement, she teased him back.

He ate one meal a day, and therefore so did I. We'd start at the cheapest local downtown diner, order blue-plate specials, and then scurry through town for one job. They'd show him an overused key, a T or an E or an O, caked with generations of ribbon fibers and ink. I'd swab gasoline across the keys with my toothbrush.

"I'll buy you a new one," Baldi had promised.

In our conspiracy, I'd also re-ink the ribbons, meaning I'd dip the same toothbrush into a jar of black India ink and smear it across the old ribbon. We'd do that job, collect ten or twenty dollars, and then fade into another town.

"Never trust anybody who talks to you with his sunglasses on," Baldi told me once while wearing mirrored windows over his soul.

Is that real advice? "Why?"

"They're hiding something, and they don't want you to see the fear in their eyes."

Something about that actually rang wise, but I regretted the so-called service we performed. *Should I help a con man, even if we both needed money to make it through each day?*

A map was posted on the wall at what turned out to be our last job, a 1920s adding machine at a mom-and-pop service station on Route 66. This time, I'd borrowed a ballpoint from the counter and drawn a map on my left hand.

We slept in his two-tone pickup. Baldi reclined in the threadbare back seat of the double cab. I unchained the tailgate and sprawled across the wooden bed.

On our third night, he apparently scratched an itch and restarted the truck. He pulled off at Bullhead City and pointed to a turnoff sign, LAS VEGAS 99. "This is where we part company, kid. But I'm gonna reward you for sticking with me." He counted out ten one-dollar bills as if they were a scandalous amount of money. "You're more than halfway to California. This is probably as good a scene as any to snag a ride. Oh, and don't forget your cowboy hat." He said "cowboy" as if it were ridiculous.

"A trucker gave it to me. He said I should protect my head in the desert."

"Don't explain, kid. People think you're weak." He shifted into first and gassed the Scout. The back tires spun.

Wait, Baldi, where's my new toothbrush? I picked up a rock and threw it, but his pickup was already too far away.

Nature called, but there was no bathroom for miles. Not one car on the road for miles, so I straddled the centerline like it was Nan's back porch, unzipped and–in my best penmanship–wrote "Baldi" on the blacktop.

Sleepy again, I rested my head in a bar ditch with only the plants and the earth for warmth. I could see no one, so I reasoned that no one could see me. That fuzzy glow on the east horizon was either the incipient sunrise or a distant town. I focused on the Big Dipper, the Little Dipper, and the Milky Way. In the desert's low humidity, I could see thousands more stars than I ever did in Oklahoma.

I added the mileage in my head. *Have I come eleven hundred miles? And how many leagues is that, Mr. Verne? A league is three walking miles, so 367?*

I dozed until daybreak, then hitched a sixty-mile ride to a truck stop in Needles. The delivery van going farther into California stopped for gas, but I saw a sign: "Showers, $3." With Baldi's ten singles, I had $24.50 again. I looked at the trucker's specials chalked on the blackboard: $2.99 for ham and eggs. Like scales, my hands weighed the choices: Food? Shower? Food? Shower? *What day is this, anyway? I left on Monday. Is this Saturday or Sunday? I'm grubby and I want to change clothes, but I'm starved. Time to splurge.*

I prepaid for a bathroom key and a locker. I unwrapped the flat, square bar of soap that came with a towel and washcloth and stood under a showerhead for five grateful minutes, steaming sand and relief from my scalp and shoulders and feet. I put on my last clean clothes and scrubbed my two dirty shirts and jeans and socks and underwear. It was too much soap and the wrong kind, so I rinsed away the residue and rubbed the clothes against each other, then hung them to dry. My hands were shaky by the time I walked inside the restaurant.

A waitress shouted across the counter: "Light where you wanna, honey!"

I looked at my watch: seven fifty A.M., but I was finally across the California border, back in the state where I was born.

"Coffee, baby?"

"Dietetic Dr Pepper."

"Fer breakfast? You must gotta cast-iron stomach."

I found myself eating fast, cramming in quarter-slices of toast slathered with butter and blueberry jam. I wished I'd ordered a real Dr Pepper. I felt like I needed more sugar.

The waitress came back. "Darlin', you a starvin' dog."

Now I had to pee again. I returned to the shower where I'd left the typewriter case and my clothes across the portable walls. Everything seemed to be there, but apparently more than one key existed. I had wanted to brush my teeth, but a trucker who watched me the whole time made me feel homophobic. My table had been cleared before I returned to my café seat.

"Darlin'!"

I jumped.

"You's gone so long, I thought you walked the check." The waitress laid a green slip on the table and patronized me with a smile. She'd charged me fifty cents for a short glass of Dr Pepper! A whole can was a quarter in any vending machine in America. And twenty-five cents sales tax. I paid with four of Baldi's singles.

"Thanks, darlin'." She slipped the money in her apron.

I waited.

"Something else, baby?"

"Uh, my change?"

She looked disappointed. "Oh. I thought you's leaving me a tip."

She broke twenty-six cents into a dime, two nickels and six pennies.

No one in my entire life had ever tipped me more than ten cents. I laid a dime on the counter, but I felt a squeeze of indecision. *Will seventeen dollars be enough to find Daddy?*

CHAPTER 25

IN CALIFORNIA

Nine A.M. must be the worst time to hitch in Needles. The few cars on the road whizzed right by. Drivers usually wouldn't pick me up if they could take me only a few blocks, so I'd have to walk through downtown. I counted the blocks: ten, twenty, forty. Traffic picked up at eleven A.M., but nobody stopped. I clomped through the last residential neighborhood at eleven thirty. The speed limit increased from twenty-five to forty-five, and still no one paid attention.

The wooden case felt heavier. Footweary, I sat on a curb so drivers could get the best look at my face. The effect was immediate. A 1963 Bel Air's taillights flashed red. It was an old couple in their fifties.

"Get in, child," the passenger coaxed. Her desiccated face was grapejuice green. "What are you doing out here?"

Practicing my future. "I'm going to California."

"Sweet, you're in California."

"Yes ma'am. To Palo Alto."

"Then you're a long way from home. We're headed to Klinefelter. Next town. We'll get you ten miles farther down the road," the man informed. "I'm taking my wife to the clinic. Get her kidney sucked out."

"The Big C." To look at me, she craned her neck as far as she could—about ten degrees. "Took half a lung, most of my liver, one whole kidney bean, and now the other one quit working so well. We drive every other day to the renal clinic. To filter my blood." She rested her head on her husband's shoulder. They seemed happier than me.

So it went the rest of the afternoon: walk a half-hour, catch a brief ride. I covered just 140 miles, according to the distance signs that had been white in Oklahoma, green in California. Then the evening sun broke through the firmament in boulevards of fire. Heat baked my face. Only two cars were parked under a neon horse's flashing head at the Golden Palomino Motel. My breakfast ham and eggs had been digested, so I needed a Dr Pepper and a Baby Ruth.

The motel guy sat in a lounge chair in the open commons. Brittle, mousy hair, but dark skin. "Evenin' son. How long you been on the road?"

"Several days, sir."

"*Teniendo mucha suerte?*"

No, I shook my head, not much luck. Days in the sun had darkened my skin so much, Mexicans automatically spoke Spanish to me.

"If you wanna spend the night, it's only five dollars."

"Thanks. I can't." I inserted two quarters in the soda and candy machines and walked back to the road. I was at the edge of town. If I walked farther, the speed limit would increase to seventy mph, and drivers would have less time to look me over. Twenty cars and trucks streaked by; none stopped. Finally, the sky lost its light; drivers couldn't make out my face. I had a yawning fit. *Quel alésage*. Exhausted, I walked back to the motel and, on the assumption I was a customer because I'd spent fifty cents, sat heavily in his lawn chair.

"Change your mind about that room?" Motel Guy's voice came from behind me.

"Sorry," I stood up. "I have to keep enough money to find my daddy."

"Where is he?"

"Palo Alto, I think."

His lips sucked in air and asked again: "How long you been on the road, *hijo*?"

"Not sure. Almost a week."

"Where you going to sleep tonight?"

"I don't know. Hopefully, I'll get a ride to Palo Alto. Does that mean Big Tree?"

"Tall Tree. ¡Qué chingados! I'm not overwhelmed with reservations." He pointed to two cars with a self-deprecating smirk. "You got a dollar?"

I looked up.

"If you want TV, it's a quarter an hour. Need change to feed the idiot box?"

It occurred to me that he'd offered hitchhikers a super-low rate before. I had a quarter in my pocket and a sudden yen to watch *Gunsmoke*. "Is Marshal Dillon on TV?"

"Yes, my young friend, the best show in America is on tonight. And Miss Kitty. I'd watch that woman act in a tow sack. You 'member the first show?" He smiled and rolled his eyes. "Yeah, maybe you're too young. That was 1955. Fella came on the set and said, 'Evenin'. My name's Wayne.' For a second, I thought the Duke was gonna play Matt Dillon. But he introduced a friend of his, and that turned out to be James Arness. They'd couldn't o' picked a better marshal. Who's your favorite character?"

"Quint." *Maybe if I got a job as a blacksmith, I'd grow muscles like Burt Reynolds.*

"I like Festus. I still 'member Ken Curtis from his singin' days."

This time, he expected the blank look on my face.

"You're just a *cachorro*. Ken Curtis was quite a musician. He took Frank Sinatra's place in the Tommy Dorsey band, then he sang country and western for Shep Fields and the Sons of the Pioneers."

Everyone knows Sinatra, and I'd heard of the Big Band leader, but Shep and the Sons of the Whoever–Whomever–must be lost to the ages.

"Okay. You look like suicide on a stick. Here's a red quarter for the TV."

I looked at my watch, and then handed him a dollar.

He glanced at my watch as he slid a key across the counter. "You're in Pacific Time here."

"Thanks." I twisted the hour hand back an hour. *Sixteen dollars left. It'll have to be enough to find Daddy.* I opened the door to my room and collapsed. The swayback bed moved every time I did. Little black pills littered the windowsills and the edges of the floors. At first I thought they were mouse turds, but then a cockroach the size of a hubcap inched onto a sill that had been blistered by a generation ciga-rette butts.

However, I didn't want my dollar back. I'd plopped on something approximating comfort, and I wanted to stay that way. I knew I'd fall asleep in a few minutes, but I was curious about a coin-operated TV, so I fed the red quarter into a slot and twisted a dial.

" . . . the way it is, May 12, 1967," said the most trusted man in America.

Then California commercials, then a program came on. "Yabba dabba doo!"

Fred. Great to see you, buddy. But *The Flintstones* had been can-celed, so–rerun.

I clicked again, heard stirring, brassy musical fanfare and saw a montage of sports clips. "Spanning the globe to bring you the constant variety of sport. The thrill of . . . "

One more twist of the knob. " . . . strange visitor from another planet who came to . . . " *The Adventures of Superman* had ended ten years ago, and I'd watched every one.

Before the red coin ran out, I found a reason to risk my own quarter. A *Stage 67* ad came on for *Noon Wine*. Jason Robards and Olivia de Havilland, but best of all, directed by Sam Peckinpaugh. A dark, twisty murder set at the end of the nineteenth century, just like *Ride the High Country*.

My room was hot, and my back had already sweat a spot onto the bed. I grabbed another pillow, rolled onto my left shoulder, and thought about California. When I was five, Mother had opened a furniture store in San Bernardino while Daddy had been stationed at El Toro. Grand and Zandy had owned the factory in Ontario, but they'd wanted to go back to Oklahoma, so they'd sold everything to our neighbors in Oklahoma, Marietta and Henry.

I had crushed on Doreen when I was eleven, but I hadn't seen her since she'd come back to Oklahoma for a family reunion. *Is Ontario on the way to Palo Alto?* A California map was thumbtacked to the bulletin board where Motel Guy had sat. I'd check in the morning.

CHAPTER 26

THE FATHER MYTH

I picked up a textbook between our seats: *The Hero with a Thousand Faces*. "College?"

"Barstow Community. You like mythology? Who do you know?"

"Thor. Hercules. Apollo. Zeus."

"From Marvel? Comics are what got me reading in the first place. You know, you're Telemachus," said my second ride of the morning.

"Who?"

"Greek myth. You know *The Odyssey*? Odysseus left home for twenty years to fight the Trojan War. Telemachus was his son. Your father was a Marine for how long?"

"About twenty years, I guess, before he retired. I haven't seen him for a while."

"Yeah, see, Telemachus had daddy issues too, and he tried to find Odysseus. How old were you, the last time you saw him?"

"Nine."

"The Greeks won the Trojan War . . . "

"Where's Troy?" I interrupted.

"The city doesn't exist today, but it would've been on the coast of Turkey."

"So the Trojans were Turks? Greeks versus Turks?"

"Modern words, but close," the driver said.

"Interesting. Before Muhammad and Christ, what were the Turks and the Greeks?"

"Turks were shamanistic–like Hindus–Greeks were Hellenic. From what little I know, Greeks worshiped nature gods like Artemis, goddess of the hunt–and they consulted oracles. Anyway, while Odysseus was gone, all these dudes had acted like he was dead. They hung around his crib, night and day, wooing Penelope. She was the foxiest babe on their island. And after the Greeks won the Trojan War, on the way home Odysseus got snagged by Cyclops. Odysseus blinded Cyclops, so his daddy–Poseidon–blew Odysseus off the sea. When Odysseus got to Circe's island, Poseidon set one last trap: the ship had to pass by the Sirens."

"Sirens?"

"Wicked-beautiful ladies. Their songs made the helmsmen steer toward the music so their ships wrecked on the rocks. Odysseus out-smarted them. He had his sailors plug their ears with beeswax. But the dude just had to hear their song–such a dog he was, he tied himself to the mast."

Sounds like the hints Mother gave us about Daddy. Catted around when he should've been home. I wondered about my driver's curly hair and deep coloring. "Are you Greek?"

"*Nyet*. Saul Zabrinski. Maat and Papa are last-generation Russian Jews, which makes me a first-gen Arizonan. Aaand–gotta cut that story short. We're here." He pointed to the highway markers. "Keep going south and west. About sixty miles."

"But why am I Telemachus?"

"His life was absurd without his father. When the mariner didn't come back, Telemachus went looking for him." He watched that last sentence hit me. "But this is America, *boytshik*. We don't have to take no crap from Papa."

CHAPTER 27

WE COULD'VE HAD THIS

After a series of rides through the morning and afternoon, a panel truck delivering fruits and vegetables to roadside stands dropped me in Ontario, next to a bank of pay phones beside the road. Henry and Marietta Hayes were in the white pages, but no one answered. I spit out the spent Double Bubble, slid the dime back into the middle slot, and dialed their store.

"Mathews Furniture."

"Marietta? This is Cutie."

"Good gracious. Are you all right?"

So, Mother did call. "Yeah, sure."

"I didn't hear a long-distance operator. You must be in Ontario?"

"Yes ma'am. D Street. There's a park behind me."

"Henry's on a delivery. I'm alone at the store, so I can't come get you, but listen, you're just a mile away. Turn so the sun is at your back. Walk east. You'll see a street sign for Vineyard Avenue. We close the store at six. Are you starved?"

How did you know?

* * *

"Sit at the table so we can talk," Marietta said. "Henry and Doreen will be here in a few. We have a swimming pool out back if you want to take a dip before supper."

A dip before supper? That's something we don't say in Hell Creek. Nice house. Almost new. So this is why Mother is so jealous. And why Nan is still mad at Grand. We could've had all this instead of our church-mouse lives.

"How often do you three eat together?"

"Oh. A lot." *Liar. We haven't eaten a meal at the table together since Casa la Bello started splitting Mother's shifts.* Biggy and I got out of school at three thirty. Biggy bottled RC Cola until seven thirty. I'd finish my evening routes by six, and sometimes I'd stay at the library until close–nine P.M.–to avoid going home. Mother didn't get home until after ten.

The door to the garage boomed open. Marietta must have called, because Henry wasn't surprised to find me at his dining room table. "Do I smell butter? Real butter makes any meal better. And bacon? Hell, Spam tastes good if you put bacon and cheese on top of it. I wish I was bacon. Then you could . . . " Marietta kissed Henry.

"Does your Aunt Zan still butcher a pig every year?" Marietta kept up the table quiz.

"Yes ma'am." Every fall, Zandy would butcher her fattest barrow, then she'd invite us to take a hindquarter; the other went to Nan and Grand's house. Mother hated Zandy's guts anyway. We didn't have to buy pork chops or hams, but Mother had to thank her sister every year. That, she said, was the high cost of Zandy.

"We was red-dirt farmers, but we shore ate better back then." Henry's voice thickened to resume an Okie accent. "Always had fat calves for roasts and steaks. These days, we buy at Mayfair. I don't even want to know how much more it costs, but shore don't taste as good, do it?"

"Nnnuh," Marietta replied with a mouthful of grilled cheese and bacon.

"The pork we raised tasted–porkier," Henry said.

"Why?" I asked.

"We blessed our swine with amber waves of grain." Henry grinned at his clever word choice. "These days, they grub 'em on dry corn and whey and soybeans. When I grew up, pork was red. Pork chops today are so white, they look bleached. I hope they never lock up cattle and make 'em eat corn. Might make 'em grow faster, but beef won't taste beefy."

Apparently, Doreen also knew I'd be here. She strode in from the garage and addressed me. "Yeah, yeah. Don't let them tell you that nothing is as good out here."

Woah, woah. Little Dorey looks like a movie star. Six months younger than me, but she already had a womanly figure, and her hair and clothes looked styled. "To hear Father Dear tell it, not one thing in California measures up to when he was a boy."

"Listen to her. It only took her fifteen years, and she's already an expert on everthang." Sarcasm leaked from his voice, but Henry's face looked proud.

"California peaches aren't as good," Marietta countered. "They're woody."

"Some peaches are woody," Doreen argued like an equal, "because they're picked green and gassed ripe. If California peaches ripen on the tree, they're just as juicy."

"You don't even remember Oklahoma peaches," Henry scoffed.

"Do too. We were back home one Fourth of July, and Aunt Ida went up to Charlie, Texas, and we picked two bushels. They were dead ripe."

"Down to Texas, Dorey," Marietta corrected. "Texas is south of Oklahoma."

"Up, down. You hate it when I argue with you, but you correct me all the time. Besides, which way is up if you're in Argentina?"

"Do you want another grilled cheese?" Marietta asked me.

Good idea. Load up on calories. You're going to miss a lot more meals. "Encore."

"Cutie, tell us about your trip," Marietta prompted as she sat down.

Doreen asked, "How many rides did it take?"

They intended to drag out my story. "To get here? Uh, a few dozen, I guess."

"Where did you sleep?"

"In a truck the first night," I said. *And a ditch in Arizona.* "In a motel last night."

"Nice motel?" Marietta asked. "Holiday Inn?"

"No. It only cost a dollar."

"A dollar!" Marietta was aghast. She and Mother were in school together, and Mother is thirty years older than me, so both must have been about forty-five. They had doughy faces and matronly bodies, and they'd married above their looks: Daddy and Henry had been slim, handsome men, four years younger than their wives.

"Hot-pillow motel," Henry smirked. He was an inch shorter than his wife, so I guessed he poodled his graying blond hair to raise himself to her height.

"What's a hot-pillow motel?" Doreen asked.

"Rooms by the hour. Pillow's still warm from the last guy. And his, uh, ladyfriend." Like Vin, Henry cackled as though he'd delivered the most insanely funny punchline on the planet.

"Ugh. So perverted, Daddy."

"Henry." Marietta's face stiffened like Mother's when Vin cracked crude remarks. I think Henry just struck a nerve. Marietta watched for signs that I was my father's son.

I think your crude husband must be related to Jonathan Robert Pye. And Vin.

"He's a roundabout," Mother had dished once about Henry. Like Daddy, she said, Henry hadn't returned home after a boy's night out, and Marietta had a come-to-Jesus with him the next morning. She threatened divorce, promised to sell the house and the store out from under him, and to move Dorey back to Oklahoma. That's when Henry had realized who buttered his toast.

"See? Be careful what you wish for." That's what Mother had always said. She and Marietta were marginally attractive wives who'd plumped out while their husbands had stayed slim. At least Henry had stuck with Marietta. Or maybe she hadn't permitted him to leave.

"So, Cutie, when are you going back home? Your mother's worried about you."

"Mother called?"

"Of course. We're the only ones y'all know out here. She's worried. Henry and I can put you on a bus. Don't you want to go back?"

How about if I open a vein instead? "No ma'am. I'm going to find Daddy."

"And what's your plan to do that?" Henry asked.

"I'm going to the Palo Alto post office."

Henry shrugged at Marietta. Their faces hid something: maybe Marietta had been talking to Mother and Henry about me, but they weren't going to let me in on it.

"Listen." Marietta's face was suddenly solemn. "Now that everyone's together, I've got to tell you something. Cutie, your grandfather died."

Disbelief shook me. Grand? They all looked at me. I was so shocked, I didn't know what to say. "Died? When? How?"

"A few days after you left Oklahoma," Henry said. "He had a heart attack in the kitchen. Nan doesn't even think he felt it. It was like he just fell asleep at the table. They took him to Hell Creek Regional, but it took an hour for the funeral home ambulance to get to the house and then to the hospital. The doctors said it wouldn't have made a difference if he'd been next door."

"Did you love your grandfather?" Marietta asked.

"He was my favorite member of the family." *I should've been there. He'd always been there for us. Now I'll never get to say goodbye.* "What about the funeral?"

"Your mother said it was nice. Half of Stephens County showed up," Marietta said.

"Dorey," Henry suggested, "why don't you show Cutie around town?"

"They want to get rid of us so they can talk about you." As if she had been waiting for this moment, Doreen winked at me, stood, and headed for the garage door.

I tried on a California word. *"Groovy."*

Her eyes were sliced kiwis: cool, pale, green with gusto. "We should make the Del Taco scene." Like a hand in a glove, she slipped into the leather driver's seat of a 1967 bright yellow Karrman Ghia. A sky blue Karrman Ghia sat beside it in the garage. She saw my look.

"That's a '66. Daddy gave it to me for my birthday, but some dude piled into it. It's going to take months to get the parts from Germany, so Daddy bought a '67. He's fixing up the '66 for himself."

For his mid-life crisis car? Mother had Henry dead to rights.

"Why did you want a V-Dub?"

"It's not a VW," she enunciated the initials. "It's a Karmann Ghia. Everyone's got a Mustang or a Camaro. I wanted something special."

Fifteen? And she drives a foreign car? "You have a license?"

"Learner's permit," she said with a haughty smile. "In California, I can drive legally with another licensed driver in the front seat. You've got a license, right? Don't tell me if you don't."

"I have a motorcycle license."

"Suits." Her eyes twinkled with evasion.

CHAPTER 28

THE SCENE

Del Taco was a happening: a fast-food drive-in parking lot populated by Firebirds, GTOs, and more Corvettes than a Chevy dealership. It was also where rich boys met rich girls to have rich babies. They drenched themselves in each other; they leaned on doors, stretched across hoods, perched all over top-down convertibles. Their radios were tuned to the same station, so the sound effect was quadraphonic.

"This is Wolfman Jack," his voice sounded full of gravel, "comin' at ya from XERF-AM, the Mighty 1090 in Hollywood, California. But just in case you're the FCC and you can't find us, we've got fifty thousand watts of boss soul power in Mex-hee-co! This is the mightiest signal in North America. Birds drop dead when they fly close to our tower."

I looked at Doreen. "This guy for real?"

"You don't get the Wolfman in Okie Land?"

"Hi, Wolfie." A teenaged giggle erupted from the radio.

"Hey, my little tomato. Are you naked?"

"Nooo!" she protested, but pleasure bubbled from her voice.

"Would you like to get naked with the Wolfman?"

Her high-pitched titter verged on silliness. "Will you play 'All You Need Is Love?'"

"That is the top song here in the Summer of Love, nineteen-hundred-and-sixty-SEVEN!"

Five feet above the crowd, a girl as tan as tea danced on a surfboard fastened to the roof of an orange 1951 Ford woody. Her knit bikini was a size six, she was a size eight, and size-ten breasts yawed from the yarn. Chance alone determined where each body part would frolic next. She grinned brilliantly and spread her arms when her left breast slipped out. Every eye was on her, the star of these follies. "Thank you, folks. I'll be here all week." After the guys applauded, she shook the unruly gland back into place and continued to rattle and roll.

Doreen anticipated my mute question. "That's Skye."

"All your buddies are socs?" I shouted above the radios.

"What's a *sosh*?"

"S-O-C. Short for socials. Society kids."

Doreen stiffened. "I don't think so."

Why are you insulted? When I live with Daddy, I want their California cool threads and their Jan and Dean hair and their Hollywood skin. And their muscle cars.

"And who are your friends?"

"Greasers."

"Mexicans?" Doreen asked.

"No. Kids who slick back their hair. You haven't read *The Outsiders*."

"I guess not."

"It's about Tulsa. Ponyboy's a greaser. He's got long hair, and he slicks it with, I don't know, oil, Brylcreem, Vitalis. Greasers and socs naturally hate each other, so they fight."

"You're not a greaser." She snorted at my hair.

True. My burr isn't even three inches long, but I sure don't identify with socs. I flinched at the honk on my side of her Karmann Ghia.

"And that is Barry." Doreen waved to the woody and added a clause under her breath, "with whom I broke up two months ago."

He shot a pained glance at Doreen.

Hmm. Poor Barry is still grieving.

The girl in the knit bikini smiled directly into my eyes. *I could get warm for your form.* Skye had vermillion hair, long and ropey, with coppery highlights that glistened from the floodlights behind her. A zodiac of freckles lent a smart quality to her nose.

A stray thought leaked out. *Would you trade O'Murphy Scott for Skye? Gee, I don't think so. Skye is Ann-Margret charismatic. But I like O'Murphy.*

Then Barry said something only Skye could hear. It crushed her essence; she was about to cry. Barry revved the engine and the metal-flake orange woody screeched rubber. The rear end fishtailed momentarily toward Doreen's car. Inches of dumb luck–not Barry's skill–kept his rear bumper from smacking the Karmann Ghia's front fender.

Doreen tried not to change expressions. "Why do you want to find your dad?"

"Nice guy."

"Your dad?"

"Your boyfriend."

"Yeah. So cool," Doreen said acidly. "You think he's still mad for me?"

I answered her question. "I really left because I hate Oklahoma."

"Hey, you guys!" Doreen shouted to a car with two boys and two girls. "Pool party?"

"Whose house?" A towhead with daisies woven into a garland yelled from a Corvair.

"Mine. Eight?"

They accepted with peace signs and gleeful smiles.

"Want a malt?" Doreen invited.

"Uh, nah." I had less than fifteen dollars left in my pocket. In defense, I crammed a plug of Double Bubble in my mouth. "Gum?"

"If you're of the female persuasion," the speakers hissed, "lay your hands on the radio and squeeze my knobs, because the Wolfman plays the best records, and then he eats 'em!"

* * *

Somebody sing "Surfin' USA." In bikinis and baggies, the eleven tannest teens on the planet swam in the first back-yard pool I'd ever seen. Doreen frowned when Barry showed up in tight white trunks, built like he'd pumped iron since kindergarten.

"Cutie, there's extra swim trunks in the pool house," Marietta encouraged. "Find something that fits you."

I looked like I'd been raised on a steady diet of fish food: thin as spaghetti and too puny to be seen in a pool, but just as uncomfortable to be staring at the swimmers. I changed and jumped in before anyone spotted me. The pool lights cast an unreal neon tint on my skin.

"You guys," Doreen introduced me, "this is Cutie. We used to be neighbors in Oklahoma."

Hands waved in the air.

"Cutie fits," I heard from behind.

Skye smiled like she actually meant it. "You do have a cute face."

"Curtis is better." I returned her smile in an attempt to charm the girl. It worked.

"And such a cute smile," she added.

Parents had spent thousands on braces for my junior high classmates. Mother couldn't have afforded that, so my incisors jutted at imprecise angles. I hid them with a neutral expression.

"Why does that blow your mind?" Skye's face was a study in round symmetry: apple cheeks, a delicate knob of a chin, and wide eyelids that revealed her entire irises.

"Well, I'm not much like your boyfriend. What's his name? Adonis?"

Skye smiled at my audacity. "What was he the god of?"

"Body toning. I think."

"Yes," she agreed. "Satan hath the power to assume a pleasing form."

"Does that mean . . . "

"It means some people regret their deals with the devil."

"Aren't you his girl?"

"That's his version."

Then you and Doreen have something in common. I couldn't resist glancing down at her floating breasts. *If you're not with Barry, I'd like to throw a saddle on you. Stop it. Think of something nice to say.* "Your swimsuit is so far out."

Her face reddened, but she looked pleased. "Thanks. My big sis knitted it. I thought it was hokey at first, but now I kind of like it. And I adore your accent. You're from where?"

"Well, the womb."

She giggled. "Immediately following that blessed event."

Wow, she responded to my joke. "I was born in Oceanside. But we're an itinerant bunch. We followed Daddy to Hawaii for a year, then Oklahoma, then San Bernardino, then Oklahoma again, then San Diego. And I just trotted in from Oklahoma. Why are you so nosey?"

"I'm showing polite interest," she grinned. "Oceanside? So, you're Navy brat?"

"Daddy was a jarhead."

"Mine's a squid," she acknowledged.

But I caught a whiff of intention: she wasn't interested in me; she was just plain nice.

"Oh well, somebody's got to swab the decks."

"He commands a destroyer group," she protested, but she smiled.

That's when an arm reached in, hooked her left shoulder, and jerked her from the water like Swimsuit Barbie. "We're leaving."

Skye grabbed at the joint where Barry wrenched her shoulder.

I felt an immediate flash of protectiveness. *Separate them, like Biggy had stepped between Vin and Mother.* I put both hands on the concrete rim of the pool, propelled up, and faced Skye. "Are you okay?"

Barry circled around to her side. "Something to say, Cuz?"

Nope. Just standing here so you'll hit me instead of her.

"She's my lady," Barry said with grim ferocity.

That's right. Drain your anger into me, Barry. Don't take it out on her.

Doreen stepped amid us. A Medusa stare turned Barry into stone. "I've said it before, but this time I'm making it clear in front of all these people. Never come to my house again."

Marietta was still on the veranda, but she didn't need to interfere.

Doreen offered her arm to Skye. "You're my friend. Come anytime. Really."

Barry grabbed Skye's arm, and she staggered away with him like a reluctant child.

Wow. There's lesson to learn: six months younger than me, but Doreen seems as confident as her mother.

CHAPTER 29

1953 VW DELUXE MICROBUS

Marietta had laundered and folded everything in my typewriter case, so I showered and dressed in fresh clothes. When I stepped into the hall, I heard voices in the kitchen.

"What are you going to do with Cutie?" Her husband asked in a low voice.

"Drop him at I-5, I guess." Henry was a little hard of hearing, so Marietta spoke loudly.

"That's what his mother wants? I shouldn't give him money?"

"She wants him to get hungry."

"But she also wants him to find his daddy?" Henry arched an eyebrow. "Now could Ginny possibly want from Jonathan Robert?"

You're a heckofaguy to ask that question. I used your bed last night, so I suppose you slept with your own wife for a change. "Good morning," I greeted both.

"Henry has a delivery, I have to open the store, and Doreen has left for school," Marietta explained from an electric skillet filled with grits, peppers, sausage, onions and Mexican spices. "What about you?"

"I'm going to Palo Alto."

"Why are you doing this?" Marietta's tone implied any answer would be wrong.

"Don't you love your mother?" Henry asked. "Surely you don't love your daddy more?"

"I don't know him."

"Truer words," Henry muttered.

Interesting. A jerk who thinks someone else is a jerk.

* * *

"Do you have a California map?"

"No ma'am."

Marietta handed me a soiled mess from under the seat, so over-used it had separated at the folds. Two fingers forked to red lines: "Here's I-5. You need to get here or here. U.S. 101 or State Road 99 will both take you north. Be careful. This is California." She bussed my cheek.

Interstate 40 was still being built; to get here I'd hitched west on two- and four-lane highways. The on-ramp sign introduced me to California's unwelcoming freeways: "NO PEDESTRIANS, BICYCLES, SKATES OR SCOOTERS BEYOND THIS POINT." Dozens of cars and trucks accelerated down the on-ramp to merge onto the Interstate 5 freeway.

I sat on the hard typewriter case and stuck out my thumb. A black-and-white with a cherry on top zipped by. Expressway drivers couldn't see me up here, so I ventured past the sign, thumb out. A second squad car roared down the fast lane, then pulled into the median's breakdown lane up the highway. Its red taillights stayed on.

A minute later, a faded red van stopped a few hundred feet in front of me. It was encased in so much Bondo and primer, it looked like an accident in progress. The VW in the circle on the back door had been repainted into a white peace symbol. Bumper stickers had been pasted on the hood, the windshield and the doors. "QUESTION AUTHORITY," one insisted. A hand-painted Earth had been captioned: "THERE IS NO GRAVITY. LBJ SUCKS." The van's passenger window rolled down. A tan hand waved at me. The cargo door opened. A sign above it read: "ASS, CASH OR GRASS. NO ONE RIDES FREE."

I'll be expected to drop an offering in the plate. Will a dollar be enough?

"Dude! Make haste. Pig'll come for our asses," the driver shouted. A Rubenesque woman on the center bench seat hollered, "Jump in, mate, afore the pig backs up."

Sammie Davis Jr., you're not going to believe this. The driver is a Negro—I guess you want me to say Afro-American—but dig this: the dude has actually got a ponytail.

A sepia-toned girl beside the driver did something else I wouldn't have believed: she stubbed a hand-rolled cigarette on the spit of her tongue, and then she swallowed it. The fine bones of her nose and the angles of her cheeks were like Mexicans and Indians, but her brown hair was frizzy, like a Negro's. No one had looked like her in our homogeneous little Hell Creek.

I tossed my typewriter case into a smoky ambiance that didn't smell like cigarettes.

The camper was a cave on wheels. A sink and a kitchen cabinet were mounted behind the driver. The center and back benches were draped with red, yellow and blue-striped *serapes*. I landed on white cotton pillows that dotted the floorboard. Windows covered with curtains surrounded every daisy-painted wall.

"Cool van."

"Far out, huh!" the driver said. "1953 Deluxe Microbus." It accelerated with the sound of a lawnmower, but the engine noise came from a compartment between the driver and passenger.

"Pig isn't moving," the woman in the back seat reported.

"Why do you call the highway patrol a pig?"

"Because authority demands obedience," the front seat girl said in a Desi Arnez accent, "but we are the people. We are the counter culture. We make our rules."

"But why pig?"

"Ever read *1984*?"

I nodded.

Back Bench Woman watched the patrol car. "All animals are equal, but the fascist pigs thought they were more equal. Are you going to Fisherman's Wharf?"

"What's at Fisherman's Wharf?"

Back Bench Woman held up two fingers. "Summer of Love, dude."

I replied with the same two fingers and a question in my eyes.

"That's a peace sign." Then Center Bench Guy drew a square in the air.

I'm can be pretty sure that means I'm square.

Back Bench Woman leaned forward and rested her hands and head on the bench between us. Her mid-winter dark hair was highlighted with molecular silver moons. Dimples creased her cheeks. "You know. 'Are You Going to San Francisco?' Wear some flowers in your hair."

That much I got. It's a hit even in Oklahoma.

"Every revolution has a song," the driver said. "That's the anthem of our generation."

"We're making the Monterey Pop Festival," said Front Seat Girl. "It's a three-day happening. Jimi Hendrix, The Who . . . "

"Ravi Shankar," the driver threw in. "Right on."

"And Janis Joplin," Back Bench Woman smiled with brown and amber eyes.

I found it impossible to guess her age.

"And Otis Redding," said the blond man on the center bench, "if you can dig that." His T-shirt revealed salt and ammonia circles under each arm, and an acrid scent emanated from his sweat. He was an illustrated man: army tattoo on his left forearm, three crosses under his collarbone, and an Incredible Hulk on his right bicep. He unfolded a plastic bag from his shirt pocket and rolled a cigarette from what looked like garden clippings.

"What's that?"

"A Glad Bag," Center Bench Woman said. "I brought it over from Australia."

"He means the dope, Dope." It seemed Hulk also shared a disposition with the wrathful asshole of superheroes. "It's marijuana."

Although she was plump, Center Bench Woman shrank into her seat.

"We're going to Haight-Ashbury afterwards," Back Bench Girl finished. She could tell from my expression I didn't know what she meant. "That's where Fisherman's Wharf is. And you—you have a Southern accent."

"Southwestern. I'm from Oklahoma."

Now she transmitted incomprehension.

"Scarlett O'Hara has a Southern accent. John Wayne has a Southwestern accent."

"I am corrected. Fisherman's Wharf is in San Francisco. All the cool people will groove there after the fest."

"It'll be a revolution, man. Lots of LSD." Hulk looked as if he'd been roasted by his own temperament: reddish-blond hair, Viking beard with golden highlights, face sunbaked to a purplish hue. He lit his roll-your-own, held his breath, and spoke at the same time. "Ohmygod. This shit is so good, they should make it illegal."

Marijuana. That's what I smell. "Are y'all hippies?"

Center Bench Woman had sucked hard on the cigarette; now she choked with laughter. She coughed: "Aye, mate, we represent an alternative lifestyle, if that's what hippie means. We call ourselves freeks or flower children." She was less attractive because she was a good twenty pounds overweight. She passed the stogie over my head to Front Seat Girl, who sipped smoke for five seconds and rasped out. She repeated the inhalation, but this time she kissed the black driver and blew smoke into his mouth.

"SHOTGUN!" The driver pumped a fist into the air. "That is boss."

"Let's hear some rock and roll," Hulk demanded.

The front-seat passenger pushed a tape into the eight-track and played the final stanza of "Incense And Peppermints."

"So," the sweet-faced girl on the back bench dimpled again, "where are you going?"

"Palo Alto."

"Why?" Center Bench Woman asked. Her anxious face seemed well used, as if life had ridden her just inches from being a barfly in a Bogey-and-Bacall movie.

"I'm looking for my dad."

"Is he lost?" Hulk snarked. It wasn't the words he had said, it was the contemptuous snap.

"'At was the sound of arrogant snide," Center Bench Woman turned to Hulk. "Can you be so uncaring as to purposely hurt the feelings of a person you don't even know?"

"Oh, hell, lighten up! I'm just joshing the *muchacho.*"

"Do you care?" It was a sincere question from the back bench.

"Crap, I don't know! It was just a question. He can answer or not. I don't give a shit about his daddy." He cut his eyes toward the woman beside him. "Don't pick a fight with me."

"Nay," Center Bench Woman said. "You stir up the trouble. And when someone calls your hand, you fault someone else, Bruce MacDavid."

That's Biggy. Picks a fight, and when it goes against him, he blames his target.

"Bummer!" Hulk sighed to me, as if he could make amends with one word.

Biggy never said he was sorry; he asked for sympathy from his victim.

The driver switched to the radio, and the Seekers sang "Georgy Girl."

"'At's me name, Georgy," Center Bench Woman turned to me. "And 'at's me song. 'Georgy Girl.' 'At's what they call it here. When I left Sydney, it were titled 'Come the Day.' The Seekers, 'at's me favorite group. They're Aussies too. Me favorite song, 'fore this one, was 'I'll Never Find Another You.' It was a hit there, ages 'fore it crossed the Pond."

"Say, handsome, what's your name?" Back Bench Girl flirted.

Handsome? It wasn't true, but I still flushed with pride. "Curtis."

"I'm Catherine. That's Bruce and Georgy. Miguel's our driver; Chica is our navigator. What," she emphasized the interrogatory, "are you doing out here alone?"

"I'm being impetuous." I looked quizzically at Chica. "Your actual name is Girl?"

"My Christian name is Aiyana."

"I call her *Caliente Piernas*," Mikey stroked Chica's bare thigh.

Hot Legs? My lips involuntarily pursed into an O.

Mikey watched me blush.

I'd never seen a black man touch a white woman, if that's what she really was. Chica looked Hispanic with an eyedropper of Oriental. And maybe Negro. There are three races: are Hispanics white enough to be white? I searched the history texts in my mind. Mexicans are Spanish, and some are mixed with Central American Indians. Spanish are white Europeans; some are mixed with the Moors that invaded Spain. And Moors came from Morocco, which is North Africa. So, Moors were Mongoloids? Or Negroids? The Black Dutch in me was rooted in the Spanish Moors. And my Native American part from Daddy would be from Asians who had migrated across the Great Land Bridge.

I'd picked up a John Birch Society magazine in my dentist's office. The Birchers had preached about the danger of whites and yellows and blacks blending themselves into a mongrel race. Xenophobia aside, Chica was an inch away from striking: a long groovy woman in a black T-shirt, fleshy lips, and arched Carmen Miranda eyebrows and cheekbones.

"Mikey, why don't we take Cortez with us to Salinas?" Chica proposed. "You'd get a couple more hours north, then you could thumb up 101 to Palo Alto."

"Or, dude," the driver glanced at me in the rear-view mirror, "do you want to hang with us? We camp in the van. *Nuestra casa es su casa.*"

"Okay. Thank you, Chica," I rolled the "ch" sound the way I was taught by Mrs. Lane.

"When you get to Palo Alto," Catherine advised, "go to a cafe called the Full Circle."

Is that jealousy in Hulk's glare?

Mikey turned up the radio and harmonized "Somethin' Stupid" with Frank and Nancy.

"It's downtown, near University and El Camino Real," Catherine said. "It's a communal restaurant. If you work, you can crash there at night."

"Crash?"

"You can stow your suitcase in the crash pad upstairs, and they'll feed you three squares, and you can clean up in the restroom," Catherine said. "And it's safe."

The radio played "Ode To Billie Joe."

"Hey, little dude," Hulk slanted more sarcasm my way. "This is your song."

"Bru-cie," Catherine derisively corrected, "the Tallahatchie Bridge is in Mississippi."

Hulk was a pure, unadulterated, fat-free jerk, but Catherine knew how to put him in his place.

I'd always heard two people just knew when they were right for each other. Catherine fit me. The library had given away little-used books last summer, and one thin paperback had been by Plato. He thought humans originally had four arms and legs. The gods had wanted to destroy us, but Zeus had split us into male and female, so we're destined to search the Earth for our other halves. *Is Catherine my other half? I like you, O'Murphy, but will you be mine if I go back?*

"How do you know?" Hulk growled.

"Bobbie Gentry says so." Catherine sang with what sounded like a trained voice, "Another sleepy, dusty Delta daaay." For me, she added, "I love a sad song."

"Me too. I mean, I love this one, Catherine."

"Do you understand the words?" Cath asked. "I've never figured out what it meant."

"I think Billy Joe loved the singer, and she must have loved him, but something went wrong. They threw something off the Tallahatchie Bridge. And then Billy Joe jumped off. So maybe it's just about the futility of life, of loving someone. To me, it speaks from across time."

"Across time? You're a poet. Everyone calls me Cath. Do you have a nickname?"

"I've always wanted something desperately hunky like Rock or Byron, but it's–Cutie."

"Why Cutie?" She chuckled. "And you–you're blushing."

"No I'm not. My older brother couldn't say Curtis. He said something like Clootie. And my last name is Pye. So my own stupid mother stuck me with Cutie Pye."

"Well, you are." Her glorious grin widened and I blushed fire-engine red, but I realized for the first time how sexy full, womanly lips can be. *I wish I knew how old you are.*

CHAPTER 3o

THE SUMMER OF LOVE

"You're a great listener," Cath said to me, loudly enough for Hulk to hear. "A skill every man should learn."

Hulk looked up and scorched my face again. *Is he with Georgy or not? She isn't old enough to be his mother, so she's either his sister or his girl.* As if to answer, Georgy reached out and picked lint from Hulk's collar and smoothed his hair. "Thanks, Beautiful," Hulk murmured.

Georgy's face stiffened. "Hardly that."

"After you find your father," Cath asked, "will you join us for the Summer of Love?"

Love. The term is overused. I've had dozens of crushes since Mary Helen, the sixth grader who'd sat in front of me. Each had been the most wonderful girl ever. Yesterday, it had been Doreen. Then Skye. Cath is no girl, she's a woman without a ring on her finger, but I wouldn't dare offer my friendship. That had always been the kiss of death. Every time I'd let a girl know I liked her, she'd snatched my heart, tossed it in the dirt and stomped it. I've always crushed on the wrong girls. Even so, I love crushes. I'd love the giddy satisfaction of bonding. And I'd love that pair-of-old-jeans comfort couples seem feel with each other.

"Are you in college?" I asked.

"And out," Cath sighed.

"What's your bag?"

"Controlling men," Hulk interjected.

Their conversation had ping-ponged for miles. "Still not sure," Cath said. "I'm an artist, so maybe I could sculpt. But I'd also like to be a poet, or a singer."

"How she's going to pay for any of that is the question," Hulk said. "Nothing but Stanford will do for her, and that's private tuition."

"What do you want to be?" Cath asked me.

"When he grows up?" Hulk inserted.

"Are you twelve or something! Why can't you just be with me?" Georgy erupted, then glanced sideways at Cath, "instead of every woman in the van?"

According to Mother and Sandy, Daddy also had Roman eyes and Russian hands. I've got a feeling he and Hulk were alike.

"Let's start over," Cath ignored Georgy. "What do you want to be?"

"Well, I've fought internationally with the French Foreign Legion." Cath smiled. *Wow. Another woman who gets my jokes.* "But I want to write." *That came out like brag, but I want Cath to marvel at me as much as I'm attracted to her.*

"I'll bet you have creative talent, don't you?" Cath chuckled and clapped her hands. "Apply early at Stanford. They have a fine-arts program. I'll be your muse."

"Once again, fair maiden fills a child's head with foolish thoughts. And how would you pay for these uber-expensive educations? Sell your asses?" Hulk said.

Georgy smacked Hulk's arm so hard, Mikey and Chica's heads turned.

"What?" Hulk said. "I'm not inferring anything heavy, woman."

Implying. You imply, and we infer from what you said.

"I'm just saying, that's what sexy women can do. They all sit on gold mines, and they sell their asses when they get married anyway, so why not earn fifty bucks an hour until they say, "I do?' Fire up another doobie." Hulk handed his baggie to Georgy and looked at me. "Pot ain't for potholes. Want a hit?"

"I don't smoke."

"You don't have to inhale, just hold it in your mouth."

"But it's illegal."

"But it'll get you high."

No, but I actually want to try it. I'm an explorer; I'm curious about anything I've never done before. "No. I don't like to lose control."

"That's the point of getting high." Hulk turned back to Cath and pimped his bright idea one more time. "You could pay tuition and bank a thousand dollars every month. When you graduate, you'd have to take a pay cut just to work at General Motors."

"What if I actually did?" Cath hypothesized. "Aren't all acts of love normal and sacred?"

"N-no," I stammered before I could stop myself. I couldn't let her advocate that. And now that I was about to speak, I was curious to hear what I had say. "You don't mean . . . I mean, you're right, philosophically, love is normal and sacred. But prostitution isn't love."

With a sideways finger roll, Hulk signaled me to continue.

"Okay, well, selling your body might be okay if your kids were starving; God should forgive a mother for that."

Where am I going with this? I'm not even sure I believe in God— not the irritable Old Testament God, anyway. Maybe the New Testament Jesus. I think Satan must be an invention. But even if there is a God, I don't admire him, and I don't think he adores me either. And if that indifferent God is righteous–if he isn't just a creator who set the earth and the heavens in motion and then took a vacation for a couple of millennia–then I'm mad at him. Why hasn't he given back my daddy? Change the topic. "So, exactly what is the Summer of Love?"

Hulk snorted. "There's a whole committee for it. The Council for the Summer of Love. They want everybody to meet at Haight and Ashbury for a love-in and a war protest."

"A lot of people will be there?"

"Yeah!" Cath inserted with emphasis. "Try to come. Okay? They'll be lots of free love."

Free love? What does that mean? I felt as dumb as the moon. "What if I don't find you?"

"We'll find you. At the Full Circle."

"Stay away from drugs, though," Mikey warned. "Young dude like you, you don't want to try the H or the acid unless you've got a guru. In case you have a bum trip."

Gooroo? H? Bum trip? I've heard of LSD, but I don't understand the rest.

The latest bump in the road bounced *East of Eden* from Cath's bench.

"Good book."

"I'm still struggling with chapter one. You've read it?"

I nodded. Mrs. Lane had said Steinbeck was a hundred pages too wordy. I think she should've subtracted another hundred.

"What's it about?" Cath asked.

"Here. Salinas. It's about sin, and I guess it's about how we can never escape evil. The characters live east of Eden which, in the Bible, is the Land of Nod."

"The Land of Nog?" Hulk asked.

"N-O-D. Means 'shaking.' Steinbeck's irony."

"Steinbeck? Wasn't he an admiral or something?" Hulk asked.

Cath rolled her eyes. "I can dig the shaking. We just had an earthquake. There was something in the Bible about Cain building his own city. Is that San Francisco?"

"Monterey. It's an anti-Eden, like Sodom or Gomorrah. And I think Adam Trask's family is trying to find their way back to the garden."

"Are you some kind of super-Christian or something?" Hulk's question showed disdain.

"I only went to church for a year, but I like reading about religion."

"Why?" Cath asked.

"I like figuring it out in the context of history. I guess I like religious history too."

Hulk snorted. "Okies read? I thought they only played shit-kicking music: Hank Williams, Porter Wagner, Woody Guthrie . . . "

"Steinbeck couldn't have said it more graciously." Georgy's tongue was a sharp Gillette.

"Dude," Mikey chided Hulk. "I dig Hank. And Patsy Cline. Ever heard 'Lonesome Whippoorwill?' 'Crazy?' 'This Land Is Your Land?' Just Scott McKenzie with a twang. Equally righteous."

Hulk's eyes smoldered. He'd embarrassed himself again, so now he was mad at me.

"So, Cutie." It was Cath's turn to change the subject. "What'll you say to your dad when you meet him?"

Chica turned in her front seat. Mikey looked at me from the rearview mirror.

CHAPTER 31

THE WAYWARD WIND

Mikey pulled over at a red-and-yellow Whiting Brothers sign. "Hamm's recycling station."

"Bathroom break," Chica interpreted. She opened her door and Mikey slid over to her side. Limb in limb, they walked like two intertwined saplings.

I popped the cargo door, liberated myself from the marijuana smoke, and tottered.

Hulk grabbed my arm. "Steady, Hoss. Got a contact high?"

This time, I felt what his flower-power jargon meant. I took a calm, pleasant, unsteady interest in Whiting Brothers. These way-stations–best seen from a rear-view mirror–appeared across the flat, cloudless Mojave. Pathfinder guarded the yards like a cigar-store Indian. However, this station's buckskin statue had been whitewashed and repainted with a Bartlesville brand. Although I'd never expected to be homesick, the Phillips 66 shield reminded me of Oklahoma. And Mother.

Inexplicably to me, we were all ravenous. Mikey, Chica and Hulk opted for more Hamm's beer. I chose the nectar of the gods, Dietetic Dr Pepper. Real Dr Pepper was like drinking a bottle of watery maple syrup, and Coke was just a harsh sugar burn at the back of the throat. Dietetic Dr Pepper was a balance of honey, citrus sour, salt and spice.

"Get thee behind me, munchies." Chica grabbed a family-sized bag of Cheetos and a cardboard carton of sour cream.

Mikey examined a package of Ding Dongs. "Never seen these before."

"Just came out," the cashier said. "Chocolate glaze. Chocolate cake. Whip cream center."

Chica's eyes widened and she lifted the package out of Mikey's hands. Two packs remained on the shelf. Cath snatched one. I grabbed the survivor.

"Mmm. You know what I learned in school today?" Georgy asked playfully. "Sharing."

I ripped the waxed paper and offered her one of my pair.

Hulk wandered the produce aisle. "Bananas are better. They're like Glad bags, but with their own little zippers." He walked to the door, spotted an ashtray filled with butts, selected the four longest, and slipped three into his cigarette pack. One long stogie had broken in half when it was stubbed, obviously by a woman with painted red lips. He twisted off the red end, lit the other, and offered it to me. "Drag?"

"Yeah, no, maybe not."

Hulk chugged the remainder of his Hamm's without drawing a breath.

Mikey refueled the van using a card that discounted the price from twenty-seven to twenty-six cents per gallon, and pasted a stamp in a booklet. I contributed a dollar. Since it was summer, a fill-up at Whiting Brothers also gave him a free sack of ice.

And the van played on. I snarfed my Ding Dong in three bites, stuffed the paper inside the empty soda bottleneck, and popped the cargo-door window.

"Dude. Don't." Mikey shouted from the driver's seat. "That's anti-ecology."

This van was an education, but I wished I had a hippie dictionary. "What's ecology?"

"It's the planet," Chica explained. "Our litter spoils Mother Earth."

"Glass is just melted sand." I felt right on this count. "It'll turn back into sand."

"Maybe, brother, but glass doesn't decompose for how long?" Mikey sounded wounded. "A hundred years? A million? Nobody knows, because three billion people haven't trashed the planet that long. Look outside. See all the paper and the cans and the bottles? See that old mattress and those tires? They aren't decomposing."

Maybe Mikey's right. Maybe what we know for sure just isn't so.

* * *

Chica had fallen asleep, and apparently Hulk couldn't tolerate her serenity. He slammed an open palm into her headrest. "Immigration! Hands where I can see 'em!"

She woke with start, assessed Hulk's expression, and just missed backhanding the grin off his face. *"Eres un cabrón!* Bruce!"

Mikey shot a disdainful look from the rear-view mirror. "So uncool, brother."

Cath leaned forward and whispered into my ear. "Aiyana was born in America, but her parents are wetback Cubans. Mikey's parents fled from Batista."

"Little Dude," Mikey called. "We're coming up on our Monterey turnoff. I'll ditch you on the turnpike so you can score an ride. You're three hours away from Palo Alto. Kapeesh?"

Chica bid goodbye. *"Nos pillamos ahora en el gao."*

I nodded. "See you later."

"If it doesn't work out with your dad, come live with us in San Francisco," Cath invited a third time. "We want to rent an old Victorian for a hundred dollars a month and sublet the rooms to all our friends for ten dollars each." She reached for my hand and drew it to her chest.

It was the first time I'd ever touched a girl's breast. My hand loitered long enough to appreciate the fullness of the organ, to feel her heartbeat, and–more magically–to sense her spirit.

"You know, we're both old souls," Cath said.

I memorized her face: juicy mouth, sugar-cube teeth, lips stuffed with maraschinos.

"Promise we'll meet again?" she asked.

I placed my hand on the empty bottle. "I swear on my sacred package of Ding Dongs."

She grinned. Her index finger pointed down, not at my knees, but higher, at my . . .

Omygodihaveastatueofliberty. I backed out of the van like a rat on ice, heels and hands and butt scraping the carpet. I had never been so embarrassed. *Please, just look away.*

She made twin bunny signs with her fingers.

I recovered enough to hold up two fingers. "Peace, Sister. Find your way to Eden."

Cath closed the cargo door, and my friends pulled away.

But I still didn't have an answer to her question. *What will I say to Daddy?*

CHAPTER 3 2

I WANT OUT

I backed down the slow lane. Traffic whooshed a few feet beside me. Cath's offer had been tempting. *Should I change course for Monterey? Could I really have her? Is she the girl for me, or is she too old? How would we make a living? How could I protect her from a guy like Hulk? But that's why I need to find Daddy.* I started up the exit a half-mile later, but a cardinal-colored '58 Bel-Air Impala ragtop stopped beside me.

"Jump in." His voice was so soft, it was hard to hear over traffic. "Where to?"

"Palo Alto."

"Sure. I'll take you."

Odd. Drivers usually tell me where they're going.

He looked angelic: skin so pinkishly tan, eyes so jaybird blue, head so wreathed with silver hair. "It's getting sunny, so I'm going to put up the top." He punched a switch, then stuck out a hand. "Francis."

I couldn't quite get my fingers around his meaty palm. "Curtis." I glanced around the car. Over seventeen feet long, this was a top-of-the-line showboat. The air conditioner contrasted with the sauna of the hippie van. Dual headlamps. Three tail lights on each fender.

"Oh, Curtis, your hand is so waaarm." His accent obviously wasn't American. "The girls must love thaaat."

I blushed, even though his compliment felt false. "Where are you from?"

"Palermo," he said with a contrast of manly beast and priss. "You have heard of it?"

"In Italy?"

"My, so young but so smart." He was fiftyish. "You are from where, and what are you doing here alone?"

"Oklahoma. I'm trying to find my father. He's a Marine." I bragged a little.

"A gyreeene?" Francis almost squealed. His reaction seemed inappropriately joyous "Isn't that a gaaas?"

My Spidey-sense tingled. *This is how Italians act?*

"He musta be *molto orgoglioso*–very proud ofa you. And you are sooo far from home."

I've always been far from home.

"Your name is Italian, you know." His round face shined like a greased pig at a rodeo.

"I thought it was Scottish, or maybe Irish."

"*Si*, but they derived it from the Romans. Roma ruled Britannia for four hundred years, no? You don't seem like a Curtis. Do you have a nickname? What does your mother call you?"

"When I was a little kid, she called me Cutie."

"Cuuutie?"

My face tightened. *I don't trust that Frankie Valli soprano.*

"I don't mean to embarrass. This is all so Americano." His voice had a comic edge. "And you've hitchhiked all the way out here? How long have you been on the road?"

"I'm not sure. More than a week." *Don't tell him more.*

He squeezed my bicep. "You have moooney?"

Our eyes met and a seed germinated. *You're why I'm afraid of men.*

He registered my distaste and took back his hand. "I justa mean— youa not hungry are you? You have money for food?"

"Yes." My seventeen dollars could last two weeks if I bought more Double Bubble. Orange groves were everywhere. I could liberate a couple for breakfast.

"*Ascolti*, I could give you five dollars. Would you taaake it?"

His question made me uneasier. "Yeah, no, I'll be all right. Almost there."

"And you're going to your faaather's house? Is that where you want me to drop you?"

"How far is it to Palo Alto?"

"Oh, I don't know. It doesn't matter. I justa enjoy being with young men like yourself. Now, you must tell me. Are you close to your father?"

Change the subject. "What do you do?"

"I wasa priest at the Vatican," Francis steered the Impala into the fast lane. "*Controllore.*"

Although he was saturated in cologne, I detected liquor on his breath. Mr. Z, our science teacher, had said that was because of osmosis. "Are you retired?"

His chuckle was an admission. "The Cardinal put it differently: s*ono senza abito.*"

"What does that mean?"

"The priest has no clothes." He grinned comically.

Defrocked? I know what that means. I've seen Richard Burton in The Night of the Iguana.

"So, you're not a preacher anymore?"

He twisted his mouth wryly like Dom DeLuise. "They acta so holy, but the Church is not without sin." He said "church" as if it were capitalized, and mimed pulling a halo from his head and flinging it into traffic. He shrieked hysterically, as if the halo had hit a car.

I smiled grudgingly. He'd be hilarious if he weren't so weird.

"Some priests, they make love to each other. All I did," he said the words innocently, as if it should have been forgivable, "was blow an altar boy. Oh well, a few. Did you know some priests use nuns for sex? Not me, ofa course. Nuns are just covens of man haters."

The Impala drifted out of our lane while he watched me instead of the road.

"Hey, if you'd rather talk, we should pull over. A nun finked you out?"

"This means nothing if you are not Catholic, but nuns are lesbians. No difference."

I nodded to agree that I wasn't a Catholic.

"They're only there to quash the joy froma holy men."

Why do you want me to know all this?

"Popes and priests are supposed to be celibate, but that's a recent contrivance. Before the sixteenth century, a vow of chastity was *facoltativo*–optional. Lotsa popes married. The Apostles were married and had families. Only the monks practiced celibacy." His tone bordered on zealousness. "The Pope St. Hormisdas–five hundred years after Christ–was widowed. He fathered another pope, St. Silverius."

"Would you stop the car? I should get out here."

"Is it hypocrisy to condemn me? In the future, I hope it will not be so much like that. Are you sure you wouldn't like something to eaaat?" The man was built like Yogi Berra, but it was creepy the way he drew out vowels. He touched my cheek, and his eyes twinkled. "We're so close to my house. I'll take you there and fixa you sandwich. Or a hot dooog."

"No. Thanks."

"Maybe you wanta five dollars now," Francis laid a bill on the seat between us.

I ignored it.

"I read the darnedest thing the other day. Open the glove compartment. Take that book." It was an old, yellowed, dog-eared paperback.

"Go to the bookmark, and read what's at the top a the page."

A father was enticing his own son by swallowing a peeled banana without biting it.

"Can you imagine? I get sooo worked up over that." Francis looked at the book, then at my crotch, then touched himself. "Oh. We are botha turned on by what is written."

Eyes on the road, Chester Molester. I drew into the space between my seat and the door.

"Did you and your brother ever play pitch and catch?"

The innuendo offended me.

Francis laughed, and I heard a forlorn softness in his tone. "For me, it was my faaather. Who did you? Was it a cousin? Maybe it was your graaandfather?"

I shook my head.

He reached down, drew a green bottle from his side of the floorboard, and unstoppered the cap. "In *Italia*," Francis offered, "we all share wine. You wanta sip?"

"No." *Time to make like a sheepherder and get the flock out of here.*

"I thinka big, striiiping boy like you has the little girls eating from his hand. So to speak." He laughed as if he had said something hilarious, and gulped from the bottle. Red trickled down his chin.

"I should doa you favor. I know a hot, salty woman in my neigh-borhood. Women and men are just alike. They aaall want to be the one who introduces a boy to sex." His eyes alternated between the road and my crotch. "I know she would like you. Let's go over to my pad."

"No." *That's the magic word.* "No. Francis, stop here."

"Cutie, it is my mission, my calling, to helpa boys like you. You need this." He giggled insanely and the red brightened in his face. The slur of his voice informed me he wasn't tipsy, he was Vin Trainer drunk. "Let me take you back to my hooouse, just a few miles . . . "

"No. Really. Let me out. Right here." *I don't think the angry God wastes his time on the likes of me. Maybe I've slighted him. But Jesus, you're the God of Love. Help me.*

The Impala slid down an off ramp.

A sigh welled up inside. *Thank you Jesus.*

The ramp was a cloverleaf, a series of right-handed curves like a roller coaster.

"Have you ever seen the Pacific Ocean? It's not that far. We can be there in minutes."

Oh no. He's headed for the coast. "I don't want to get off course."

"You can swim. Won't that be a treaaat?"

"No, I don't have a swimsuit."

"Don'ta worry about that. No one will see us."

"No, Francis, I've got to get to Palo Alto. My father's waiting for me." *He's going to know that's a lie. I've already told him I'm trying to find Daddy.*

His eyes shifted to my crotch. I covered it with my hand.

"Let me touch it. Once. *Per favore.* You will enjoy more than I."

"No! I don't want to." It'd been a mistake to set my typewriter case on the floorboard. Nothing between his Marlon Brando arms and me. Pushing him away had no effect; he just popped my hands into the air and went for my crotch again.

"I show you what girls want. When you learn this, you will have one thousand girlfriends. You will be the most popular boy." He giggled continually. "You will screw everything . . . "

"Francis, no." *What is he going to do to me? Jesus or God, I don't know whose shift this is, but I need help.* "Stop. Stop the car! Let me out!"

"Oh well, I think we're on the wrong side of the highway now. You don't want me to put you out here. Let's get back on *il nord* side." But instead of pulling over at the northbound ramp, the Impala sped up and veered into an inside lane.

My hands trembled. *Now I know why he put up the top. No witnesses. No escape.*

He handed me the five dollars again. "Here. Pleasea take this. Let me put this in your pocket. It's yooours." Instead of aiming at my front pocket, he rubbed my crotch with the bill.

I wedged my butt into the space between my seat and door. "I'm not taking money."

The crumpled bill fell between the seats. "Oh, you don't take it yet. Why?"

This is a Hobson's choice. The correct answer is no choice at all. "Francis, let me out."

He pinched my nipple hard enough to make my eyes tear.

"Shit, Francis, that hurt. Don't do that again."

"Sorry." And he genuinely looked apologetic. Then he rubbed himself fast. A spot appeared on his pants and spread into a pool. He wasn't wearing underwear. Nothing between him and me but a sheer layer of silk.

He looked me in the eyes, licked his lips, and tried to force my head down to his legs. "I know, Cutie, you want to taste a man. Isa okay to put me in your mouth."

I slipped under his hand and retreated to my corner.

"Look at me." He looked like a snake ready to devour a mouse. "Open you eyes. I'ma gonna have you tonight if I have to knock you out and carry you inside. So say yes and enjoy it."

I couldn't stop trembling. My teeth were clenched; my eyes were wide. He saw my fear and his tone became gentler. "I know what youa thinking. It's a going to hurt. Having sex witha man will make you queer. No. I myself am not a homo. I'ma omni. You know what that means?"

I shook my head. "Francis, I'm a virgin."

"It means I screw boys, girls, animals, anything."

Scarlet anger misted my eyes. It took a long time to get me mad, but when I finally snapped, my anger was unmanageable. I hiked my boots onto his white leather seat and drew my knees up to my chin. Then I picked up my typewriter case from the floorboard and set it on his wrist, which was encroaching across the console.

"*Ahia*!" The wooden box dug into his arm. "*Amico*! I'ma gonna need that arm to drive."

I raised up a little. "Promise to leave me alone."

He withdrew his arm with alarm, and his demeanor changed from angry to apologetic. His voice was contrite. "Okay, Cutie, I see. I'ma sorry. *Siete buon ragazzo*–a good boy."

"Let me out of this car." I balanced the typewriter case in my left hand and pointed it at his head. The steel in my voice sounded as if it was coming from someone else. "Right now."

Suddenly, his falsetto deepened and his accent was American. "Whoa, kid. You'll get us both killed."

"I don't care. I'm fixin' to hit you so hard, it'll kill the whole screwed-up Vatican."

He looked in the rear view mirror, measuring his chances of moving across five lanes of congested traffic to stop on the right shoulder. "Okay. Just not here. We're in the inside lane."

"Yes. Over there." I pointed to the narrow breakdown lane on our left.

He whipped onto the narrow blacktop and braked. "Now what? You can't get out on your side; those cars will take off your door. And I'm too close to this fence. I can't open mine either."

Cars breezed within inches of the coupe. A driver laid on his horn.

Yeah yeah! I'm trapped in a car with a man who's trying to rape me. Nothing in the back seat. I pitched my typewriter case close to his ear. He ducked, and I dove over my seat. I touched the rear-window button, tossed out my typewriter case, and scissored my left leg outside.

"Hey," he watched the traffic. "You don't have to do this. Come back. I'll drive you to an exit. I'll take you to Palo Alto. Just get back in the car."

I snatched the five-dollar bill between the seats. Then I banged my case on the post between his face and the back window. "I've got two words for you: Tag. Number!" I took the BIC Stic from my front pocket and walked behind the Impala.

Francis rammed the gearshift into reverse.

I jumped into the chain link fence. The tail fin grazed my stomach and a whitewall tire rolled over my Wellingtons. A second later, the Impala jerked forward. Francis was gone.

CHAPTER 33

CAUGHT

A trucker honked four times. "Get off the median. Asshole!"

That's my fondest desire. Rectum. Another Hobson's choice: I could dash across four lanes of traffic and encourage every southbound car to play rush-hour dodgeball with the geek. Or I could scale an eight-foot chain-link fence topped by two strands of galvanized wire.

More horns blared. Okay, what if this was *Combat*? What if Sgt. Saunders had ordered Little John over this fence, right now, to save the entire squad? He'd double an army blanket under his body and throw himself on the wire. I don't have a blanket, but if I balanced my typewriter case on the chain link? Maybe I could roll under the barbed wire.

I tried to visualize it. *Impossible.*

Well, try. I wedged one boot toe into a diamond-shaped fence hole and grabbed another hold two feet up. Tiny shards of zinc poked holes in my fingers and my boot, but another step raised me a foot higher. I jammed a second square boot into one more diamond toehold in the galvanized steel. The second barbed strand was now chest high. One, two more steps, and I summited the cyclone fence.

And that's precisely when a black-and-white blew by. *So sorry. You're southbound, and I'll be northbound in a few seconds.*

I couldn't wriggle between the strands of barbed wire. Turning back would be easier–maybe smarter–but I hoisted the typewriter case to the bottom strand of barbed wire. I wrenched the case so it would stand up. Steel barbs ripped cloth that had been glued to wood, but the case bowed a two-foot gap between the top and bottom wires. *I'm going over, Little John.*

My stomach grazed a barb, and I felt cool air when a second barb scraped my shirt's back. *Go. You've got more shirts.* I somersaulted and whammed down on the other side. "Awhhh!" I kneecapped myself. I straightened my right leg to climb again and retrieve my case. A barb had stuck in the wood. I opened the case, pulled out the U.S.M.C. spoon, and pried out the steel.

Four lanes of I-5 traffic were in front of me again, but at least I was headed towards Palo Alto. Gashed typewriter case against my chest, I limped into the fastest lane of traffic and looked down the other three. The fast lane was clear for the moment, but not all four. Just then, both fast lanes cleared and a space opened in the two slow lanes. I pushed off from my right knee and stepped into the inside lane. The knee crumpled. I spun back onto the median so fast, the spoon fell out of my shirt pocket.

"Whoop! Whoop! Whoop!" A highway patrol car swung from the slow lane across the three faster lanes like Tarzan on a vine.

I grabbed the spoon.

The trooper avoided a dozen cars and made it look easy. His Plymouth Fury entered the breakdown lane thirty feet past me and halted without the screech I expected. The siren silenced, but the cherry strobe still rotated on my typewriter case and torn shirt. The cyclone fence allowed his front door to open with just enough clearance to exit with the radio mike in his hand.

"Walk to my unit," a loudspeaker on the roof commanded with the strident voice of a god.

I shuddered from the intensity of the sound and trudged to the passenger-side back door. *Caught. A few hours from Daddy, and I'm going to jail.*

"Set your suitcase on the ground!" His voice sounded like the Great and Powerful Oz. "Put both hands on the car! And drop the flatware!"

Time slowed. The spoon clattered to the concrete, bowl first, then handle, bowl, handle, bowl, handle. Handle. My hands had barely touched the hot trunk lid before the trooper was behind me, hands patting my breast pockets, sliding down my jeans.

Eat your heart out, Francis.

"Do you have a driver's license?"

I showed him my motorcycle permit. The thick card had been bent and worn and scuffed from nine months in my billfold, but the name, address and dates were legible.

His voice was no longer Olympic, but it nevertheless ordered me. "Get in the back door. Buckle your seat belt."

I grabbed my spoon and imprisoned myself inside the cruiser.

He checked the rear and side-view mirrors and dove into a vacant spot in the fast lane. My neck snapped back an inch. The Plymouth Fury accelerated from zero to eighty in what must have been eight seconds. He steered for the next exit, and the unit coasted into a convenience store parking lot. He opened his door, then unlocked mine.

"Why were you on that fence?" His tone changed to a strict parent. Tall, fit, his face looked thirtyish, but white hair salted his temples.

"I had to get back on this side."

"Why couldn't you do that at an exit?"

"That's where he left me."

"Who?"

"The guy who picked me up."

His voice softened and filled in the details. "You were hitchhiking? Someone took you the wrong way? And then he dumped you in the inside lane?"

"Yes sir."

"Why?"

"He was . . . He wanted to . . . "

He leaned back against the patrol unit and cocked his eyes toward my torn shirt. He lifted my shirt tail. "You've got a scratch. I'll get the first-aid kit. He tore your shirt?"

"I . . . I . . . "

"Easy. It's all right. Just tell me. Why did you get out? He tried something?"

It galled me to rat out anyone, but I nodded.

"Get his tag number?"

I shook my head and stretched the toes Francis had run over. They felt bruised.

"Make and model?"

"A '58 Impala convertible. Red."

He nodded, swabbed alcohol on the scratch, and applied a Curad.

"Why did he let you out?"

I tapped my typewriter case.

His smile widened with involuntary admiration. "While he was driving?"

I nodded.

"Glad it didn't come to that," he chuckled. "I'd have spent the rest of this shift sweeping up the roadway." The trooper had one of those high, square foreheads that suggested intelligence. In a mythology book I'd read at the library, the Greeks had thought beauty equaled goodness, that handsome men and beautiful women were morally upright. It wasn't true. Gatsby was good looking. Scooter is good looking. O'Murphy is good looking.

"Okay, I need to ask you a question. Be sure now. Where'd he touch you?"

I didn't answer, but he saw shame in my eyes.

"He assaulted you?"

"Not really."

"Son, let's be a hundred percent," he said with an honesty that sounded habitual. "Did he put his hands on you? Anywhere. Even your face, your shoulder?"

Instead of making eye contact, I stared at the outline of his undershirt against his short-sleeve uniform. Francis had been strong but soft in the gut; this CHIP was a Charles Atlas comic book ad. He could've beaten the dog out of Francis.

Why had Francis picked me? Did I look like the sort of boy who would've accepted? He never would've molested this trooper. I looked at the brass nameplate above his left pocket. Ronald Stanhope.

His eyes watered. He tentatively placed his hand on my shoulder. "Son, are you okay?"

I nodded.

"What did he do? Did he put his hands down your pants? Did he try anything sexual with his hands or his lips or his penis?"

"He touched me." *I wish I were dead, right here, right now.*

"He touched your penis? Son, I know this is tough, but you have to be precise."

"Yeah. He touched my . . . the outside of my pants." My throat constricted, but I controlled my emotions long enough not to choke on the words. "And he tried to make me . . . "

I concentrated on Ron's hands. Long, lean. They looked like they could've played piano, but they had an athleticism. Maybe he'd been a wide receiver. We were standing in the open. *What if Francis had followed us?* My head swiveled in both directions. I didn't see the '58.

"Okay," Ron seemed relieved. "I'm going to make a few phone calls. You're gonna stay with me, right? Until we square a few more details?"

I'm not going anywhere. Francis could be waiting.

" . . . going to look for the perpetrator, and if we can find him," the trooper's voice faded in and out " . . . ID him for me. Can you..."

I nodded. *I want to call Mother, or Nan, or Daddy. Come get me. Tell me it will get better.*

" . . . complaints in this area about molestations," Ron stuck out his hand. Veins bulged in wrists that were twice as thick as mine. " . . . more guts than I do, kid . . . how fearlessly you're standing up to all this. It took courage to do what you did. I'd have been bawling . . . "

Me? No one had ever praised my bravery, even though I'd stood up to Mother when she was wrong and fought Biggy. He had always taunted me, but he was the real coward. Biggy never fought kids who could kick his ass; he'd always picked on me or someone smaller.

"Let's take a booth in back." Ron looked so heroically groovy, he could've co-starred with Broderick Crawford on *Highway Patrol*. "You're probably hungry. Grab yourself a Coke and something to eat. By the way, did he tell you his name?"

"Francis."

A hot deli was filled with trays of fried chicken, French fries, even mozzarella on white napkins to absorb the yellow-brown grease. I chose three wings–my fave.

Ron came back. "Where can I get in touch with you?"

I shook my head between bites. "I'm going to meet my dad in Palo Alto. I have his post office box. You could write a letter, I guess, but I don't have Daddy's phone number."

Ron's eyes winced in disbelief.

"He doesn't know I'm coming." *Okay, got the message: Gil, Marietta, and now Trooper Ron. Nobody thinks taking off for California without Daddy's phone number is a good idea.*

He sighed. "Well, good luck with that. I gotta get back on patrol."

I dug into my right front pocket.

"No, you're my guest." He produced a five-dollar bill and his business card. "I'd give you more, but this is all I've got until payday."

I touched Francis' five dollars in my pocket, and held up my hands in refusal.

"You take that," Ron assured me with a smile. "If you were my son, I'd want someone to give it to you. Really. I've got a Diner's Club card, and you don't know where your next meal is coming from. Put that in your pocket. Now listen. I know kids don't think anything can happen to them. And Francis really is just an old queen. But an honest-to-gosh killer is out here. A mass murderer. A hebephile–one of his vics was twelve, three were thirteen, fourteen. We think he's kidnapped a dozen boys already." Ron reached for my shoulder.

I shifted away from his touch. Mother issued the same sort of dire warnings. As if a killer were going to find me in a state with twenty million people.

"The kids we're finding have high levels of liquor and tranqs in their blood. We think he drugs them, or gets them drunk, and ties them up while they're passed out. But here's the part you want to pay attention to." He reached for my arm with a wide, hairy hand.

I drew back again. *Why do you want to touch me? I can't even stand to smell a man's breath.*

"He knocks them out cold. Probably slips a Mick in their booze."

"A Mickey Finn?"

"Yeah. How'd you know that?" He looked at me in the eyes. "Don't drink anything someone offers you."

"It's a great advantage not to drink among hard-drinking people." I quoted Gatsby.

Trooper Ron didn't catch the reference. "But don't just look out for one bad guy. We don't know if he operates alone. Maybe he's got a young guy with him. Maybe a woman. All we know is that we find the vics bitten, bound, tortured."

Apprehension crawled up my neck.

"They're strangled or bludgeoned. Although, for at least one, it was pharmaceuticals. And one V was stabbed to death."

"Victim?"

"Victim. Discarded–although not always–along the roads. It's why we call this unsub the Freeway Killer. But that could be misleading. There could be copycats."

"Unsub?"

"Unknown subject."

"Here?"

"All over California. But the Freeway Killer ranges as far north as Oregon. The detectives think the unsub drives vics into a garage. That explains how he can burn them with a car cigarette lighter without anyone seeing or hearing."

Francis tried to get me to go home with him.

"Several vics had extensive blunt force trauma to their face and head. If you get a whiff of some guy who seems sexually interested, do what you did. Bail."

"Is a queen a homosexual?"

"Yeah. But Francis isn't really a homo, he's a pervert, so he's dangerous to young boys. He may try again. I think Francis is done for today, but if he stops here, run." He pointed to the convenience store. With that, he stopped at the on-ramp and issued a final order. "Don't walk past that sign. Stand here. It's the best place to get a ride."

I wasn't the sort to make emotional gestures, so I just said thanks.

"I should take you to the station, but you're just a few hours from your dad. If anyone with a badge gives you a problem, though–you've played Monopoly, haven't you–my card is your 'Get Out of Jail Free.' Tell 'em to call me."

The highway patrol car started forward.

"Wait! Is this the way to Palo Alto?"

CHAPTER 34

THIS CLAY MUST BE YOUR BED

"Back to your mama . . ."

"Boykie. BOY."

Something touched my shoulder. I recoiled against the passenger door.

"Sorry. Didn't mean to startle you. Dream?"

"Something like that." *And I wish I knew what it meant.*

A middle-aged man with a gray goatee and a precise South African accent tapped his watch. "Five A.M. This is as far north as we're going."

"Where are we?"

"Big Sur," Marilee interjected.

"Big Sir?"

"Off your route. We ran into a detour last night. I kept going." Marilee saw alarm in my eyes. "We're not far from where you want to be. We must drop this refrigerator unit in town, pick up an empty reefer, and deadhead to Fresno State College. It's not where you are going, so we drove a few miles out of our way. Big Sur is an ocean town. You

may sleep on the beach. No *braais*, no lights, no music, and the *kêrels*–
the police chappies–won't bust you. Roll down your window. You must
be awake to hear this: the sun rises from the east over those dunes.
Follow it to Highway 1, then turn north to Carmel and Monterey. Keep
going until you reach Gilroy. From Gilroy, you're not more than, oh,
one-hundred-twenty miles south of Palo Alto."

"Thanks, Marilee." I memorized the towns: Carmel, Monterey,
Gilroy, CMG. I'd pass by Cath and the gang in Monterey.

"Hope you find *ou toppie* soon." *Ou toppie*, Bokamoso had said
before I went to sleep, meant old man.

My boots stepped on sand instead of dirt. I looked up as Bokamoso
and Marilee's semi lumbered away. The moon was a great silver fact in
California too, but it was just an inch above the ocean horizon. I wish I'd
asked this in science class, Mr. Z, but why is Earth the planet and Luna
the moon? Because Earth is populated and Luna isn't? But that can't be
right. If Phobos is inhabited, are Mars and Deimos her satellites?

It'd rained last night, so the air smelled crisp. I lay on a dune and
studied the one-eighth cameo. *Where does the shadow come from? It's
not Earth's shadow, or this would be an eclipse. Hmm. I create my own
shadow. Maybe the moon's shadow is from the moon itself.*

The cold moon and the warm ocean communicated with an intimacy, an understanding, a celestial wavelength when the time of reces-
sion had been required. The crescent finally dipped into the ocean. I
half expected to hear an icy sizzle.

No one was around and the Pacific was a courteous invitation,
so I parked my typewriter case among the dune grasses, shucked my
linen and dove in. I closed my eyes and floated. *A guy could live like
this. I wouldn't need money. I could fish and crab and oyster and boil
seaweed. I could bathe and brush my teeth. But that wouldn't get me*

closer to Daddy. Or save O'Murphy from Scooter and Spit. I waded back to my clothes, dressed and splatted onto the beach.

* * *

We passed a narrow green sign: GILROY 2 SAN JOSE 60.

"How far is Palo Alto from San Jose?" I asked as I stepped from the pickup.

"Long way," my ride said. "Durn near forty-five miles."

My imagination leaped ahead. If I could get to the Palo Alto post office by five, the postmaster could tell me Daddy's address. I could sleep in a bed tonight, or at least on Daddy's couch. I'd be indoors. I'd be safe.

But no car slowed. It'd taken four hours to walk backwards, thumb out. "GILROY POP. 7,348," a sign finally greeted. One-horse town. No traffic lights.

The sun squatted low. Wow, I was tired. A westerly breeze had felt tropical at first, then an unruly north wind had stolen my warmth.

Thumb out, I continued through town and hoped against forlorn hope I'd get one more ride before it got so dark drivers couldn't see my face. Down Sixth Street, I could make out Gilroy City Hall, not gothic but nonetheless foreboding. A motel advertised its nightly rate: twelve dollars. *No way. I can eat for days on twelve dollars.* And besides, I wanted to meet Daddy with money in my pocket.

Another mile and I was north of the town limits. The pasture looked warm and flatulent from the summer's day, but the sky faded into haze, and minutes later I walked in the dark. The blacktop road felt spooky. I sat on my suitcase, thumb out. Mist turned to drizzle. Still, I faced the opposing headlights, shirt clinging to my back, right thumb out.

I should be happy. I turned my face toward the sprinkles and stuck out my tongue. I'd rather walk by myself in the rain than kill myself over Biggy or Pickle. No one hurts me here. If I don't count Francis. But no way he can find me in for-God-sakes Gilroy.

I decided to be optimistic: the past had deserted me, and the future was taking its sweet time to find me, but when was the last time I'd expected a good life? I checked my watch: nine P.M. Thirty minutes ago, the clouds had been a study in gray scale. Now they drained to silhouette the trees and the fences and the grass, and the night turned as cheery as a graveyard.

I pulled my CPO shirt from my case. The wooly Pendleton prickled my skin, but at least the drizzle wouldn't penetrate. *I've got to get inside.* A brooding, silent lea lay to my right. Was that an upside-down water tank? I climbed through the barbed wire. Lambs loped backwards. I kept my voice low. "Easy, girls. I'm not in the mood for mutton. You know, 1967 is the Year of the Sheep." Fat raindrops plunked rudely onto my nose. My ears picked out the creatures of the gloom: the deer browsed for tender shoots, the rabbits for wild oats, the mice for seeds. That "yip yip yip" in the distance was probably a coyote browsing for the deer, the rabbits, the mice.

Close to the fence, the overturned bottom of a corrugated livestock pond had rusted into Swiss cheese. I raised it into a standing position. No bigger than a round kitchen table, but it looked uninhabited: no spiders, no ants, no snakes. I shrugged. *I've got to sleep somewhere.* I lowered my shelter over my head. I could still smell animal musk in the dirt. My shirt and jeans and hair smelled wet. I needed to shower; my underarms stank. I stuck a finger inside my mouth and sniffed. Ugh. I hadn't brushed my teeth since I'd left Marietta's.

I quieted my mind by reciting a stanza of something we'd sung from the church hymnal during my only year in Sunday school:

"Princes, this clay must be your bed,

"In spite of all your towers;

"The tall, the wise, the rev'rend head

"Must lie as low as ours!"

CHAPTER 35

THE FILTHIEST BOY

A rustling sound.

I woke.

Skunk? Dog? No. It sounded bigger.

Did something see me come here? Easy. Don't Bosco in your boxers.

Something tried not to make a sound. Then it inhaled. And it snorted.

People don't make noises like that. Maybe a bull.

I raised the tank about twelve inches.

A Mia Farrow-sized doe leaped into a defensive stance and trembled with anticipation.

We had a five-second staredown. "Hey, girl. Just me. No pointy weapons."

She spun and . . . blink. A football field away, she sprang over a four-string barbed-wire fence with no more effort than I would use to step over a curb.

Gee. Teach me how to do that.

* * *

Rain had dripped through the stock tank's rusty holes. Mud had caked my back. Not a dry spot on my clothes. *I should've changed in the pasture. No one will let me in their car.*

The first car of the morning was a rural postal Jeep with a right-side steering wheel. I stuck out my thumb, but the postman smiled and pointed to a sign on the rear quarter panel: "FEDERAL VEHICLE NO PASSENGERS."

I walked, thumb out, and thought of Mikey and Chica and Cath at the Summer of Love. I sang in my head. *Who am I this time, gentle people? Right you are. Mr. McKenzie.*

The rolling hills and the ponds and the cows and the farmhouses looked just like Oklahoma. A tractor towing hay bales rolled toward me and stopped. I ran to the passenger side, but the farmer rode on the only seat.

"You a purty mess. Did ya camp out here last night?"

"I–uh–how far are you going?"

"Twenty miles, straight ahead." He nodded toward the trailer. "Ride on the bales."

At least you can't molest me.

We made it to Los Paseos in fifty minutes. "Am I still on Highway 101 to Palo Alto?" I asked when the farmer stopped at an Esso for diesel.

"Durn near home. Thirty miles'll do it fer shore."

I waved my thanks.

A woman about the age of Mother pulled up to the gas pumps in a turquoise '66 Thunderbird. She looked me up and down, then glanced doubtfully at the gas attendant.

He winked at her.

Yeah, I know. I'm the filthiest boy in the history of filthiest boys. I walked up to the attendant in a khaki shirt, bow tie, and Esso uniform cap. "Can I wash up in your bathroom?"

"You may." He emphasized the correct word while he looked me over. "But trade me a favor. There's a broom and a mop in there. Clean up after yourself? Rinse the sink?"

I nodded. "Of course."

It took ten minutes to rub my entire body using only my hands and liquid soap from the dispenser, change clothes, and spiffy the restroom. I passed a pay phone on the way out. *See, Gil, I was right; now a call will cost a dime.*

"Information. What name? What city?"

"Do you have a phone number for Jonathan Robert Pye? In Palo Alto?"

She paused several seconds. "What is his street address?"

My heart sputtered. *You won't give me the number unless I know his address?* "I have his post office box number."

"In Palo Alto? Sorry. No Jonathan Robert in Palo Alto."

"Do you have any Pyes? P-Y-E. And is San Francisco anywhere close to Palo Alto?"

"I don't have San Francisco." Another pause. "Could he spell it another way?"

"No. Thanks." I hung up. I was just thirty miles away from Daddy. If he actually lived in Palo Alto, I'd be there by dark, even if I walked all the way at two-and-a-half miles an hour.

Turned out, that wasn't necessary. T-bird Lady must've waited for me. She pulled alongside, pushed a button, and the driver's window whirred down. "*Where* are you going?"

"Palo Alto."

"Get in," she said, as if she had made a grudging decision.

I walked around and opened the passenger door. *White drop top. Leather seats with biscuit pleats. Leather on the doors. Chrome on the console and the instrument panels. Custom T-bird floor mats. Close to five thousand dollars here.*

"Where in Palo Alto?"

"The post office."

"Downtown? Or one of the branches?"

I deflated. "How many are there?"

"At least a half-dozen. It's a Palo Alto address?"

"Yes ma'am. A P.O. box."

"Good. Then it's not Menlo Park or Mountain View. I'm going to Pacific Bell, downtown. You should start at the main post office. They'll direct you to the right one."

Doorstep delivery.

"What is your name?" Her tone seemed gruff.

"Cuti…" *Time to get rid of your stupid nickname.* "Curtis."

"My name is Louise. Where did you come from?"

I stiffened. After Francis, I wanted to avoid details, but I needed this ride.

"And why are you out here hitchhiking?"

"Looking for my dad." I felt offended by her presumption that I should answer to her.

"And why do you expect to find him at the post office?"

And why do you suppose I can't? "I have his box number."

Louise shot a look of motherly disapproval. "And you are from . . ."

"Oklahoma."

"You surely haven't hitchhiked all this way?"

I nodded. *I surely have.*

"How long?"

"A week." I'd lost track of the days. "Or so."

Louise was chagrined again. "Where is your mother, that she lets you wander about the country like this?"

"Oklahoma." I felt compelled to defend her. "She didn't know I left."

"I shouldn't think so. And your father? Does know you're coming? Am I just supposed to drop you at the post office and allow you fend for yourself?"

And why is this your bee's wax?

"Don't Let the Sun Catch You Crying" played on her radio. One of my all-time faves. Gerry and the Pacemakers had sung it three years ago on *The Ed Sullivan Show*. With paper route money I'd bought their first album, "Ferry Cross the Mersey." I'd loved it, even more than "Revolver." I'd taken their song as a profound instruction: boys don't cry. And if they do, they don't let anyone see their fear.

A few minutes later, Louise parked in front of the downtown post office. Her voice mellowed. "Sugar, if you don't find your daddy, tell me where will you sleep tonight."

"It's okay. I can take care of myself." My tone sounded affronted. *I'm a salty dog. Sugar. I sleep in ditches. I'm the most invisible kid in the history of most invisible kids.*

She brought out her checkbook.

"No, please. I don't need . . . I have money."

She looked miffed, but printed numbers on a deposit slip. "Here, my work phone at the telephone office. I'm the office manager. Sugar, if you need help, you call me. Hear?"

Thanks, but I've got it from here.

CHAPTER 36

NEEDLE IN A NEEDLESTACK

I set my typewriter case on the post office steps. I went through every pocket of every pair of jeans and of every shirt. Even though they'd been worn and washed since I'd left, I pulled out all my clothes. The Marine Corps envelope from Mother's closet wasn't there.

I panicked. *Where's that letter?*

P.O. Box nine-something. 956? 969? I'd hitchhiked seventeen hundred miles, and now I didn't know Daddy's post office box number? I should've memorized it. I didn't cry, but I was miserable enough. A sharp-faced postman passed. I opened my mouth, but he was already gone.

In the lobby, dozens of rows of vintage brass post office boxes with two combination locks had tarnished into black. I peered into 969, but I couldn't read the names or addresses on the letters. The highest number was 999. Getting to Palo Alto from Oklahoma had been like finding a needle in a haystack. Finding Daddy's box now would be like finding a needle in a needle stack. And I might not even be at the right post office. I hadn't expected Daddy would be standing here when I arrived, but I had imagined that maybe he'd get off work around six P.M., pick up his mail, see me, and say how sorry he was for not coming around the last six years.

I emptied my typewriter case and searched again. It had to be there. Although I'd worn them on the road, I turned every sock inside out. No letter.

Should I call Biggy? He'll find the address, but he'll be an assho— don't cuss. He'll be an anus about it. I'd rather ask Mother, but I'm not going to. I'll just sit here for two days.

I peeped into the windows of Box 959 and Box 956. No way to see the recipient's name or address on the letters. The same hatchet-faced postman walked by again and caught me staring into the boxes. "Sir?"

He ignored me.

"Sir?" I followed him.

He cut into an interior entrance: Employees Only Past This Point.

"Sir! I'm looking for my father."

"Does he work here?" He spun around. His look defined the difference between ignorance and apathy: he didn't know, and he didn't care. "Are you lost?"

"No sir."

"Then why are you here?"

I felt bewildered. "I think Daddy may have a box here. Jonathan Robert Pye."

"You don't know?"

"No sir. This isn't the only post office, is it?"

"In California?"

Quel jerk. "In Palo Alto."

"No, this is not the only post office." He assumed an air of polite exasperation. "Don't you have his box number? You're going to need a few more facts."

Here's a fact: your mama wishes birth control pills were retroactive. "I can't find it."

"Well. Then, I suggest you go home and get it. Then I can help you." He shut the door.

I trudged outside, plopped onto the steps, and looked at my watch: eleven thirty. I read the hours on the door: nine A.M. to five P.M. Five hours and thirty minutes to find Daddy.

Another blue uniform passed me; this postman was middle-aged, but with a two-inch blond ponytail. Must be a California thing.

"Sir?"

"Yes, young man. How can I help you?"

"When the post office closes, can people still get in?"

"Our windows close at five o'clock, but yes, the lobby is open from six in the morning until midnight."

"I think my daddy has a box here."

"And you're waiting for him?"

"Yes sir. Do many people come here after five to get their mail?"

"Oh, I'm not here then, but yes, many of our patrons can't get here during business hours, so they come before work or after they get off."

Bank on that. "Thank you."

"You're most welcome, young man. Hope he comes soon."

I sat down by the main entrance. *With any luck, Daddy will walk right past me. And I'll recognize him.*

* * *

The pony-tailed postman left for the day at five-fifteen P.M. "Glorious day to be alive."

I hadn't noticed, but I nodded.

"You picked the right place. The post offices back East are all Federal or Colonial. Spanish motifs and flat roofs are the rage here in

California, and this was the first." He sat down and recited a five-minute history. Then he looked me in the eye. "Sure your dad's coming?"

"Sure." *Are people ever really sure when they say sure?*

"What's your name?"

Don't say Cutie. "Curtis."

"The federales here call me Chick." Made sense. He was about five feet six, skinny, with a bowed chest. He rubbed my hair.

Thanks, Chick. But please don't touch me next time.

I waited another four hours until no one else passed by. Then I had to find a place to sleep. I didn't want to go far, though. What if Daddy had worked the graveyard shift and came to get his mail before he started work tomorrow morning? I needed a place where I could watch who came and went. The bushes wouldn't do. Too scratchy. Too visible. Well, Chick said the roof was flat. I picked up my typewriter case, walked around the building, and found a ladder attached to the wall. I don't like high places, but which would be worse, climbing up to the roof or being discovered by cops? Or Francis? I'd told him I was coming to Palo Alto.

The temperature plunged all night. I shivered. How cold was it? Into the fifties, I was sure. I put a pair of jeans over my jeans, socks over socks, shirt over shirt, and threw my CPO shirt onto the black tar roof to make a bed. I'd find him tomorrow.

CHAPTER 37

THE ATTITUDE OF A CIVIL SERVANT

The stars eroded as postmen met the dawn, parked, and walked into the back entrance.

The tar roof had dusted my clothes like lamp black. I'd wallowed in mud the night before, and now I looked like I'd been attacked by a charcoal grill. I wanted to climb off the roof before anyone realized I'd slept there, but should I wait on the post office steps looking like–well, like a charbroiled hippie? I shed the blackened layer and wore the last of my last quasi-clean clothes.

The back parking lot finally emptied for a moment. I swung my right foot over the parapet, reached for the ladder, and discovered that down was harder than up. I couldn't force my right leg over the side. Each time I lost my nerve and rolled back onto the roof. How would I get down?

It was seven A.M. The lobby had been open for an hour. Dozens of customers had already collected their morning mail. I might've missed Daddy already. I walked around the rooftop. There was no other way down. It was this ladder or jump. What if I lay on my stomach and swung both legs over at the same time? I could hang onto the parapet with both hands. I looked down at the ladder, then the ground below. The top step of the ladder was two feet down. A fear of falling dictated that both feet must touch the ladder at the same time.

As cold as it was, I sweated and heaved. My hands were moist. I moved backwards an inch and forced my right hand to let go of the ladder so I could grab the typewriter case. My left foot slipped an inch, and I shrieked like a ten-year-old girl.

* * *

Chick was sitting in my spot when I walked around the building. "I wondered about you. Your dad didn't show?"

"Not yet sir."

"Where did you come from?"

"Oklahoma."

"You're not old enough to drive, are you?"

"No sir. I hitched."

"Well, wait until after morning rush. About ten o'clock, come in and speak with the postmaster. Ask if he'll help find your dad. Understand now, don't ask for your father's box number; don't ask for his street address." He looked me over. "Where did you sleep?"

I was afraid to answer.

"Curtis, that's dangerous. There are creeps out here. You don't know."

Oh, but I do. I've met Francis. "Where should I sleep?"

"Soup kitchen around that corner," Chick pointed. "Three hots and a cot."

My hands trembled like a geriatric Chihuahua.

"You hungry?"

"No sir," I lied. The chicken wings two days ago had been my last meal. I needed sugar, but I'd swallowed my last two pieces of Double Bubble yesterday.

"But they won't serve until noon. There's a McDonald's a few blocks away. It's cheap. Burger, fries, and a Coke for fifty-nine cents. You need money?"

"No sir. I still have twenty-five dollars." Counting the two fives from Francis and Trooper Ron.

"Don't say that out loud." He looked concerned. "Curtis, you're getting thinner right in front of my eyes. Go. Eat. See you in a couple of hours."

* * *

I craved sugar, so I ordered a real Dr Pepper.

"Doc-tor Pep-per?" The counter girl smirked with the cool conceit as Doreen's California friends. "McDonald's doesn't serve Doc-tor Pep-per. Do you want, like, a Coke? Or whatever?"

Actually, I'm desperate to eat. Right now. "Okay. Coke. And a cheeseburger. And fries." As soon as she laid my tray on the counter, I crammed a half-dozen French fries into my mouth.

"Dude. They're straight from the fryer. Three hundred and seventy-five degrees."

I fricasseed the roof of my mouth. My eyes watered. I fanned my mouth with my hand.

"Here." She handed me a paper cup and a slogan. "Things go better with Coke."

"Thanks." I spoke through soggy fries. I sat down in the first available booth and stuffed in the burger. I looked at the bun, amazed at the expanse of my own bite. The food was gone before I'd tasted it. I slurped the rest of the Coke and belched. "Sorry."

The counter girl watched me. "No waaay! Do you want, like, a second order?"

I could have eaten three, but I wanted to be there when Daddy showed up.

"Sure, when this place is civilized and gets Dietetic Dr Pepper."

"*Doc*-tor *Pep*-per." She shook her head, but this time she was teasing.

I waved her off and walked to the men's room, typewriter case in hand. This was my chance to brush my rotten-smelling teeth before I met my old man.

* * *

I hoped Chick had eased the way with the postmaster, who turned out to be the ferret-faced man.

"Sorry." Another brusque refusal.

"Why?"

"Why can't I help you?" His eyes shifted fast from me to Chick and back again. "How do you want me to help?"

Walk a mile in my Wellingtons and see how it feels. "I need his address."

"His street address?" He dragged me into the rhetorical trap Chick had warned about.

"Jerry," Chick soothed, "how about if this young man writes a card to his dad? Tells him he's here? That okay?"

"And what shall we do with this heartwarming missive?"

"Post it in his daddy's box. That is what we do."

"Only U.S. mail goes into the P.O. boxes."

"Curtis," Chick turned to me. "Have you got ten cents?"

I nodded.

"Give it to me." Chick dropped my dime into his wooden drawer and produced a stamped post card. "Write your note. I'll post it in his box. Okay, Jer?"

The postmaster heard sarcasm in Chick's voice. "That's giving him the box number."

"Jer, you've got the attitude of a civil servant." It didn't sound like a compliment.

Jerry's face flashed as red as a neon Coke sign. "Oh, I'm the rat? How do we know who his father is? How does he know if he's even at the right post office?"

"Jer," Chick laid a friendly hand across his boss's arm, "if this were your son, if he'd walked halfway across the country to find you, would you want your postmaster to help? What are we here for, anyway? Curtis, what's your father's name?"

"Jonathan Pye."

"Middle name?"

"Robert."

"Jerry, just whisper it to me. Do we even have a boxholder named Jonathan Robert Pye?"

Jerry looked uncertain. "Back in a minute." He returned with a folded slip of paper.

"Thanks, Jer. Maybe this solitary act of charity will get you into heaven." Chick flipped my postcard and wrote P.O. Box 989 on the address line.

That's it. I remembered as soon as I saw the numbers. He slid my card into Daddy's box and winked through the glass door. I peered inside: a manila envelope wrapped around smaller envelopes – two, three, four, five, six, seven. More mail deeper in the box.

I walked outside, took my spot on the steps, and waited. I dozed in and out of sleep and glanced at my watch several times throughout the day. At eight P.M., I went inside and looked into Daddy's box. His mail hadn't been disturbed.

Daddy hasn't been here in a while. So, decision time. I can loiter all day and every evening on the concrete steps of the post office, but I need a place to sleep–preferably ground level, since I'm not on the best terms with gravity. And I need clean clothes.

A lady stomped by, punishing the concrete under two-inch pumps.

"Excuse me. Ma'am. Is there a laundromat around?"

"Thataway." She pointed in the same direction as the soup kitchen. "Two blocks."

Kill two birds. I cruised by shelter. Bums waited in line, some bearded, some dirty, some in clothes that had been wrinkled since forever. From the stench, some needed a few personal hygiene tips. I peeked in. Wall-to-wall bay. No privacy. *Anyone could crawl into my bed.*

I found the laundromat. I plugged a quarter in the washer and spent a dime for a box of soap, sized for one wash. Bowl-shaped chairs were fastened into benches. I started yawning. The problem was remaining upright. I could feel myself sliding as I dozed. I wanted to lie down, but the slick chairs made that impossible. I finally curled into the middle one, rested my head on a first seat, and hung my ankles over a third.

I woke when the ridge dug into my side. My washer had stopped. I reached into my pocket. Dimes, nickels, pennies and a Liberty half-dollar. No quarters. No change machine.

I woke again to the flashing red cherry of a police car. A spotlight shone in my eyes. I sat up, the spot clicked off, and the unit drove away. I dozed off.

An hour later, I was in an exhausted REM sleep when a flashlight tapped my chair. "Son," a man's voice said. "Wake up! You can't loiter here."

My eyes were dry and scratchy. I could barely focus on my watch. Two A.M.

"You awake? Look at me."

My eyes fixed well enough to verify I wasn't drunk. Or high. "I'm washing my clothes."

"And sleeping for three hours. Vagrancy is against the law. Finish and go home."

"I don't have a quarter."

"For what?"

"Dryer. For the dryer."

He fished into his pocket and snagged a quarter. "Need change?"

"Yes sir." I traded my dime and three nickels.

"Dryer takes forty-five minutes. I'll be back. Am I going to find you in this chair?"

"No sir."

"Good boy." He returned to his squad car.

I fed a dryer, moved behind two rows of washers, and curled up on the floor. The buzz of the dryer woke me this time. I folded my clean clothes, then glanced at the bathroom. A chance to change. And brush my teeth twice in one day. I locked the door, stripped, and remembered a dingy washcloth in a pile of left-behind clothes.

I put on clean white Fruit of the Looms, unlocked the door, and peeked into the laundromat. No one. I tiptoed out, liberated the faded washcloth, and grabbed a not-too-grubby tie-dye T-shirt with the silk-screen message, "Make Love Not War." The abandoned washcloth was stained, and the terrycloth was frayed and pulled into a dozen strings, but it was nominally clean. *No time to be squeamish.* I rinsed the cloth in the bathroom sink, scrubbed my underarms and my neck, sat on the stool, and scoured the soles of my feet. I rinsed the cloth twice and repeated. This time, I massaged my scalp with the soap mini-bar I'd saved from Needles. Not enough bubbles for shampoo, but my hair didn't feel greasy anymore. I tossed water on my face and torso, used the cloth as a towel, and hung it to dry on the side of the sink. Now it was mine.

I sat on the toilet again. *Running away from home is dirty work, but at least I'm clean for a while.* The only satisfying thing to do now was to finish sleeping. The hard tile floor was nasty and I was in clean underwear. I spread the socks, shirt and pants I'd just taken off across the floor and draped my wool CPO shirt over me like a blanket. My hands were my pillows.

I checked the door. A latch had been added, but the wood was splintered and the screws had pulled out. I wedged my feet against the door and my head against the cinderblock wall.

CHAPTER 38

THE GANG'S ALL HERE

"Don't you know . . . "

How long had I heard the pounding? Time hung between the purple of night and the pink of dawn. I wasn't quite awake, yet I knew I was dreaming because I couldn't move. Someone was knocking, and I heard him speaking. He sounded frustrated. Was he disappointed that I had come? Finding him seemed to be what I'd done wrong.

Then I was two people: the one in the dream watched my sleeping self on the bathroom floor, head against the wall, feet blocking the door.

" . . . the hell are you doing in there, for Christ's sake? Open up!" The door pushed against my feet. The fingers that reached inside were so unclean, the cuticles looked underlined with mascara. The face that looked in was the toffee color of decayed leaves. Most of his hair had fallen out. He looked as if he'd missed a few rounds of penicillin.

I was finally awake, but I was naked except for my underwear. "Hey, wait. I've got to get my pants on." I closed the door and rolled yesterday's clothes I'd used for a mat and shoved them inside the typewriter case.

He intruded into the small room and looked me up and down. "What the hell are you doing in here?"

"And I said wait a minute! I have to get my stuff." My turn to be bad tempered. I reached past him for the clothes on the floor. I grabbed my typewriter case–and the washcloth–and pulled the door closed with him inside. I was still in my underwear.

What the hell am I doing? I'm going to wind up raped, or the cops are going to find me in an alley breathing through extra holes in my head. My watch said five thirty A.M., and my stomach was vacant. I hadn't eaten since yesterday morning at McDonald's. Worse, if I didn't eat a meal before stationing myself in front of the post office, and it might be another eighteen hours before I could eat again.

No one else was in the laundromat, so I dressed and took a different route back to the post office. A half-block away, a couple with their backs to me panhandled for spare change in front of a restaurant. Then I saw the sign promoting the eatery Cath had told me about.

The Full Circle turned out to be an ingenious combination of cafeteria, coffee house and people's library. Sheetrock had been excised from the hall walls; the pockets between the studs had been repurposed as shelves for hundreds of books and magazines. Sheetrock rectangles had been painted, framed and hung to advertise cafeteria line offerings: Cereal 40 cents; Milk 35 cents; Fried Egg 45 cents.

The couple in front of me had chosen two slices of toast.

"No butter, no jelly?" the cashier asked. "They're just two cents each."

"No." The man turned. It was Hulk. He nudged the woman beside him.

Cath squealed and ran to me, arms outstretched as if I were her oldest, dearest friend. As her breasts bounced, I realized what a gravity-defying mystery of physics mammaries really were. "Cutie!" She enthusiastically poked her bodice into me. A sexual charge giddified me and filled a void. This happy pressing of chests could become addictive.

"How are you!"

"Better. Now." *The truth is, Sister, I'd need plastic surgery to smile any wider.*

"Have you missed me frantically?" She looked at me in a way all guys want to be looked at. "I am sooo delirious to see you again."

My jaw dropped a smidge.

"Kiss me!" she whispered.

Uh, no. Not with Hulk standing right here. This is how I wound up in California in the first place.

She slowly closed her eyes and gave me a wet, open-mouthed, eyes-closed smooch.

Supernovas don't get this hot. "Who are you?"

"The wrong kind of girl for you?"

"Now you tell me."

And then she smacked me harder, fuller on the lips, with even more passion.

"Hey! Careful," I whispered. "I only have one heart."

Hulk looked pissy. "Are you going to eat, or honey up to Opie from Oklahoma?"

Cath leaned into me for a second hug, and I felt her bones. It was as if she hadn't eaten meat since Gerber Chicken and Rice. Finally, she backed away and stomped a gleeful dance. "I just kneeew I'd see you! How long have you been here? Were you looking for me? Did you find your dad?"

"Cath!" Hulk commanded.

She paid little attention to his tone and grabbed my hand. "Join us."

"Okay. I have to order first."

"Eggs?" The cashier asked. "Fried? Scrambled? Bacon? Ham? Sausage?"

"Two looking at you. Bacon."

"Two?"

"Four."

"Toast?"

"Two."

"Butter? Jelly?"

"Yes. Yes. Two. Two."

"Coffee?"

All this will add up. "Water."

"Take a glass. Anything else?" The clerk keyed a stand-up cash register, a machine taller than her with buttons that forced up little price tags. "One dollar and ninety-three cents."

McDonald's is cheaper. Am I going to run out of money before I find Daddy? I walked to Hulk and Cath's table. Like a couple, they sat side by side and slathered their toast with ketchup and mustard. My dismay must have shown.

"Never had ketchup-and-mustard sandwiches, dude?" Hulk asked.

I shook my head, embarrassed to have been caught disapproving.

From the sugar dish at the table, Cath crushed a cube with a spoon and crumbled granules onto her toast. She squeezed four free lemon slices into her water, then sugar coated the bottom of her glass with more free cubes. "Voila! Lemonade!" Whoever said beggars can't be choosers had never met Cath. "So, where are you staying?"

I was a little ashamed of what now seemed like my excess of food. But I like excesses. I'm attracted to outrageous girls, to short shorts, and to intellectual humor.

"Have you found your dad yet?"

I shook my head.

"Then where are you sleeping?" Hulk prodded.

"Wherever."

"You can crash here! Just go ask! You can work here too!" Cath squealed as urgently as a six-year-old. Every sentence was an exclamation.

Why is she so wild today?

Her face seemed flushed, her pupils big like she'd spent a week in a dark room.

People must be staring.

"Don't sleep on the streets." Hulk was calmer, but his pupils also seemed oversized. "The manager isn't here this morning, but ask him for a job this afternoon."

"Are there any openings?"

"Don't matter. It's a commune. He hires everyone."

"Far out!" Cath grabbed both my hands as if the matter had been settled.

Uncomfortable, I withdrew my hands. "Do y'all work here?"

"No, man." Hulk seemed contemptuous of the idea. However, he winked, "but when you do, you can toss us a steak every now and then."

"Ugh! The carcass of a dead cow?" Cath stuck two fingers inside her mouth. "So, Cutie, tell me! Do you have a girl back home?"

"Yeah, no. Sorta."

"Sounds like you covered all three bases." Hulk smiled for the first time since we'd met.

"O'Murphy's not my girlfriend. She's–somebody else's."

"Love triangle?" Cath explored.

Never thought of it that way. "Kinda. She dates an actual rectum."

"Handsome fellas get lots of girls," Cath told Hulk.

"Gotta drain my lizard." Hulk finished his toast and stood up.

"So, tell me more about O'Murphy." Cath intended to sluice out my bio, drop by drop.

I didn't want to tell, but she seemed so interested. I opened up for five minutes about the Pretty Girl, even if she wasn't the Smart Girl or the Good Girl. But we got to the point where Cath had been heading.

"So if O'Murphy is there, why are you here?"

"I'm sorta hopeless."

"Of course you aren't. You just need a little boost. You'd feel confident with O'Murphy if you had more experience. If you knew how to love her, you wouldn't be afraid." Cath pointed out the heart of my fear and squeezed my hand.

My hopes were energized—electrified, actually—by her touch.

Hulk had moved to Georgy's table in the back.

"Is he your boyfriend, or hers?"

"We have open relationships."

Something else I've never heard of, but Jonathan Robert Pye would surely advocate it. I must have looked disappointed, because Cath defended the concept.

"Fidelity isn't for everyone." With a playful glint in her eye, Cath added. "After they get married, five out of ten people get divorced. The rest die."

Hulk moved from Georgy's table back to Cath, so I excused myself and took the opportunity to get to know a member of the van gang I hadn't connected with.

"Nobody will play with you?" I teased. "Are a bad girl?"

"I can't compete," Georgy said.

"Are you sad today?"

Her voice had a hostile edge. "I'm not. But I guess I am depressed."

"How long have you been here? I mean, in America?"

"Oh. A few years, I guess. I've lost track. I've long overstayed my six-month visa, 'at is a certainty." As Georgy's voice filled with anxiety and emotional turmoil, her Australian accent seemed more pronounced.

"Why don't you go home?"

"To what?" Georgy said sharply. She had bought two enormous slices of German chocolate cake, perhaps one for herself and one for Hulk. She had polished off the one on her side of the table, and kept glancing at the other as if she couldn't decide. "I ditched me mum and me da' and me lovely sis in Sydney."

I wonder if you're a younger version of Mother. "Let me guess. You and Sis aren't buds?"

"Would ya be friends with ya brother after he rutted after ya girl?" she asked.

Actually, I have an answer for that.

"The little sheelagh nabbed me fiancé. She's younger, she's prettier, so she merely inserted a ring in his nose and led him to her bedstead. In fact, my da and me mum approved."

"Surely he didn't like her just because she was prettier. He chose you first."

"Probably wanted her all along." Georgy seemed unable to accept a compliment or see herself squarely. "Even me mum always loved Sis more, I can be certain of that. And she was the apple of me da's eye. She could do anything she wanted."

"And you?"

"Lumpy, frumpy me? I don't think anything was ever expected. Except that I would become a dumpy house mum with three or four dingoes." She attacked the second slice and looked at me miserably. "I know. I should 'ave offered this to ya. I can't help it. Eating makes me feel better."

Now I'm curious. "You're eating it, even though you're not hungry?"

Georgy's grimace was just a flicker. "Ya too young to know this. No doubt ya will learn it later in life. For a few of us, food isn't about food. It's about boredom, or problems with ya sister, or ya failure to earn a mate." She glanced at Hulk and Cath.

CHAPTER 39

COMMUNE IN A CAFETERIA

I sat in front of the post office with my thoughts. *My first mistake was not bringing the Marine Corps letter. And Gil was right, I needed Daddy's address and phone number.*

"Curtis? Still waiting for Daddy?"

"Hi, Chick. Yes sir."

"I don't have the card he filled out when he rented his box. That's in the postmaster's office, and Jerry isn't a charitable bastard."

"It's okay. Daddy will show up soon." I ducked Chick's reach to rub my hair.

Chick's eyes quizzed me with an odd look, but he moved on.

I rummaged *The San Jose Mercury* from the trash and spent the morning reading: Johnson had stationed a half-million troops in Vietnam, so he was now sure the U.S. would win. Governor Reagan had legalized abortions in California. And for the first time ever, the Denver Broncos, an American Football League team, had beaten an NFL team, the Detroit Lions.

By three P.M., I was stiff from sitting on concrete. *Where will I sleep tonight? I won't climb onto the post office roof again, the thought chilled me of curling up on a laundromat chair and waking to police lights, and I sure don't want a hobo reaching through the bathroom door.*

I took a shortcut through an alley to the Full Circle and, twenty feet in front of me, a dumpster lid rose. Eyes periscoped up. He realized I'd spotted him, so Dumpster Guy climbed out and stalked away. I looked inside. Cardboard boxes. Office paper. But Cath's suggestion sounded more appealing. If I worked at the Full Circle, I'd have free food and a temporary address. When Daddy found my postcard, he could bounce over and meet the son he hadn't laid eyes on for six years.

I approached Chick's window. "I want to write another card to my dad."

"Got another dime?"

"Daddy," I wrote. "I'm in Palo Alto. You can find me in front of this post office, or the Full Circle. Your son, Curtis."

"Can you replace the first postcard with this one? I want him to read this one first. He needs to know I'm working at the Full Circle."

Chick turned to his boss. "Jer, suppose I tape the second card on top of the first?"

Jerry exhaled in mute frustration.

* * *

I leaned against the post office stucco and warmed in the June sun. I felt more hopeful than I had since the moment I'd stuck out my thumb in Hell Creek and caught the first ride. Daddy had what he needed to find me. But now I had to get that job.

"Donald," the manager introduced himself. With coal black hair, wide muscular jaws, and a beard like a frazzled push broom, he looked as friendly as a gorilla in rut.

"Do you have any jobs available?"

"What's your name?"

"Curtis Pye."

"Don't ask if a job is available; that puts me on the spot if I don't want to hire you," Donald instructed. "Introduce yourself. Then tell me you're looking for a job. How old are you?"

"Fifteen."

Donald shook his head.

"And a half."

"I can't." He drummed on the adding machine keys. "You have to be sixteen."

My face fell. *Oh no. Can I take back that second postcard?* I stood up.

His face softened. "Stop. Sit down. What's the matter? What's so important about working here? Do you live around here? Where are you from?"

"Oklahoma."

"You a runaway?"

Should I answer a question like that?

"Okay. Be honest. You need to stay here?"

I nodded.

"Okay. California won't allow me to pay you. But you can volunteer. What can you do?"

"Anything. Prep. Make salads. Wash dishes. Fry burgers . . . "

"All that?"

"I worked at the Freeze, and I threw paper routes. And I cooked at home."

"Yeah, well, put in one hour a day here. Do anything. Push a broom. Pick up trash. I don't care. Then sleep here at night. I should keep track of you. Deal?" He stuck out a hand.

I shook and smiled. *I feel safer already.*

He frowned. "What's in the typewriter case?"

"My clothes."

"Well, let's take it upstairs. I'll show you our crash pad, then you show me what you do."

"Thanks." I was tired of lugging a wooden box everywhere I went. I stowed it against a wall and came downstairs. Dinnerware and silverware lay on tables and in bus tubs. *Are they lazy, or does earth's gravity have a stronger effect on California restaurant workers?*

"I should bus the tables first. Then mop the floors."

Donald pursed his lips as if he hadn't expected initiative.

The sinks were full, so I emptied glasses and coffee cups, then dragged over a trash can and filled it with bread bones and half-eaten meals. I stacked the dishes, then I washed the glasses first, since they needed clean, soapy dishwater more than plates and bowls.

It took an hour to empty the sinks. The customers had gone, so I took my time with the tables; I scrubbed each top with an abundance of soap and water, something that hadn't been done for a long time, judging from the salt and the crumbs crusting around ketchup-bottle circles.

"Impressive," Donald said from behind me. "It's too late to sweep and mop. I'm turning out the lights. I'll leave a note for the morning manager."

What had been the manager's office this afternoon was a second-story happening tonight. Two dozen come-as-you-are hippies were strewn across the shag carpet, four more on one couch, two on its arms, and five on the two armchairs. One couple sprawled across a desktop, face to intimate face. The rest–including the cooks and counter help I'd seen downstairs–had staked perimeters on the carpet with their bedrolls, or tossed backpacks against the walls.

"I sleep under my desk. You can crash anywhere else," Donald invited.

Got to be better than sleeping in a laundromat. Or even my own private dumpster. I sat on my typewriter case. My eyes roamed from conversation to conversation until I spotted Mikey, Chica and Georgy. Hulk saw me, and Cath followed his eyes. Her smile was broad and immediate but Hulk didn't release his hold on her waist, so she beckoned with a one-handed wave. The van gang was presumably back from the music festival.

"It doesn't have to mean anything." Hulk sounded as if he were losing an argument. "Sometimes a cigar is just a cigar, and this time a red hat is just a hat. Salinger keeps bringing it up, but if it has any meaning at all, it's to make Holden seem ridiculous."

"That's just wrong." Chica waved her copy of the book at him.

Cuban kids read *The Catcher in the Rye* too? Or maybe she'd been schooled here?

"What does it mean then?" Hulk's tone suggested he wanted to be the authority.

"It's sexual," Chica contended.

"How do you know that?" Hulk's question was an assertion.

"Everything is about sex," Chica grinned, "except sex. Sex is about power."

That rings true. "It's a symbol," I butted in. "Mrs. Lane, my sophomore lit teacher, said when something–like a color–appears over and over in a literary novel, it's almost always a symbol. White usually means innocence or purity. Red is for blood or war or aggression."

"You've read *Catcher in the Rye*?" Cath asked.

I nodded.

"Did your teacher say what the red hat symbolized?"

No good would come from challenging Hulk, but this was my chance to impress Cath. "Mrs. Lane said it's about being different; it's how Holden chooses to stand out. And Phoebe and Allie's have red hair, so the red hat is Holden's red hair–his connection to his sister and his dead brother. All three of them are innocents, I think."

"And innocence is the absence of sex," Chica said.

I half agreed. "The whole book is about sex. And women."

"The whole book," Hulk repeated. "Is that your opinion, Encyclopedia Brown?"

"Okay, I overstated, not the entire book. Holden keeps trying to get away from sex, but it's everywhere he goes."

"Wow. Great. Junior High is going all Professor Salinger on us. Should I write this down? I wrote a term paper on this when I was a senior. In college." He attempted to trump me. "How is it all about sex? Name three times *Catcher in the Rye* mentions sex!"

"On the school walls. In the window across from his hotel. And Holden tries to have sex."

"I'm holding up three fingers." Cath's smile challenged Hulk.

"It's in the way he thinks."

"Four." Cath sprang a little finger.

"You know what Holden Caulfield thinks? Are you a mind reader? What am I thinking, right now?" Hulk's scorn said he didn't want to respect my opinion.

"Holden's a prude, like me."

"What do you think, guys? Four and a half?" Cath's thumb went out.

"He hires a prostitute, Quiz Show." Hulk pointed his sarcasm at me.

"But then he doesn't want casual sex, so he can't do it. And then he tries to have sex with a girl he likes, and he can't go through with that either."

"Because he's queer as a choir boy," Hulk asserted.

"Is that six or seven?" Cath asked Hulk.

By now, people around us had tuned into our conversation.

"Because he thinks casual sex devalues women. So do I." *That won't make me popular with this free-love crowd.*

Hulk rolled a finger, a signal to continue.

I looked at Chica and Mikey. "I don't want to offend. That's just what Salinger wrote."

They nodded.

"And I've only got ten fingers." Cath looked awed. "You got all this from Freshman Lit?"

"Sophomore. But I read it in the eighth grade."

"Yeah?" Cath nodded. "I got that you read a lot."

"Two, three books a month."

"And you understood it?" Hulk snorted in disbelief. "On your own? This world-famous novel with such deep meaning?"

"Actually, I didn't, so I went back and I asked the librarian. She gave me a study guide."

"Ah. So all this actually comes from *CliffsNotes*," Hulk challenged.

"Some. And *American Lit Review* explained the Robert Burns song."

Mikey smirked. "Brucie here's a gen-u-ine college grad-u-ate. Just thought everyone ought to know that. Berkeley, wasn't it?"

Hulk turned third-degree red. His eyes had smoldered at me, they flashed fire at Mikey.

Cath whacked Hulk's shoulder.

"And the song is about sex," I added another straw to the camel's back.

Hulk sagged.

"Do you think *The Catcher in the Rye* is a tragedy?" I asked.

Hulk looked thankful to agree.

"Holden misunderstands the rhyme," I said. "His little sister has to correct him. He wants to be the catcher in the rye–to catch children before they jump off a cliff. But he doesn't realize that the cliff isn't real; it only represents virginity. I think that's why it's a tragedy. Because Holden's world became so . . . "

"Sexualized," Chica grinned at Hulk.

"And the Robert Burns poem is about sex," I said.

Hulk looked puzzled now. "That's bullshit! It's a just Robert Frost song about a girl, walking though a field."

"Burns," Chica reminded.

"Burns. Yeah, yeah, Robert Burns. But how do you know the song isn't just about some chick walking through a field?"

Cath turned to me.

"Jenny has sex," I said.

Hulk's finger circled impatiently, coaxing me to the point.

"Frequently."

Mrs. Lane had required everyone to explain a poem. I'd chosen "Comin' Thro' the Rye," because it was short.

"Jenny likes to meet her boyfriend in the rye field. They do it in the dew. So the song makes fun of her for being wet all the time. But it also defends her . . . 'Gin a body meet a body.' Can't a person meet a person? 'Need the world know?' Is it anyone else's business who has sex?"

Chica intimately pecked Mikey on the mouth. He ran one brown hand across the delta where her bare thighs met. He looked at me apologetically and his hand dropped to her knees.

I wish I weren't so bothered by their interracial relationship.

"Dude," Hulk challenged. "Do you actually know crap about sex?"

Mikey objected. "If he's a virgin, his opinion is disqualified?"

Hulk rolled his eyes, but that was his last salvo.

CHAPTER 40

BROTHER LOVE

When Nan and Grand had taken Biggy and me to the Woolworth cafeteria, they expected our best manners. California coffee-house etiquette wasn't up to Woolworth standards.

Cath was sitting in Hulk's lap at a corner table when I returned from another fruitless week at the Palo Alto Post Office. Hulk seemed delighted to bum spare change. "With your baby face," he had suggested to me, "it's what you ought to do. You'd collect a dollar a day, easy." But if they'd been too lazy all day to beg for spare change, they'd filch used coffee cups from a table and make ketchup soup by adding salt, pepper, hot sauce, and warm water. Or they'd pay for one cup of coffee and share all day. Or without even washing a used tea glass, they'd make a hippie milkshake: add sugar to creamer from little chrome pots on the tables, and consume enough calories to last the day. I'd seen hippies sit at a dirty table and finish a half-eaten meal.

Hulk could've had free food if he'd just worked five hours a week at the Full Circle. So why would a beauty like Cath make him her Mr. Right? Darwin seemed to know the answer. My biology teacher had said female guppies preferred males with longer tails or ostentatious orange colors because they would produce prettier minnows. "But they provide no resources for raising those children." *Right on, Mr. Z. They father good children, but they're no-good fathers.*

Bumming made no sense to me, so I walked to the food joints along El Camino Real and stopped at Onionheads–a burgers-and-dogs eatery with fifty-pound sacks of onions and potatoes stacked in the aisles. I asked for the manager. Should I offer to shake hands with a woman? "Howdy. My name is Curtis Pye. I moved here two months ago, and I'm looking for a job until I start school next year." *Which might actually become true if Daddy ever collects his mail.*

A tallish, slender, pleasant woman stuck out her hand. "Sue Randall. Hmm. I could use some help for the rest of the summer. Judging from how old you look, have you any experience?"

"Yes ma'am. I'll be sixteen soon. I worked for the Freeze."

Sue's eyes widened. "Have they no child labor laws where you're from?"

"Oklahoma? Nobody ever mentioned it."

"Well, for a certainty, California does. When will you turn sixteen?"

I looked her in the eye and fudged a month. "Two weeks." *Okay, two months.*

"Have you a driver's license?"

"Yes ma'am. From Oklahoma."

"Very well. Come in tomorrow. Will you be here at nine A.M.? Sharp? I can give you a one-day tryout. Minimum wage."

A dollar an hour? I'll be here early.

* * *

I felt blue about not finding Daddy, and watching Mikey and Chica make out had contributed to my depression. Worse, I hadn't see Cath, so I dropped a quarter in the jukebox and punched in five songs.

"You're screwing up my sequence!" Jerry's salt-and-pepper mustache was almost invisible, but his eyes shone like black marbles in the dark dining room. Judging from how red-faced Vin got when he'd been drinking, I guessed the ferret-nosed postmaster shared the same disorder. He sat across from Chick at a chessboard painted on the picnic table.

My first selection was my favorite song last year, "Solitary Man."

"Righteous tune, *amigo*," Chick countered.

Jerry's eyes flashed at him, then stared me.

Neil Diamond's lyrics hit hard: he'd almost given up hope of ever meeting the woman he'd love. Wow. I thought only I was that hopeless. Louis Armstrong was next up. "What a Wonderful World" would be my all-time number-one fave. I sat beside Chick.

"*Kibitzers*! Can we do without the *kibitzers*!" Jerry grumbled loud enough for me to hear.

I looked for interpretation.

"Jer–for whom someone should invent a chill pill–doesn't like anyone watching his chess game, *compadre*. Want to play me?" Chick pointed to a second board painted on the same table.

"I don't know how, Chick."

"First-class mind like yours? Time to learn."

"But you're playing Jerry."

"I can do both. By the way, my given name is Martine Loving." He pronounced it with a Spanish accent: mar-TEEN loo-VING. "Chick has been my nickname since my *padre* first laid eyes on me. But I'm a street pastor, so the flower children here at the Circle call me Brother Love." He cocked his arm for the hippie handshake. While his game demoralized Jerry, Brother Love explained how pawns, knights, bishops, rooks, queens and kings move.

In an hour, I was playing novice chess.

"You're a natural," Brother Love said. "In a few months, you'll be up with Jer."

The postmaster scowled.

"How long have you been without your father?" Brother Love asked.

"Six years."

He stroked a salt-flecked Green Arrow goatee. "Then you probably know more than anyone, fatherlessness creates an emotional hunger, doesn't it?"

True. I can hardly look at a man Daddy's age without sizing him up as a father. I'm doing it with Brother Love at this moment.

"I work at the post office for fun and profit, but one of my degrees is in psychology. I read tons of books, so on Sunday and Wednesday evenings at the homeless mission, I nourish wounded souls and expound pious-sounding thoughts."

"My brother also expounds pious-sounding thoughts, but he doesn't read much."

Brother Love's eyes were mirthful. "The men I minister to at the soup kitchen–many, it turns out–have daddy issues. You should come with me some time."

Maybe. I'd feel safe with you. I marveled at his ability to shuffle jobs. If something needs to be done, give it to a busy person, Mr. Presley had always said.

"Before you hear it from someone else, I should also tell you I'm gay," Brother Love said.

"Gay?"

"Homosexual," Brother Love said. "No one has ever introduced himself to you as a homosexual?"

Francis. "Why don't you say that instead of 'gay?'"

"Negroes prefer black or African-American because Negro has been besmirched. For the same reason, 'queers' and 'homos' favor the word gay describe their orientation."

"Okay. But I should tell you that I'm afraid of homosexuals."

"You're homophobic? Had a bad episode with a gay man?"

I nodded.

"Yeah. So have I. But there's a distinction to make. Gay men are attracted to other men. Men who prefer boys are just perverts. I'm not a pervert."

"Let's change the subject."

"Six years since you've seen your dad, huh? Sociologists could fill an ENIAC computer with statistics on the sociological plight of fatherless boys. It affects the whole country. Eighty percent of the men in prison have no dad at home. Fatherless boys are more prone to fight," Brother Love said. "Fatherless boys are arrested in most assaults and homicides."

That's Biggy. And the Andersens. I know lots of boys—and girls—who don't have fathers.

"Something like sixty percent of teenage suicides are from fatherless homes," he recited.

Did Daddy's absence have something to do with my suicide attempt? Think on that.

"And it's all because boys lack a solid male mentor for guidance and discipline at home," Brother Love said.

I agree. Vin had been of little help to Biggy and me. And Daddy had sired us, but in what other sense had he been a father?

"What unholy shit is this?" Someone shouted from the hall in front of the men's bathroom. It was Donald. He waved a bent, blackened spoon. A syringe and a strip of red-and-white checkered napkin were in his left. "What if narcs found this? Do you H freaks want to get our pad busted? You know how the Man yearns to bring us down."

Hulk and Cath started down the stairs, but reversed course.

"Why's Donald so mad?" I asked.

"That's a drug spoon," Brother Love muttered. "Bad juju. Looks like someone cooked a hit, shot up in the restroom, and just tossed their spoon and their noose on the floor."

"*Dragnet* didn't complete my education."

"Sprinkle heroin or coke or speed in the spoon." Brother Love filled in the details. "Add water. Boil it with a match. When the match flames out, your rocket fuel is go for launch. Suck the liquid into a syringe. Tie that strip of napkin around your arm to plump a vein, inject it, and release the noose. You're on the moon."

"Stab yourself? In your arm? Not my idea of a swell time. How do you know this?"

"The mission. Come with me next week. You could help a young man in some pain."

"How?"

"Just listen. That's the best therapy. Boys at the mission are so invisible."

Invisible. That's me. "OK. I will."

Brother Love stood up. "Well, this is bringing me down, and tomorrow's a school day."

Somewhere inside, I resented feeling grateful that Brother Love had spent so much time with me. "Thanks for showing me how to play chess."

"No worry, man. I dig helping. Where're you staying?"

"Here."

CHAPTER 41

FREE WILL

Another day at the post office. The same mail had been in Daddy's box for three weeks. *Answer a nagging question, Jesus, and be honest: did you let me go on a fool's errand?*

Chick sat beside me on the concrete steps. "Good news. Marines get their retirement checks next week. He'll be here for sure."

"Another week? That's good news?"

"I know. But the end is in sight."

* * *

I spent the morning at Onionheads frying steak burgers mounded with minced onions. That evening, Mikey and I tag-teamed Brother Love at chess. "Can I ask you a question? People say, 'I prayed and God answered.' But how do they really know that?"

"They don't, Miguel," Brother Love said. "For some, faith means crediting good things to God, and blaming bad times on the Devil."

"My church, they expelled my mother. She's a white Cuban, and she married an American Negro," Mikey said. "Ask why, and the bastards always–always–quote the Bible."

"Those are pseudo reasons," Brother Love opined, "made up by people to justify their own discrimination. They're not necessarily bad people, they just think George Wallace gives them permission to hate. But if you think Jesus would condone those wrongs, you need to go sit under a tree and give it more thought. What happens in your life isn't caused by God. In your case, Cutie, why did your mother leave your father?"

"What do their choices have to do with God being fair?"

"Exactly. God granted free will to every man, every woman, every child. But people conflate self-determination with freedom of choice. God doesn't send a drunk driver to run into a car with three Girl Scouts, nor does God save one scout and kill the other two. The drunk chose."

"I think someone wants your attention," Mikey said.

Cath sat one table to our left in a skirt so tight the Jaws of Life couldn't have wedged her knees apart. She looked at me and smiled a come-hither.

Daddy was a dog, and so am I. I moved to her table. "Where's Hulk?"

"I hope he's working."

That would be news to all.

"Do you want to make love?" She asked in the same voice she would've used to invite me to a party.

Cath defined big brown eyes. They were merry. They requested the pleasure of my company. But if she had casual sex with me, I'd think less of her. My groin said yes, yes. But my brain said no, no. Besides, I'd feel stupid. I wouldn't know where to start.

Mikey castled his king too late in the game, I thought. Brother Love pushed a pawn and blocked the rook's attack. "Cutie? Go with me to the mission at lunch tomorrow?"

"Sure." When I turned back to Cath, she stood up and took my hand.

"There goes Cutie," I heard Mikey say as Cath and I walked upstairs.

"And there goes his virginity," Brother Love said softly.

"I lost mine to Cath too," Mikey said. "I don't miss it at all."

Brother Love raised his beer bottle. "I've given up dancing, drinking and illegal drugs, so here's a toast to the only vice I have left."

* * *

"The first time I had sex, it hurt," Cath whispered in my ear. "We're not going to do it rough, like you see in the movies. You're going to learn foreplay. We're going to make love together, soft and slow."

I nodded in the dark of the upstairs crash pad, deserted except for us.

Cath kissed my lips, then sucked on my earlobes and softly nibbled my neck. "Now you do the same," she instructed. "Take your time."

I bit below her ear and she groaned; gooseflesh popped up her back and left arm.

"Don't 'wham, bam, thank you ma'am.' Ask what I want."

"Was that good? You really did like it?"

"I did. It was sensual. Touch me. Stroke my hair, and move your hands."

I stroked her hair, caressed her neck, and held her head. She followed suit.

Donald walked in but said nothing. He gawked at Cath's body, a younger, slimmer version of Elizabeth Taylor.

"You should have cleared your throat." Cath admonished Donald.

"I couldn't. My heart was in it." Donald grinned. "Maybe go out and come back in again?"

"Yeah. But give us thirty minutes," Cath said.

Donald kept his eyes on Cath, but he closed his office door.

She kissed my nose, sucked my earlobes, and thrust her tongue inside my ear.

I spasmed from an unexpected burst of pleasure. I explored with my hands and mouth at the same time. She groaned and guided my hands to her chest. I caressed and gently tweaked, imitating her at first, but what I was doing felt natural within a few minutes.

"Good. You're learning what intimacy is." She rubbed my bare chest. "You like that?"

"Mmm." I went under her blouse with both hands, but I didn't know what to with her bra. "Is there a trick to this?"

"Find the clasp in the center. When I arch my back, just snap your fingers to unlock it."

My left hand moved to her back, and bingo, her breasts jumped free.

She pulled off my pants.

* * *

Cath was gone when Mikey woke me.

"So," his eyes twinkled. "What did you learn from Cath?"

I blushed with pride.

"Time to introduce you to marijuana. You up for it?"

I shook my head. "I don't smoke."

"Yeah, well, how about an Alice B. Toklas instead?"

"What's that?"

"A brownie. With an amusing ingredient."

That didn't sound as bad as smoking marijuana. "Well, okay. Just one." *Holy feces, I have improved my station in life: I just had sex, and I'm about to try marijuana. This is how God meant for man to live.*

CHAPTER 42

SOCIAL COMPOST

"Johnny," Brother Love said, "has been at the mission a month. His head was shaved when he got here, so he probably just got out of the military. That's about all I know."

I walked up to his cot and held out my hand. "My name is Curtis."

Dumpster Guy just looked at me.

I sat down. "I think the usual courtesy is for you to tell me your name."

"John," he said warily, as if I would try to trick him.

"Brother Love thinks you're just out of the military." Get him to volunteer something, Brother Love had instructed me. A few words. Whatever starts him talking.

Nothing.

"Where did you come here from?"

Nothing.

"Pendleton?"

"MCRD. San Diego."

"Boot camp?"

Nothing.

"What's next?"

He shrugged his shoulders and opened his hands. "This."

"You're staying here?"

"I don't know." He looked despondent.

Brother Love watched us.

Good, because I may need a little help. "If you could just wave your hand–like magic–and make everything the way you wanted, what would you do?"

"Well, I can't do that, now can I?" Ice was in his voice.

"None of us can. But we have to think, and then we have to try, don't we?"

"I tried to be a Marine."

Were his eyes watering? "What happened?"

"I washed out."

"How'd that happen?" I leaned forward. I wanted him to sense that I'd settled in, and that I wanted to listen to his story.

"It was my fault. My drill instructor came into our barracks one night. Drunk. Woke us up about two o'clock, screaming 'Reveille, reveille, reveille! Enemy attack! Out of your bunks.'"

I nodded, but I didn't understand.

"We had to stand in front of our bunks. Surprise inspection. Gunny ordered the key man–the private who locks and unlocks our barracks door–to run around the room, fast, and jerk the lock of every foot locker. And my lock fell open."

My eyes asked for more explanation.

"When reveille blows at five A.M., we have ten minutes to roll out, make up our bunks–Marine Corps tight–and fall in for inspection. We don't have time to try the combination twice. We dial in the first two numbers at night, so when we get up in the morning, all we have to do is turn it once to the right number. The lock opens. Simple. But the night before, I dialed mine too close to the unlock number, and when the key man jerked on it, it fell open."

Doesn't sound like a big deal.

"It was my fault, but key man's responsible for every lock inside our barracks. The drill instructor went batshit crazy on us." John imitated his D.I.'s voice. "'You slimy, syphilitic, puss-sucking pieces of shit. You two privates have exposed the entire Marine Corps to enemy sabotage. Now they can steal uniforms and subvert the Corps from within. Plant bombs. Cause mayhem. Kill your fellow recruits. And then who will defend America? No one! Because all the Marines are dead! Because of you two!'"

"Sounds like your D.I. was a few beans short of a combination plate," I said.

"He made examples of us. He made me step up on my footlocker. I had to stand at attention and hold my M-1 in front of my nose for–I don't know–maybe ten minutes. I wasn't allowed to move. I had to hold my rifle–ten-pounds–straight out in my arms."

I nodded.

"That's when I screwed up the second time. He counted on me to lower my rifle. Then he could punish me."

"It was your fault that your drill instructor was embarrassed? What did he say?"

"'Where is the sight of that barrel supposed to be, Private?' Screamed it into my ear. 'Sir. Between my eyes, sir.' And it was. But he pretended it wasn't, and he stiff-armed the front sight right into my face. It's the hardest I've ever been hit in my life. I thought I was going down for sure. But I kept my feet."

"That's against the law," I informed John.

He paused and thought about that. "So he makes me do the first half of a jumping-jack on the footlocker. That means both my hands are above my head; both my feet are spread apart. He ordered the key man to punch me in the stomach. He had to keep punching me. But didn't hit me hard, and that pissed off the D.I.

"'Key Man,'" John imitated the D.I.'s guttural voice, "'if you don't actually knock the breath out of that blood-bag in front of you, you're gonna stand on his footlocker, and he's going to knock the wind out of you.'"

"What did you do?"

"I couldn't let the key man take my punishment, so I nodded to him. Get this over with."

Ten minutes of being beaten in the stomach with your hands over your head? Not allowed to move? And I wanted a Marine to train me? "So . . .

"The D.I. demonstrated. Punched under my ribs. Knocked the breath out of me."

"Did you really have to let him do that?"

"You'll find out, if you ever join. Or get drafted."

"How did it end?"

"He punched me so hard in the kidneys, I finally made a noise. I didn't cry or anything—I wouldn't give him the satisfaction—I just grunted. And that's what he wanted. I guess."

"Were you okay?"

"I was sore next day, yeah. But I pissed blood the third day, so I requested to go to Sickbay. And my staff sergeant—we had three D.I.s who rotated twenty-four hours on, forty-eight off—made me tell him why. When he realized the gunnery sergeant had beat the shit out of me, he wouldn't let me go. Said Gunny would be back in two days, so I should ask him for permission."

"Did you ask?"

"I had to. I was scared. I didn't know how bad I was hurt. He acted like nothing happened. Said he was just toughening me up. That it would be a lot worse if the Viet Cong captured me."

"I have a brother like that. He thinks screaming and humiliating and bullying builds character. It doesn't. I have a character. He needs character."

John's eyes agreed. "It got worse. The night before I went to the chaplain, I saw another D.I.–not my gunny, but one from another platoon–rape a recruit."

"Where?"

"In the head." John saw my question. "Navy and Marines call the bathroom the head. I went to the head that night and saw this D.I. order a private to bend over and grab a urinal."

"Did you . . . "

"No. See? The boot–he saw me. He begged me with his eyes to do something. If I had, that D.I. would have gone to the brig. So I did nothing. And I didn't report it to my chaplain or my colonel. That proves I'm a coward. Marines live by a code. 'Respect human dignity.' Marines help others. We don't leave our buddies on the battlefield. But I did."

"You didn't know the guy?"

"He was a Marine," John said. "He needed my help. He was my responsibility. It was my duty. That's why I don't deserve to be in the Marines."

John was right on that point, of course, it just took me a moment to realize how much honor meant to him. "What about you? Were you bleeding internally? From the beating?"

"Yeah. My urine turned orangey at first, then it was bloody red. I was really scared. Before noon mess, the platoon had to report to the chaplain. We had to write down our religion so they'd know what to do if we came back from 'Nam in a bag. And in the space where it said, 'DO NOT WRITE,' I wrote that my D.I. had beat me up and wouldn't let me go to Sickbay."

"Are you okay now?"

"Yeah. But they kicked me out of the Marines."

"Why?"

"I don't know. Because I turned him in?"

"But it wasn't your fault. You had to see a doctor."

"Yeah. So the chaplain said. My stomach and back had turned yellow and green and orange and red. And the doc ordered me tell him the truth. The chaplain sent for the sergeant major—the top enlisted man for my battalion. He ordered me to lift up my blouse. Sergeant Major turned red, and he had to notify the battalion commander. Colonel made me lift up my blouse. My stomach and my sides were so bruised by then, I looked like a rainbow trout. Colonel sent for my D.I. Demanded to know how those bruises got there."

"He said, 'We have to motivate them, sir.'"

"'Not this way, Gunny.' Colonel gave me two choices: I could file charges, but the Gunny would be sunk—court martialed. Lose his pension after eighteen years in the Corps. He'd served two tours in Vietnam. That's probably what made him a crazy drunk. My second choice was to go back to my platoon and forget everything. But I knew Gunny wouldn't let that happen."

"So what are you doing here?"

"I took the third choice. General discharge. So I can't go home. My pop will kill me."

"No, he won't. You did it to save your D.I."

"You don't know my dad. He was a World War II leatherneck. He knows I'm out. Mom said Pop thinks I've disgraced the family. She wants me to come home; he doesn't."

Wow. What will Daddy think of me, losing two fights? "What're you going to do?"

"Stay here."

Live at a soup kitchen? I thought my life was bad. "Look, your colonel was right; your gunny was wrong. A Marine who leaves his footlocker unlocked doesn't deserve to be beaten up. Marines don't deserve to be sodomized. Marines who are injured have a right see a doctor. When your dad knows that, he'll be mad at your D.I., not you."

I took the last five-dollar bill from my pocket. I didn't want it anyway; it had belonged to Francis. "This may buy you a couple of days to think about it."

* * *

Brother Love and I walked back to the post office. "Still want to join the Marines?"

"Wait," I stopped in my path. "Is that why I'm here? You want me to make a connection between John and . . . "

It was true. Because he was a Viet vet and had an eighteen-year career, the Marines had rallied around their gunnery sergeant, but they'd left John behind. Had Daddy left Biggy and me behind? *My family always rallies behind Biggy, and the school rallies behind the Andersens. Does society usually stick up for the abusers?*

"Did you serve?" I asked Brother Love.

He nodded silently. "And if you join, and if you get into trouble, you're going to find that you probably won't be court martialed. Marines use superior officers as a defacto judicial system. They give non-coms far too much decision-making authority. Marines have a culture of abusing recruits. Sometimes it's supported by officers. After a few months in Nam, the scareder I got of the Cong, the more I hated the Marines. I was ashamed of my fear, but I couldn't humiliate myself in front of my buddies. The whole time I was in country, I felt like I was hanging onto my honor by my fingernails."

CHAPTER 43

MY FULL CIRCLE

Laundry night. My clothes had spent thirty minutes in a washer, and now they were in a dryer. It gave me an hour to think. These months away from Hell Creek had been my chance to listen to the quiet voice inside me. Being on my own at fifteen was something few kids got to try. I was free to come and go for the first time in my life.

So why am I not happy? The truth is, I'd make a great recluse. All my life, I'd wanted to connect with people, but I had watched from outside the window. Now I'd become part of a commune. This odd assembly of men and women and girls and boys had become my full circle. I liked watching the romantic couple here, the panhandler there, the mother with her brood of children. I could join their lives for a moment and turn with them into a day care, a jewelry store, a dentist's office. Sometimes, they saw me watching and they smiled.

Of course, that's when I was loneliest; that's when I knew needed a life with someone. I'd felt a secret thrill when Cath had sat with me yesterday. But Hulk had walked in, and Cath had gone to him. Then I'd felt worse. *Maybe that's the trouble. When I do connect, I fail. Maybe I'm destined to wander this life alone. The few relationships I've tried always ended in disaster.*

The night was foggy as the future by the time I got back to the loft. The room lights were off for the night, but the neons along University Avenue shone into the double-bay windows. I curled into my spot and slept so heavily, I was surprised to wake two hours later.

Others had been watching. The moon's steady strobe and the street signs flashed behind Cath. Her shoulders and breasts were bare, body bent into a graceful letter "S." Two hands, incandescent in the electric blue, stroked her hair and her shoulders. Polished by moonshine, they pressed together like tarot Lovers. But of course, the meaning of tarot cards comes from within–we see what we want. To me, Hulk and Cath represented the base instincts that drove the first humans from Eden. I abhorred their moral nakedness. *Why are they doing this in front of us? Oh well, I guess it takes two to see-saw.*

Cath's breasts trampolined into the voyeursphere, defying gravity, higher and higher, never seeming to come down. The moon's incandescence revealed a body more generous than I'd realized two nights ago. Cath had taught me about sex, but nothing had prepared me for how wanton a woman's body can be.

Some averted their eyes; others watched openly. "Get a room!" someone shouted. "Perverts!" someone shouted. Some watchers laughed at the public sex show. Why would a woman make herself into such a spectacle? Where was the dignity I'd seen in Mikey's van, when she'd been so contemptuous of Hulk? How could she be so gratuitous now?

"Cutie!" Mikey whispered at the top of his voice. "You shouldn't watch this. Let's go downstairs."

Faces turned, and I felt an instantaneous blush. *I'm grateful that Cath made me more than I am but, Neil Diamond, does this prove she's not the one girl who'll love me, right or wrong?*

"Little dude." Mikey pulled my hand. When I didn't move, he slipped his right arm under my knees and stood. He was even smaller than me. I wouldn't have believed he could pick me up, much less carry me down the stairs.

He dumped me into a chair and came back with a round tray of leftover coffee, milk and a lemon pie. "Forgot the forks. Oh well." He grinned and picked up a slice with his fingers.

* * *

I took out my disappointment on Mikey the next morning, but my words in my mouth tasted like vinegar. "Interesting. You're the guy who made out, pretty shamelessly, with Chica at this very table, in front of this entire restaurant, but you didn't want me to see Cath and Hulk."

"True. But it isn't the same. We made out; they made whoopee. And you're fifteen." Mikey looked at me evenly. "You really like Cath, don't you?"

"Yeah. She's the kind I can't stop thinking about. But," I paused, "is she a bad woman?"

"It's a good question about any woman. Or man. Are Cath and– sorry, what's her name, the girl you left behind . . . "

"O'Murphy."

"O'Murphy and Cath, and your mother and mine, are they bad women because they chose bad men?" Mikey asked.

"I know O'Murphy and my mom made bad-boy choices. Maybe I made a bad-girl choices." *I know we're wrong for each other, but I'd felt gravitational pulls from O'Murphy and Cath from the moment I'd seen them.*

"Pretty ironic." Mikey pondered. "Boys brag about who they get to home base with. And when they're done, they cast yesterday's girlfriend as tomorrow's slut. Does that mean it's okay for guys to choose bad girlfriends?"

Brother Love overheard our conversation and joined us for breakfast. "Convenient double standard, isn't it? Guys don't have to pay for their bad choices. We can even keep making them. It's actually a point of honor for men to have a sordid history."

"My mother left Daddy because he kept doing it with other women," I said. *Mother had said I'm just like Daddy. Am I doomed to repeat his bad judgment? If want to be better than him, I need to make smarter choices.*

"You look glum," Mikey observed.

"I'm thinking about my mother. She's probably wondering about me. She blames herself for everything, so she probably thinks she's responsible for me running away."

"Yeah," Mikey turned introspective. "I ran away too. Black and white wasn't a problem in Cuba, but people here looked down on Mami. I knew she'd never have a chance to remarry here in the States if she had a black son, and my big brother and sister are white. If I beat feet, Mami could get a job. Put a roof over their heads."

Mikey gave up his home so his mother, brother and sister could have a better life? What have I ever sacrificed? "I feel worse every day about what I've done."

"Yeah, we're all wondering about you. Are you gonna stay here, on your own, the rest of the summer?" Mikey asked. "When's the last time you talked to your mother?"

"I don't know. Months."

Mikey winced. "What if you don't find your Daddy soon? Are you going to let a year to go by before you pick up the phone?"

"I wanted to wait until I found Daddy. I never thought it would take this long. You're right, I should call, but she'll beg me to come home. And she'll cry. It's Mother's secret weapon."

Cath and Hulk came downstairs for breakfast, and she ostentatiously plopped down in his lap instead of a chair.

Maybe girls like Cath are better admired from a distance. "Why do women go for the wrong men?" I lowered my voice and we started a whispered conversation.

Brother Love shrugged. "Everyone has issues."

Something else that had never occurred to me. O'Murphy and Cath have boyfriend issues. I had brother issues. Biggy has Daddy issues. Mother and Nan and Marietta had husband issues. "Yeah. Marybeth–a friend back home–said the girl I like has her mouth set for the wrong sort of boy. I just realized I'm guilty of the same thing"

"We all fall into our own traps. Some men only go for loose women. Ask yourself, do you want to fix your bad girl?" Brother Love was unnervingly right. He pushed a pawn, an invitation to play. "Some girls want security. They latch onto the first man who can provide. Some girls want to tame the most dangerous guy, so they're infatuated with bad boys. But remember, when they're ready, the right girl brings the good guy home to mom and dad, and they raise children with him."

"How do we tell people they deserve more?" Mikey asked.

"Cath?" Brother Love stood up. It was time for him to report to the post office.

And O'Murphy. And Mother. Three complicated souls.

"Here's my real answer to both questions: we receive the love we think we deserve. First, understand that our time with each other is limited, so use that time wisely. Don't tell O'Murphy, show her you understand. She may stick with the lousy bastard; she may be won over."

Mother, I wish you'd heard that.

Spit planned to assault O'Murphy on her birthday, this is September. *Should I go back? Without Daddy's training, what help could I be if I found Spit and Pickle raping her? Well, I have to try. Helping others isn't just the code of chivalry. It's my code.*

"Been thinking," Mikey said. "What have you done to find your daddy?"

I went through the list: waiting at the post office, searching the phone book, calling Information.

"Maybe they misspelled your daddy's name in the phone book," Mikey said. "Half my teachers got my last name wrong. They ever misspell yours?"

So we searched the Palo Alto phone book under Pie. Or Pyle. Or Pile.

"Maybe he has an unlisted number?"

"I tried that. The operators said there's no unlisted number in his name." A light bulb turned on. "You know, a lady who works for Pacific Bell gave me a ride. She gave me her card."

"Dude. That chick has the keys to the kingdom. Ring her up."

What was her name? And where had I put her card? I went upstairs and poked though my typewriter case. There's Ron Stanhope's get-out-of-jail-free card. *I have to be more organized.* And there was a white paper the size of a personal check.

I walked to the post office and sat in my usual spot. *How much longer can I keep this up? When will a truant officer ask why I'm not in school? I've gotten used to living on my own. But Mikey, you're right.*

CHAPTER 44

ALIAS DADDY

I walked into Pacific Bell and asked for Louise Sawyer. The receptionist pointed to the desk farthest in the back.

Louise watched as I approached. "Still looking for your father?"

I nodded.

"Wait here." She was attractive in the same way as Mother: a former hotty who'd gained too much weight to interest any but an over-the-hill man. She was back in a few minutes. "Your father's full name is . . . "

"Jonathan Robert Pye."

She winced. "You're cold. Does he have an alias?"

Like a criminal? "No ma'am. He's a Marine."

"What's his address?"

"P.O. Box 989 is all I know. Here in Palo Alto. You're warm."

She switched to a filing cabinet of index cards. She found something, but she looked as if she couldn't say it straight out. She handed me her phone book: "Try again."

Have I missed something?

"What do you see?"

"There aren't any Pyes at all."

"What's his middle name again?" she asked.

"Robert."

"Now you're getting hot. Do you see something close?"

"J. Bob Pyne?" That clue made sense. Jonathan Robert Pye.

"And what's that address?"

I read from the phone book: "309 Cherry Tree Drive, Apartment 369."

She wrote the address on the deposit slip she'd given me months ago, and opened her purse. I thought she wanted a handkerchief, but she offered me a five-dollar bill.

"There's a McDonald's around the corner."

"Yes ma'am."

"Eat something. You've lost weight. Call a taxi. Go to that address. All that will cost about four dollars, so you'll have a dollar left."

"Thanks, really, but I don't need money. I work."

"Then get a haircut. Look right for your daddy." She looked back at me, then dabbed her eyes with the tissue. "If you tell anyone I gave his address, I'll probably lose my job."

I looked her straight in the eye and drew a line across my mouth. "Lips. Zipped."

"I hope you find a wonderful life."

I heard doubt in her voice, but I looked up and smiled.

"It's the first time I've seen you smile. Do that more often."

* * *

His neighbor told me how to find Sarge–that's what she called him. He was a groundskeeper at a Mountain View golf course, and she looked up the phone number.

My dialing finger trembled. I forced myself not to hang up. *Cath, what am I going to say to my daddy? That my life is feces? That I hate Hell Creek because it's the most boring town in the most boring state*

*in the Union? That a day without Biggy is like a day without darkness?
That I want to start over? That I'm nearly sixteen and I really, really,
really need to live with my Daddy if I'm ever going to become a man?*

"Ale House, this is Walt." He said it brusquely.

"Is this the golf course?"

"Yep. Nineteenth Hole. I'm the barkeep. Can I help?"

"I'm trying to find my daddy."

His voice gentled. "Who's your daddy?"

"Jonathan Robert Pye. Maybe you call him Sarge? Or J.
Bob Pyne?"

It seemed as if Walt might not answer, so I blurted the
CliffsNotes story.

"So that's why he changed his name," Walt said, as if what he'd
just heard had explained everything. "I never knew he had kids. But
he's gone for the day. He always gets here early to avoid the heat. He'll
be back tomorrow morning. And Jesus, you hitchhiked by yourself,
clear from Oklahoma, just to see your old man?"

"Yes sir."

"Sarge is going to be blown away. What's your name?"

"Curtis."

"Wow. You must be some kid. I won't tell Sarge you're here. You
should surprise him."

CHAPTER 45

DADDY'S GOT A GIRLFRIEND

After I hung up the phone, I had two choices: because she rarely saw him, the neighbor lady had said Sarge probably lived with a girl-friend, so he wasn't likely to come home tonight. I could sleep at the Full Circle, but meeting Daddy again would be the most important moment of my life. I wanted to be at the golf course when he got to work. I started walking.

Maybe O'Murphy and I could live at Daddy's apartment. I could swim laps at the pool and lift weights until I had Popeye forearms.

I have the sense of direction of a scrambled egg, so I got lost at the start. A sign in the evening fog said I was at the city limits of Menlo Park.

"Is Mountain View this way?" I asked two teen girls. They gig-gled as if I might be crazy, but one pointed in the opposite direction. Mountain View was behind me.

I sat under a redwood with two trunks. The tree had its own name: El Palo Alto. A plaque told the story of the Portolà expedition from San Diego, almost two hundred years ago. Old Portolà had gotten lost too. He'd overshot Monterey, camped here, and discovered this giant tree. And San Francisco Bay. Now I didn't feel so bad. I walked a few blocks and then confirmed with a man in a business suit. "Is Mountain View this way?"

"South down El Camino Real," he assured.

It was getting harder to see. Sunspots–that's what I called floaters in my eyes–blocked my central vision. My hands shook. I'd eaten pie this morning with Mikey, but I hadn't eaten lunch or supper. Walking had made me shaky. There was a McDonald's sign, but I wanted to meet Daddy with as much money as I could. One emergency ration remained in my typewriter case. I took the red-and-white can of Campbell's Vegetable Beef and set it on the park bench. I slumped low so the bench would support my head, and I napped while the sun warmed the soup.

* * *

"Haven't you got any gumption?"

I woke from the dream that had repeated ever since I had left Oklahoma. The shaking had gotten worse. *You've got an emergency ration. You'd better eat. Now.*

I dug the can of Campbell's soup from my typewriter case and positioned the blade of Grand's Barlow knife on the rim. Using the flat of my hand, I hammered until the point broke through the lid, then sawed tin until I could bend back the lid. I was ravenous. I couldn't pour soup into my mouth fast enough. The jagged top poked my eyelid, and my lower lip hung on a shard of metal around the rim. I emptied the condensed soup, but I couldn't stand up yet. *What is wrong with me? Why do these shakes come on so suddenly?*

Pedestrians must have thought I was drunk. Or drugged. I walked the rest of the way to the golf course. It was eleven P.M., and the road entrance was locked. The sign said the country club would open at seven A.M. Where to sleep? The ditch on the opposite side of the road was grassy. It would be soft, but it wasn't secluded enough to avoid being seen by passing cars. I could camp on a rough, but how would it look if Daddy found me on the course? There was a water tower up the hill. No one would see me there. Nobody human, anyway.

My mind raced so I couldn't sleep. I took the island-fighters photo from my typewriter case and stared into Daddy's eyes. I wished I could turn back time twenty-six years and go to war with him. Courage and character couldn't be faked in battle. I'd never known this self-assured Marine, but he was the kind of cocky other warriors wanted to be with.

What had happened between the years this photo was shot and Mother deserted Daddy? How are Daddy and I the same? His eyes look like my eyes, but I've never had his self-assurance. God, I sure could use a sign. If not a burning bush, at least a little conversation.

CHAPTER 46

ONE HEROIC SON
OF A BITCH

" . . . gumption? Don't you know I don't wan . . . ? " My eyes opened at seven-fifty A.M. I walked to the country club with gumption–the word I kept dreaming about–stuck in my mind.

Last night's dirty dishes and beer mugs littered the tables inside the clubhouse while Simon and Garfunkel crooned my favorite lyrics about rocks and islands.

Will I even recognize Daddy? I sat at the bar on a Naugahyde captain's chair and studied the island fighters photo.

"Curtis?"

I'm pretty sure that's not Daddy.

He reached to shake hands. "I'm Walt." His face became solemn when he saw the photo. He sat without looking and almost missed the stool. "I haven't seen this picture in–this is '67, so–twenty-three years. Your old man wound up with it? I thought it was lost to the ages. Wow. I see the resemblance now. You look like him on the day we met. You don' t know how glad I am to meet his son."

In Walt's doughy mug, I could see the bony, rabbity, teenager's face that dwelled inside the photo.

He studied the photo. "All dead. 'Cept me an' Two. We called him that because he was a two-striper then. I'm the bastard at the end. With the BAR."

"It doesn't look like a machine gun."

"It wasn't. After Adolph took over the world, Ordnance realized everybody else had a portable machine gun, so they converted these, chambered for a .30-06. Hellava recoil. Tail Man had a BAR too, but by the time this pic was taken, our thirteen-man squad was down to six. And I'm only alive because of Two. He never told you?"

I shook my head.

"Never talks about it to me, either. This was taken just before the worst day of the war. We–1st Marine Division–were assigned to seize an airstrip on this pimple of a coral island. Rupertus, our genius major general, predicted we'd capture it in four days. Neither side needed it, but by then the Japs had to protect Tokyo, so they fortified against us. The only reason we even went there was that Dugout Doug got all wet-eyed about retaking the Philippines, but MacArthur wouldn't go anywhere the Marines hadn't already been, so he sent us to Peleliu and Angaur."

A foursome moseyed in to pay for their rounds of golf.

"Japs had maybe ten thousand men, not enough to stop us at the beach. So those canny bastards buried mines and artillery shells on the beaches, fuses up. Exploded when our landing craft and tanks rolled over them. Killed three thousand of us right when we came ashore."

"Got some two-piece Spauldings?" A golfer interrupted Walt's story.

Walt handed over a box with a dozen balls, collected five dollars, and continued. "Japs blasted into the ridges overlooking the beaches.

Built pillboxes and placed twenty-millimeter cannons inside with four gunners. Then they sealed the pillboxes. Left those poor bastards there to die. Want a Coke?"

I shook my head.

"Finally, our rifle squad crawled up the mountain. Honeycombs under it, five hundred caves connected by mine shafts. The 1st Marines had to push into Umurbrogol; the 7th had to clear the south end of the island. Chesty Puller—our colonel—damn near bought it. Artillery round hit his LVT, but it was a dud. We all should've died. And we would've, but your Daddy . . . "

"What did he do?"

"He was one heroic son of a bitch."

I guess every kid wants to hear that about his dad.

"Last day of the battle, gun cave pinned us down. I got it in both legs. Five left in our squad—three too wounded to move. Two, he figured out how to assault a gun cave. He traded his .30 caliber popgun for my BAR, took our grenades, and attacked like a red-assed rooster. Blinded 'em with smoke. Then he scooched up and slipped a grenade down the slit. Killed all four Japs with their own munitions. He went nuts, and we lived."

"Daddy? I mean, he was a typist."

"Yeah. After the war. Nobody never told you that your daddy's a gen-u-ine war hero? The things sons don't know, huh? Anyway, Sarge is going to be jacked to see you. He's out there now on the eighth. Hear the mower?"

I walked to the eighth hole, where his tractor clipped towards me but circled.

Surely he saw me. Did I make a mistake?

The tractor circled a third time, and this time I got a good look. I remembered that hair: curly and thick and gray with so little black, it was as if the strands had been forged from tarnished spoons. *Every time I see a man with hair like that, I wonder if it's Daddy. I even think that about Robert Mitchum. Mother's right: I have Daddy's straight nose, his long earlobes, his green eyes. And that balloon chest. Will I have that big trunk someday?*

Finally, he braked the John Deere and took off his red cap, a yellow eagle, globe and fouled anchor above the capital letters, "SARGE."

I smiled.

Daddy's lips tightened as if he were trying not to say what he wanted to say. He seemed pained to get off his tractor. He didn't look me in the eyes.

Do you think I'm here to beg you to restore our allotments? I'd try, if it would get rid of Vin. Come to think of it, maybe that's why Mother hadn't sicced the cops on me. To be rid of Vin. Maybe that's why Marietta didn't send me home on a bus.

He bit his lip and looked up. I saw his vulnerability, his refusal to sanction my uneasiness. His fists balled, as if he had to defend himself. *Are you going to hit me?*

"Haven't you got any gumption?"

Gumption. I swallowed hard. I was blinded by dread. The hair stood on my neck. I sensed my mouth was open. We were face to face, blood to blood, in a slow-motion tragedy.

"Don't you know I don't want you? Go back to your mama."

I took one long last look.

Without even saying hello, my own father just left me standing there, flat footed, too stunned to speak. In the next moment, he was back on his tractor. The engine started, and he rode away. His mower cut a swath as short as the greens across the rough.

The island fighters photo slipped from my hand. It would've been my proof that I was his son. Still too stunned to think, I trudged back to the clubhouse.

Walt could sense something was wrong. "You found him? What happened?"

I shook my head. "Nothing."

"Nothing? What the hell does that mean? What did Sarge do? Aww. Naww. Piss on my Post Toasties. I guess Jonny Bob is out of the running for Father of the Year."

I hadn't let my eyes tear, but Walt did. He paused, took off his New York Giants baseball cap–a ten-year-old relic–and held it to his chest, as if paying respects to someone who had died. "I never would've thought that. Sarge is one of my favorite people in this whole freaky world. So, what'd he do, just toss you a wad of cash and tell you to snag a bus back home?"

"No."

"That son of a bitch!" His eyes widened and his lips parted in surprise. He reached into his jeans and brought a money clip with a five and some ones. "Here. I'd give it you more, kid, but I'm tapped. That's every dollar I got."

I shook his hand. "It's probably time to get back to Peaceable River."

"No, no. No! Take this. I'll make that sociopathic prick pay me back. And here." He dropped the bills into a brown bag with his sandwich, a Coke, and a package of M&Ms. He tossed in a paperback, *To Kill a Mockingbird.* "You won't see your dad in there, but maybe you'll find the one you deserve. Maybe Atticus will help when it's time to raise your own kids."

If I had opened my mouth again, he would have heard me choke up.

"Kid? Don't let yourself be . . . " Walt's eyes glimmered again. "Everyone's got a cowardly flaw. Sarge is scared that people will need him."

I started the two-mile walk back to the Full Circle, and I cried for the very last time in my whole screwed-up life.

CHAPTER 47

WHAT NOW?

I'd hitchhiked seventeen hundred miles to find him, and in twenty words or less, Daddy had sent me packing. *And exposed my most cowardly quality: I don't confront people. I should've made him talk to me. I should've forced him to learn who I am.*

But I didn't judge him. That's what Biggy had done. To him, Daddy was the worst father in the history of worst fathers.

"People don't change unless they want to," Mother had said about Daddy. Maybe I hadn't listened because I had such great expectations.

Who did he reject? Okay, whom. It couldn't have been me; he probably hadn't thought about me since I was nine. He had gotten me wrong a few minutes ago. I'll be honest when I tell Mother and Biggy about him, but they'll probably get him wrong too. No one will ever understand why he left me standing here.

So, what am I supposed to do now? Pull out Grand's Barlow knife and open a vein? That sounds funny in my head, but I don't suppose anyone else will get it. I don't want to hitch a ride back to the Full Circle, I want to walk and plan my future. Where should I go? If I go back home, can I take two more years of bullying from the Andersens? Will Mother understand why I left and make Biggy leave me alone?

It would be two more years before I graduated from high school. People say I'm special, but not enough to overcome two more years of backing down. The good news was that Biggy would graduate next year. Then he would join the Marines. Maybe I would too.

And then what? Will I become you, Daddy? Why did you reject me? Why haven't the last six years changed you into a better father, a better husband, a better person? A better question: Why haven't I changed?

Suddenly, I was furious. *Why do I keep screwing up my life? No. Don't get mad. Change.* I willed my thinking to slow, and I received a moment of clarity. I was unprepared, untrained, and unskilled at everything but flipping burgers and throwing newspapers at porches. I came here because I'd wanted Daddy to change me. Could I change without him? I loved learning. Would I need Mother to start over as a freshman in high school, here in California where no one knew me? Maybe I could enroll early in college. But was college just a high school with ashtrays? Would college kids act differently?

I felt more depressed than ever. Was there still time to be happy? Loneliness fell on me like a disease. I didn't want to stop the tears. Meeting Daddy would become a memory I'd want to forget. The journey would have to be enough.

CHAPTER 48

THE CHESSMASTER

I had advanced through the ranks, so today I'd play the chessmaster for the Full Circle championship. I tossed my *Time* magazine on the table, opened with a pawn, and challenged with a smile: "I'm gonna beat you like you stole my dog."

"You can't bluff in chess." Brother Love opened with his queen. "I see by your outfit that you are a cowboy."

"What's that mean?" Hulk asked from behind me.

"'The Streets of Laredo.'" I stuck out a Wellington boot and tapped Gil's black Stetson.

Hulk's look questioned Mikey.

"Ballad about a dying cowboy." Mikey prodded. "Marty Robbins."

"I don't like cowboy music."

"We've heard." I loped out my king's knight.

Brother Love needled Hulk. "Bruce, we're five minutes from Stanford and forty-five from Berkeley. We don't admire the unknowing." He castled his king's rook, then tapped the cover of my worn magazine. "'God Is Dead.' You believe that, my Huckleberry friend?"

"I haven't read all of it. Has he been sick?" I smiled up at Mikey and Chica. "Old joke. Preacher, you trying to take my mind off the tournament?"

Brother Love leaned back in his chair and grinned to himself.

"You really want to know what a fifteen-year-old thinks?" I baited his rook with a pawn. "I probably have this backwards, but one thing I learned in Sunday school is that God granted us free will, and when we didn't use it the way he wanted, he got pissed and destroyed stuff. Five times. Noah's flood, the Egyptians, the Canaanites, and New Mexico from the looks of it. Sodom and Gomorrah used free will to get drunk and make whoopee, so he only rescued one guy, and he turned that guy's wife into a salt lick. So maybe the 'God Is Love' types shouldn't ignore that."

Brother Love's rook moved up three rows to target my pawn. "How long have you been playing chess now?"

"Four months. You taught me."

"Hmm. The student may have exceeded the master." His rook snatched my pawn. "Bottom line—was Nietzsche right?"

"Nietzsche told *Time* that the world will become less religious, and that atheism will—well, make people less moral."

"And are people less moral?"

My eyes swept the cafeteria. Hippies in T-shirts; one read, "Off the Pig." Girls in short shorts. Restrooms hazy with doobie smoke. "I can't help but think that everything is less moral. My church wouldn't even let a woman run a Sunday school class. Used some Bible quote: 'Do not permit a woman to teach or to have authority over a man.' Is that moral?"

His incipient queen crashed my rank of pawns. "So if God is dead, where do you think we go when we die?"

I swung my queen's knight in an L and shrugged. "Where are we now? By the way, is your name really Loving?"

"Lovinski. Grandpapa changed it. His family hid from the Spanish Inquisition in Mexico."

"Is that Christian?"

"Jewish. But I'm non-denominational. So what did the Baptists lay on you about Jews?"

"My preacher–ex-preacher–claimed a lot of things. Like all Jews go to hell."

Brother Love didn't appear surprised. "Because?"

"He always thought God should've come to him for advice. He said God's chosen people are imperfect Christians because Jews aren't baptized, they don't pray to Jesus, they can't go to Heaven." I pushed another pawn. "So is God dead? I don't know, but if I go to Heaven, I hope it's after God's had his coffee."

Brother Love's queen took my pawn.

"That's what I've been waiting for." I trapped his queen with my red bishop. *En garde.*

"Stunning," Brother Love studied the board and pursed his lips in mock chagrin. He tipped over his king and waved me away. "Go child, and sin no more."

CHAPTER 49

WHY AM I STILL HERE?

That afternoon, I spent a dollar and climbed to the balcony to watch the five o'clock matinee, *To Sir, with Love.* Sidney Poitier played a teacher in London. His students were disrespectful. They disrupted his classroom. One burned her Kotex in a classroom grate.

I got drowsy after Lulu finished her song, which was number seven with a bullet on the Full Circle jukebox. I slept better in the theater than I had on Full Circle's carpet, so I settled back into that soft chair. I woke again in the middle of the next show.

* * *

"They just left!" Chica said.

Hulk slumped at the front table, his back against the wall. His left hand pressed a white towel to his temple. "I'm okay," he assured me with a chuckle. "We're okay. Some biker freek rabbit-punched me. Broke the skin, that's all."

"Are you sure?" I asked. "Can I get you a brain surgeon or something?"

"I think I'll survive." Hulk grinned while Cath stroked his arm.

"Is everyone else all right? What happened?"

"They just left!" Chica repeated.

"Who?"

"Ángeles de los infiernos," Chica fumed.

"Angels of the inferno?"

"Hell's Angels," Cath translated. "They stomped in, grabbed food off the cafeteria line, trashed the kitchen, picked a fight with Hulk . . . "

"They ordered beer, and it was coming," Donald explained, "but for some . . . "

"They were trippin' on acid," Hulk interjected.

" . . . reason," Donald continued, "they stuck their heads right under the spigots and . . . "

" . . . drank from the taps," Mikey finished.

"He wouldn't let them touch me." Cath encircled his right arm.

"Uno de los Ángeles de los infiernos agarró su teta," Chica spurted.

"A Hell's Angels grabbed her . . . " I blushed.

Cath pulled down her blouse and showed me the insulted breast.

"How long were they here?"

"Donald," Hulk said admiringly, "came running down the stairs from his office. Screamed 'The pigs are coming.' The Angels rabbited."

"So where's the cops?" I asked.

"Maybe I was premature," Donald laughed.

The group chuckled at the manager's gambit. Too many customers held heroin or pot. If the place had been searched, it would have been disastrous for the Full Circle.

"Check your stuff," Cath took my arm. "Some of the biker bitches raided our crash pad."

I ran upstairs. My typewriter case was open; my clothes were strewn across the floor. I'd stashed Trooper Ron's five dollars and Walt's eight dollars in the breast pocket of my CPO jacket. Except for the few bills in my pocket, I was destitute again. And Gil's hat was gone. I felt violated. I'd wash everything tomorrow.

I sat on the case. I loved this cafe. I cherished the maturity I'd found here. But where had it gotten me? I had considered living the rest of my days in our communal loft, but was that possible? I returned downstairs to think. *I've found Daddy; why am I still here?*

"You never said what happened last week." Brother Love sipped his coffee. It was a blessing to have a listener and a mentor, so I spilled my guts. Not just about Daddy, but Mother and Biggy and Pickle and Spit's plan to assault O'Murphy–now just a few days away.

"You and I are more alike than we realize," Brother Love said. "I thought about you a few days ago when I read a study. It said one in four of us are angry at our mothers. The rest of us are pissed at dad. I could write Hallmark cards from that study. 'Dear Mom: I hope you die, but I still want your approval.' Or 'Dear Dad, you reprehensible bastard, wish you were here.'"

I couldn't help but grin at the irony.

"I can't remember when I wasn't mad at my dad. My parents fought every day."

Astonishing. If Brother Love didn't have a normal childhood, who did?

"I blamed my unhappiness on Father," Brother Love said. "I don't know why now, but I wanted Mom to divorce him. As a kid, it never occurred to me that half of their problems must be her fault. And you know what mom told me, many years later? She was happy with her life. Yeah. They're still together. They've fought for thirty-six years, but Father said he might have killed himself if she'd left him. They weren't perfect role models, but you gotta love them."

"My Daddy was a bastard. It crushed him that he never knew who his dad was," I said. "My mother thinks I've already turned into Daddy. I just hope there's still time to reinvent myself."

"You'll realize this someday, but our fathers live inside us," Brother Love agreed. "We become more like our dads as we grow older, but no one is a genetic time bomb."

"How can you be so sure?"

"You think you know who you are? You have no idea. I'll tell you how I know: you're a better person. Your conscience won't allow you to do to your son what your dad did to you."

I wanted to agree.

"But you need to forgive him anyway."

I don't forgive. And I guess Daddy didn't either.

"Curtis, are you going to keep chewing on that pain or swallow it? Ask yourself again if you can forgive. These young days will never come again."

Forgive Daddy? Forgive Biggy? Forgive the Andersens? I'd rather forgive the Devil.

"Tell me, did someone do something bad to you in the first grade?"

I nodded. "A girl named Peewee. Stabbed my hand with a pencil. She was such a terror, everyone was afraid of her. Even the teacher. Even the principal."

"Do you still hate her?"

"I haven't seen her for ten years. I guess she moved."

"You don't know this yet, but some people never forget school-days injuries, even though they're successful now, married, have kids of their own. Do you plan to hate Peewee when you're eighty?"

I scoffed at the thought.

"Seems silly, doesn't it? You may never forget your turdhead father's most egregious offenses, but I think you'll find it easier to forgive him than to carry a lifetime burden of disappointment. This is going to come as a surprise–it does to most boys with crappy dads–but sometimes it's the role of the son to redeem the sins of the father. Are you wondering why this happened? Why God visited this pain on you?"

"I guess I deserved it."

"Not in the way you imagine. Have you heard the parable of the beggar?"

"I think I'm about to."

"Jesus passed a blind beggar on the road," Brother Love said. "His disciples asked: whose sin blinded him, the beggar's or his parents? Neither, Jesus said: the beggar had been blinded so God's works could be revealed. Jesus placed mud on the beggar's eyes and told him to wash in the Pool of Siloam. And the beggar saw. You were blind when your journey started. Now you see. Like the beggar, your pain has revealed what you need to learn."

True enough. I've learned about Daddy. And people. And courage. And I've learned that a lot of what I know just isn't so.

"Ever heard of anagnorisis? It's the moment when someone recognizes they've committed an unforgiveable wrong. But they can't ever take it back. All fathers make mistakes. Even God."

WHAT HARRY HARLOW FOUND

The next morning, Brother Love got to the point of our impromptu counseling. "Children are born too soon–they don't stay in the womb long enough. That's why our father-mother-child unit remains bonded for years–physically and psychologically. Been around many babies?"

"Seven girl cousins."

"Then you know what happens when a baby realizes its mother isn't there?"

"It cries?"

"Because separation from a parent causes anxiety." Brother Love sipped his coffee. "Babies cry to express loneliness. And if Mother doesn't come . . . "

"It screams." *If you're talking about Daddy or Biggy, I know where you're going.*

"If Mother doesn't respond, Baby gets more aggressive. What do we do when we feel anger? When Baby screams, its hands bunch up. How does it know to make a fist?"

"That's my brother." *Daddy hadn't paid attention, so Biggy had gotten belligerent.*

"What about your mother? Does she want her husband to return home?"

That's always been my question: what does Mother expect? She lost weight. She didn't remarry. Does she pine for Daddy? I guess we're nobody till somebody loves us.

One night, we'd gone to Marsha's house in Comanche. They'd kept their voices low in the kitchen, but I'd overheard snatches of conversation from the living room.

"He was the love of my life." And, "He's such a charmer, he could talk his way out of an earthquake." Mother hadn't been talking about Vin in that tone. "He could make anyone like him, and he could make anyone believe in him."

"Biggy always worshipped Jonathan Robert," Marsha had said.

"And Jon was so partial to Biggy," Mother had agreed.

"So, let's get down to it," Brother Love's tone changed from professorial to friendly. "Why do you think your father sent you away?"

"He doesn't want me."

"But why? If your mother were sitting here, how would she explain that?"

"Nan always said Daddy was so self-centered, his ambition was to die in his own arms."

"Fascinating. What do you think that means?"

"I don't know, but Mother says I'm self-centered too. And she says I never react to anything. She can't read my face. She never knows what I'm thinking."

"You're emotionally inscrutable. You keep your face impassive—never smile, never show your emotions. Other people show what they're thinking. They frown when they don't approve; they smile when they find joy. If you wonder why you're a loner, that's one reason. If you don't open up and react to people, they can't reach out. But you're the most mature fifteen-year-old I've ever met. What is your father like?"

"Nan said Daddy is a Peter Pan–a boy who never grew up."

"Freud would want to know about his relationship with his own mother."

"Daddy never knew his real parents. He turned seventeen right after Pearl Harbor, and he joined the Marines. But they wanted his birth certificate. That's when he found out."

"Bastardy was the ultimate ultimate in those days."

"Mother thinks Aunt Frankie is really his mother. But she wasn't married, so Mother thinks Frankie gave Daddy to her sister, Gianna. His stepdad was probably really just a live-in lover." *Like Vin.*

"So who was his natural father?"

"Mother thinks Whitey Pye was out of the picture very quickly. If he was Daddy's father."

Brother Love saw the light bulb go on in my head. "You made a connection?"

"Daddy was rejected by his father. Biggy thinks he was rejected by Daddy. Is that why they're both jerks?"

"Is that what you think?"

I didn't answer, but the way Biggy bullied me had sabotaged what should have been the best times of our lives. He had turned our brotherhood into civil war.

"That similarity is quite clear. Your father didn't get the love he needed, so he rejected the love of his wife and the love of his children. Your brother seems to have rejected his father and his brother. What about you? Do you reject love?"

Before anyone rejects me.

"I should tell you about Harry Harlow's rejection experiments. He separated rhesus monkeys from their mothers. He was heartless, even for a researcher, but his data revealed so much. He placed monkey babies with two substitute mothers. One was a wire doll, it offered no comfort, but a nipple was attached so infants could drink as much milk as they wanted. Or, the baby monkey could choose a foam-covered doll. Foam offered comfort, but it dispensed no milk. And do you know which the babies chose?"

"Babies only know what they need. Milk?"

"So we supposed. But Harry Harlow's experiments were about needs. A baby's needs are more complex than hunger. After the baby monkeys suckled from the wire mothers, they jumped back to the foam doll because they needed–not wanted, but needed–comfort. We need food first, but after we feed, we need mother's love. Harry taught us that nursing serves two necessary functions: nutrition and parental bonding. That's what your daddy was up against, and your brother too. The need for love is imprinted on primates."

So we actually, desperately need love? Somehow, that sounds right.

"Your daddy had a shitty pop. Which is why you have a shitty dad. And a shitty brother."

"Hit that nail right on the head, Brother Love."

"I've always wanted to ask: how smart are you, Curtis?"

I've learned not to talk about this, but . . . "My IQ score says 135."

"Top three percent? What a gift." Brother Love thought for a moment. "Were your top marks in word skills?"

I nodded.

"Lots of math questions on your IQ?"

"A whole section. "

"And how did you score there?"

"Fifth percentile."

"Bottom of the scale?" His eyes narrowed. "And yet 135 is your average score? Then you must have tested higher in soft skills. English? Vocabulary? Reasoning?"

"Ninety-eighth percentile in word skills. High nineties in reasoning. But so un-swift in mechanics and science."

"And did your counselor explain what that means?"

"She said I'm a word-hungry young savant."

"Agreed. You are next-level smart. You may be a true genius in soft skills. You're an excellent listener, so don't be surprised if you turn out to be a psychiatrist." His face changed. "Nah, it'll be impossible to get into med school without hard-science skills, but psychology or sociology, they may accept you. What does your mother say?"

"I'm always reading books. She thinks I should be a librarian."

"Tell your mom a fence isn't built on one post. I think you'll do lots of things, and some will be bigger than shelving books. More likely, you'll write books."

"I don't know how to write. Books, I mean."

"I imagine no one does before they write one. But why do you seem disappointed in yourself?"

"I do things I'm not proud of. And no one likes me."

"Life puts us in a corner, doesn't it? But you think no one likes you? Has someone taught you to hate yourself?"

Biggy. I always thought being smart would make him proud. It makes him jealous.

"Well, you are liked. I like you, and so do Mikey and Chica and Cathy. Hulk would never say it, but he admires you. And I think your brother and your schoolmates would too, if they gave you a better chance. And you tried to kill yourself once? But you really didn't want to die."

"How do you know?"

"Because you're not dead." Brother Love looked me in the eye. "You know, there comes a time in our search for the meaning of life when we realize there are no answers. At night, as we drift into sleep, our souls wonder if this is all there is. But when morning comes, we wake up and we live our lives. You did this morning, and you will tomorrow. And when you come to the horrible realization that there are no answers, you'll accept it, and you'll stop searching. So let's get honest: why did you leave home?"

I'll be half-honest. "I wanted out. Because of a problem with my brother."

"He picks on you?" Brother Love smiled. "That doesn't mean he hates you."

"You haven't met my brother."

"I've seen some research that you probably already know a lot about. It shows that a third of older brothers and sisters bully their siblings. Some bullying is so hateful, it changes the way the younger child acts, and they become targeted by bullies at school. An awful predicament, because there's no escape for us younger children. We usually develop emotional problems. The victim is often depressed and hurts himself, even as an adult."

My mouth opened a little. "You got picked on?"

"Absolutely. My big sis put so many knots on my head, Mother sent her to *bais ya'akov*."

My look questioned the term.

"A girl's school for Jews. In Brooklyn."

"I didn't know girls bullied boys."

"Oh my, yes. My sister's a middle child. Desperate for people to notice her. Takes charge of the whole family. Pays for everything. I tried my best to get along with her. I think she's always compared herself with me–you know how sibling rivalries work by now . . . "

I do.

"But instead of learning discipline, she took her revenge. Beat the shit out of me every time she came home. Every time. If sibling bullying persists long term, it damages their adult relationships. Sis and I haven't spoken in years. She had to be better than me, but found herself lacking in every way. She felt better about herself if she could push me around. Finally, I left home, just as you did, because I'd rather cut myself off from family than fight with her. She did become much more successful than me. But don't do what I did. Stand your ground with Biggy."

"I can't win."

"I'll bet he taught you to believe that. I thought I couldn't win. Which is why we both failed. In families, there is no winning. Only respect. Did your brother call you a coward too?"

I nodded.

"The courage of the brave coward." Brother Love shook his head in disbelief. "You're fifteen; you left home, you hitchhiked across the Great Plains and the Desert God Forgot, you found your father. How much scratch did you start with?"

"Twenty-five dollars."

"Curtis, you have more guts than I've displayed in my entire life. I wish I'd done what you did. You have the pluck of Lewis and Clark. Look around. Who's the youngest person here?"

I didn't have to. "Me."

"How many in this room take care of themselves? And I don't mean panhandle. Do you think your brother could have done this?"

Alone? Biggy? I chuckled. "He never would've tried."

"Why?"

I smiled again. "Maybe he has better sense than me."

"Fear lies." Brother Love stared into my eyes to make sure I understood. "Fear says, 'You can't do this.' Fear said you couldn't possibly make this trip."

I nodded.

"And yet, here you are. Fear always says, 'You're going to lose.' Courage says, 'If you try, if don't give up, you'll win.'"

I nodded.

"I'm going to finish eating, and then I've got to go. But I have an important question: do you have what you came for?"

It's the only question left. Well, if I'm not going to live with Daddy, my place isn't here. I want to go to college. I don't want to be afraid anymore. That about covers it.

"I believe you've got a girl to go back to?"

"Maybe. Probably not."

"But you like her?"

"O'Murphy. I really don't have a chance with her, though."

"Why? Tell me about her. Is she pretty?"

"So pretty, the world is divided into two parts, where she is, and where she isn't. But I could never be–I don't know–good enough for her."

"Don't put a period where God has placed a comma. Would you like her better if she were a beggar maid?"

"You lost me."

"Shakespeare, Shaw, Graham Greene, they all wrote stories about kings who weren't attracted to women until they saw a beggar."

Hmm. I could imagine MBe and me or Sammie and me, but never O'Murphy and me.

"And I think you've realized that, like Dumbo and Dorothy Gale, you don't need a white feather or emerald slippers."

I nodded. "There is no magic. Just me to fight my battles."

"Do you want a ride somewhere?"

"How far are you going?"

"How far are *you* going?"

"Could you take me out to Highway 101?"

"It's just a few miles from here. But if you're heading east, I'd rather take you here," he sketched a map on a napkin, "across Dumbarton Bridge, and let you out on Interstate 880. You can take that over to 580, then down 5 to I-40."

"Better. But I've got to get my typewriter case. And I have to call Onionheads."

When I returned from the upstairs crash pad, Brother Love stuck a forefinger in his water glass, touched my forehead, and swept his arm across the dining room. He must have talked to everyone about this, because they stood up. Mikey and Chica and Hulk and Georgy and Cath surrounded me for a group hug.

Brother Love's voice rose, and he intoned slowly, ceremonially:

"For ye shall go out with joy

"And be led forth with peace

"The mountains and the hills shall break forth before you into singing

"And all the trees of the field shall clap their hands."

"Sounds groovy," I grinned my embarrassment. "What does it mean?"

"Isaiah 55:12. It's an anointment by God. And an invitation to the needy."

BOOK 3

"We are going back from whence we came."
JFK

CHAPTER 51

REVERSE COURSE

I'd failed to connect with O'Murphy, I'd failed to connect with Biggy, and I'd failed to connect with Daddy. I'd drifted away from Oklahoma because of the sad things that happened, and now I'm drifting away from California.

My first ride on 880 lasted just twenty miles, but it got me to San Lorenzo. Hours after dark, an electric window rolled down on an aging, gunboat Lincoln with faded black paint. "Alight, my young brother. Monroe France is the name. And how are you this glorious Monday morning?"

It must be after midnight. Which means I'll be sixteen tomorrow. "Curtis Pye. I'm just ginger peachy. How about you?"

"Ginger peachy! Well, I'm on my way back from a Sunday-night revival at the Lord's chapel, so that's a ginger-peachy day. And I've got Jehovah's music on tape. What more could an old man want?"

The eight-track clicked to a song I'd never heard before. "What a voice. I thought you meant church music. This is . . . " I searched for the word.

"You modern cats call it rhythm and blues, but it's soul to me." A black leather case was behind the driver's seat.

"You're a guitar player."

"By avocation, but I make a little spundoodelus sometimes, jamming with my brothers, white groups, whoever needs me. Last year, I grooved with the cats that opened for the Monkees at the Cow Palace."

"The Monkees Monkees? Micky Dolenz and the Monkees?"

"Yes sir indeedy. And Michael and Peter and Davy Jones."

"Where?"

"The Cow Palace is in Daly City."

"Cow Palace. That sounds like a . . . "

"Livestock arena. On the coast. January 22, 1967. My, the girls were just hysterical. It was the biggest show I have ever seen. The Monkees even changed costumes during the breaks."

"I wish I'd been there, Mr. France. What did they open with?"

"Last Train to Clarksville."

"My fave. Except for 'I'm a Believer.'"

"That was their curtain call. So, where are you going?"

"Oklahoma."

"Is that so? Micky said they had just played Tulsa."

"So I heard. Did you like them, Mr. France?"

He flashed a knowing smile. "Well, let's just say they needed a session crew a lot more than their fans knew."

"I heard they don't really play their guitars."

"Young Mr. Nesmith asked for my help. He said his promoter wanted them to sing and act, not play. But they were trying to learn."

"So it's true?"

"It was worse than that," Monroe said. "It was dishonest. What they were required to do on stage was to duplicate the recordings made by session musicians like me. And they didn't have the skills, except for Peter. But they were learning."

"Wow. Did the audience know?"

"The crowd was ecstatic just to be there. Micky said to me, 'We're like Leonard Nimoy, trying to really become a Vulcan.' It frustrated them. But they cared, I can tell you that. Now you won't believe this: the cheapest ticket was five dollars," Monroe shook his head. "Five dollars. Some people paid seven. Might have been worth five if Jimi Hendrix had opened."

"Who's Jimmy Hendericks?"

"A truly talented young guitarist. Micky said Jimi joined them in July, but the audience wouldn't listen to him. He said Jimi would stoke up the amps and fire into 'Purple Haze,' but the kids would drown him out with 'We want Daaavy!' Embarrassing. He dropped out."

"So who do you like?"

"Curtis Mayfield and Sam Cooke and Otis Redding, they my cats. I don't just appreciate their music, they touch me. Don't need no ticket, I just thank the Lord for Curtis," he said. "You little white cats grow up and never know Mr. Mayfield. After he listened to the Rev. Dr. Martin Luther King deliver his *I Have a Dream* speech, Mr. Curtis Mayfield, on that very August day in 1963, led 250 thousand people to sing 'We Shall Overcome.' He wanted to write a great gospel song. And he did. Two years later, we all heard 'People Get Ready.'"

"What's it about?"

"A most excellent question. You a cat who studies lyrics?"

I nodded.

"Well, it is celestial poetry. Nothing less than salvation for every believer. It says 'People get ready,' because the Prince of Peace is aboard the Rapture Train. 'Don't bring your baggage' means you we can leave behind our troubles in life. It encourages the black man, beaten down since the time of slavery, to lay his difficulties before the Lord."

"It's about redemption? So is Woody Guthrie's song, 'Bound for Glory.'"

"No ramblers, no gamblers, no two-bit liars," the driver confirmed.

"Nothing but the righteous and the holy." I quoted Woody's lyric.

"Right on. These are songs about rising above Earth's pain."

So many stories were about redeeming ourselves: *Huck Finn, Catcher in the Rye, Gone with the Wind, The Grapes of Wrath.*

Monroe drove a couple of exits out of his way to put me on 99. "Young brother, you can either stand at I-5 exits and wait for a ride, or you can walk right down 99, where it's legal. Straight ahead, probably three hundred miles. Turn left at Bakersfield and head for Barstow."

And 99 would make it clear to drivers that I was headed south, not somewhere in the web of roads that circled San Francisco and San Jose and Sacramento. The rides were short. Modesto, Merced and Madera. Then Fresno, and then another narrow green sign: VISCALIA 20. I just needed to get to Barstow, and then I could turn east for home.

* * *

I wanted to crawl into a ditch and sleep a few hours, but if I didn't get back to Hell Creek in two days—which might be an impossible task—O'Murphy might have no one to defend her.

About six A.M., a car halted a few yards in front of me. It was a strippy: a cheap, white, Ford Galaxy with a sun-faded red interior. I was surprised because the sign on the passenger door said: "No passengers. California Department of Motor Vehicles." Maybe that's why I got inside without looking at the driver. "Do you know much farther it is to Barstow?"

His face was turned toward his left mirror as he concentrated on traffic behind him. When he saw an opening, he gunned the engine and darted into the slow lane. The speedometer raced to eighty miles per hour. "Oh, not faaar. A couple of hundred miles. I'll take you there." Francis smiled like the big bad wolf.

My head spun like a balloon in the breeze. *Danger, Will Robinson!*

"Tell me again, Cutie. How old are you?" Three months after our incident, his face was still as red as a wiener.

"I'll be sixteen tomorrow." *That means O'Murphy's birthday is two days. You have to get there before Spit attacks her. Don't ditch this ride.*

"Oh, that's *sooo* young. You're still a pup." His smile was carnivorous. "Ah, the romance of being a young man on the road in America. Ah, California."

"How old are you, Francis?"

He laughed. "Hey, I guess that's fair. I'm thirty-nine."

Liar. You couldn't see fifty if it was written on your rear-view mirror.

"Stick with me this time. I'll introduce you to some boys your age. Girls too. Young. Whatever you're into." He noticed my hands shaking. "Hey, don't be afraid. It only hurts the first few seconds. After that, it's a pleasure." He chuckled at his own ridiculous innuendo.

The trooper is right. This guy is dangerous. If you stay in this car, you may not get home. "I think I should get out here."

Francis kept driving as if he hadn't heard.

Time to use my get-out-of-jail-free card. I fished into my type-writer case. "You know, I found my dad. You may know him. Ronald Stanhope. He's a sergeant in the Highway Patrol."

"All I want to do is give you a blowjob." He held up his hands and giggled.

"Why is that funny?"

"Because Ron works in my district. He's queer too. Or didn't you know? The boys in uniform are in the closet. What are you doing with Ron's card?"

Is he telling the Big Lie? Lie to him too. And make it big. He's more likely to believe if it's outrageous. "I found my dad. Ron Stanhope's my father."

"I know what Ron looks like. So unless you're his long-lost bastard, you're no relation."

I felt color drain from my face.

"So tell me the truth this time, why do you have Ron's card?"

Mix your lie with a powerful truth. "He picked me up after you let me out."

Francis giggled insanely. "Yeah, I know. What did you tell him?"

Mix the lie with the truth. "That I made you let me out of your car."

"And he said, 'Francis? That old queen.'" He offered a smile to a vanquished foe. "So yes, Ron knows me too. I'm DMV's chaplain for this district."

"Ron told me to call him if you gave me any more trouble." I held Ron's card between us like wolfsbane. "If you lay a finger on me, I will."

Francis raised his fist to cover his mouth. "Oh. No. Please. Have mercy." Then he smiled again–a mirthless smile this time–and snatched Ron's card. He held it an inch from his wing window and let the wind suck it out. The card wheeled and soared and danced in the eddies on the trunk, then plopped onto State Road 99.

Anger rose in my face. "Go ahead. I don't need it. I memorized the number. I'll call from a pay phone. Sounds like the Highway Patrol knows where your office is." *I see it in your eyes. Checkmate.*

"You want out, *ragazzo*?" He steered the Galaxy toward the right breakdown lane more suddenly than I had anticipated.

My jaw hit the typewriter case and I saw stars for a moment.

His right hand took the wheel and his left hand went toward his door pocket. He giggled.

Quel creep. Then my vision cleared. A black .380 automatic appeared in his Francis's left hand, and it was leveled at my face.

"Bail." Trooper Ron said in my mind. *Now.*

Is he the Freeway Killer, Ron? Then I have nothing to lose. I'm going to stand up to this guy. "Is that a chocolate gun?"

Francis's eyes formed a question.

"Because you're going to eat it." In that moment, my forearm and bicep pistoned upward, my left arm fully extended. I felt the typewriter case smash his pistol into his face.

He slammed on the brakes.

My eyes were fixed on his hands, but my right hand knew where to find the door latch. I backed out of the car, and his engine roared even before the door shut.

CHAPTER 52

GINGER PEACHY

It took more three rides to get to Bakersfield, and one more to move halfway across the Mojave Desert to Edwards Air Force Base, but that was the end of my luck for two hours. I walked past two dozen strip joints and decided to eat at a truck stop.

"How's it going, Kid?" the truck driver next to me asked.

"Ginger peachy."

"Ginger peachy. I like that. What does it mean?"

"I guess it means I'm peachy, but I've got a little extra spice. How about you?'"

"Me? Not that original." By then it was six P.M. He exhaled a yawn and set his empty Thermos on the counter. He looked at my case. "I used to have a typewriter just like that."

"It was a typewriter. Now it's my suitcase. Do you know a trucker named Gil LeBeouf?"

"Cajun? Goes by the handle Coon Ass?"

"Yeah. He told me if I talked to another trucker, to ask if he's around."

"Why? You need a ride? Where you headed so late?"

"Oklahoma."

"The Sooner State? Well, I gotta haul my patootie to Needles by eight thirty. I could get there a smidge faster," his eyes twinkled a proposition, "if the CHIPs are sleepy."

"I can keep you awake."

"Read my mind. Let's reload the caffeine. I'll get the check. Darlin,'" his eyes twinkled at the waitress, "a Thermos of coffee for me, and bring this boy–I'm Papa, what's your moniker –the biggest go cup you can find. Fill it full of . . . "

"Dietetic Dr Pepper. My name is Curtis."

"You heard my deputy driver. And honey, shift 'er into overdrive if you wanna earn a small fortune in silver." He flipped a Kennedy half-dollar on the counter.

The waitress snorted her contempt, pocketed the coin, and grabbed the flask.

* * *

"Find a new station. This one's a fadin' fast."

I did, just in time to hear the last stanza of what I thought was my favorite folk song. "That's not Joan Baez."

"You're thinkin' of '500 Miles,'" Papa said. "This is Hedy West, but they're both singin' 'Railroader's Lament.' Lotsa different versions: Peter, Paul & Mary, Bobby Bare . . ."

"Lament? Is it blues?" I asked.

"Sorta," Papa said. "A blues song usually starts with a lament. Then the singer grieves again. Then comes the answer. Hedy starts with an extra-long lament."

"Are you a musician?"

"Truckers know their music. We listen eight, ten, twelve hours a day. But yeah, I sang before I became the successful commercial trucker you see today. And played the guitar, and the harmonica, and the drums. Wadn't makin' much of a living, so I sorta fell into trucking as a way to move from one gig to another. But I made a ways more money as a trucker, so now I am what you see. '500 Miles' is a song about you. Read the lyrics sometime, if you ever find the sheet music. It's about a kid, not a penny to his name, to ashamed to go home."

I know. We fiddled with radio knobs, sang country songs I hated, told every joke we knew, and slapped our thighs and faces to stay awake. Papa dialed the cab lights low. "Take a fifteen-minute nap if you can. I'm gonna need some conversation later just to stay awake."

* * *

I woke when Papa geared down and rumbled onto a newly completed section of I-40 at Barstow. We competed in the license tag game. Before his Peterbilt overtook a car, we guessed where the plate was from. He'd played a lot longer than me, so when he saw a '66 Impala SS with red letters on a white tag, he said, "That un's goin' your way." He was right. The plate bragged "Oklahoma Is OK." He pulled alongside in the left lane. "Who's drivin?'"

I saw nothing but rich red hair. "Girl."

"Boyfriend?"

"Can't see the passenger seat."

"Anybody in back?"

"Packed with stuff. She must be moving."

"Lemme talk to her for a minute." He flashed his lights and blew his air horn until she pulled over. "I'll see if she wants some company."

It was more like five minutes, but Papa came back on my side of his truck.

"Grab your typewriter, Pard. You gonna ride this muscle car to Elk City, Oklahoma."

We walked back to the driver's side of the Super Sport.

"Sherilyn, this cub is my friend, Curt. If you can help git him home, it shore would be a load offa ole Papa Bear's mind."

She still looked dubious. "I'm planning on stopping soon."

"No need. You're outside Needles–sixteen hours away from home. Curt just woke up from a nap, so he can help you tool straight through. You'll eat breakfast in your own kitchen."

"Can you actually drive a car?" Sherilyn asked. Her scent whiffed by me. Youth Dew. Apparently it's the groovy new perfume. Lots of girls wore it in Palo Alto.

"I'll turn sixteen at midnight. I have a motorcycle license. I've driven Mother's car. And my Nan's. And my Grand's pickup."

"Well," she sighed, "you're as cute as a six pack of puppies. What's your name again?"

"Curt," Papa inserted.

She wrinkled her nose. "I'll try to remember. Why are you going to Oklahoma?"

"Yes ma'am, well, I gotta get back to Peaceable River."

"Don't 'ma'am' me. I'm only twenty-two. You know where Elk City is?"

"Sure. I passed it on my way out here."

"Can you shift a four-on-the-floor?"

"Nan's Impala has a three-on-the-tree."

"So you can work a clutch?" she verified.

"Sure, I just don't know the gears on a floor shifter."

She shrugged. "That I can show you. Okay. Climb in."

"By the way," Papa goodbye hugged as if we were old friends, "I heard Coon Ass on the CB after you got to sleep. Told him you were my seat cover. He said to tell you, 'Hey, Boo.'"

Sherilyn set the volume at seismic. This time, it was Bobby Bare singing "500 Miles."

CHAPTER 53

THE ROAD HOME

Sherilyn stopped every two hours across Arizona and New Mexico–usually at a Whiting Brothers–to reload her coffee mug, refill my Dietetic Dr Pepper, and refuel the big block 396. She pulled over just after we passed the Texas line. She popped a wide-open yawn. "I guess I'm gonna to have to let you drive. If you get sleepy, pull over at a rest stop."

No. I have to get to Hell Creek. But I need some conversation. "Do you go to church?"

"Me? Naw, church ain't for redheads." Sherilyn snuggled her face into a pillow and dozed off in seconds.

Farm-to-market roads on my left and right led to Borger and Pampa and Panhandle and Clarendon, but after we left Amarillo, there was just one tiny town, Groom. Then the dark closed in, and I drove one of the loneliest, the blackest, the most boring stretches of U.S. 66 in the Wide Wide West.

In science class, Mr. Bettz had shown us a documentary about road hypnosis. Stare long enough at the fence posts or the white line or the black top, and drivers will mesmerize themselves. I rolled down my window, rolled up my window, turned off the heater, turned on the air conditioning, turned up the radio, played the license plate game by myself, and swigged Dietetic Dr Pepper until the straw gurgled hollowly, but my eyelids stayed as heavy as silver dollars. With no one's voice to keep me awake . . .

I woke when the tires on my side rumbled on gravel. I jerked the Chevy to the right, stomped the brake pedal, and the tires screeched into a death spiral.

Sherilyn screamed into my ear. "Let off the brake! Take your foot off the brake!"

Time divided into microseconds. *How will that help?* But arguing seemed counterproductive. I commanded my right foot off the brake.

The car stopped spinning, but now we sped backwards down the highway. "Pump the brakes!"

I ignored my fear and eased the brakes down and down and down, and we halted askew the centerline. If a semi had been behind us, we would've been bugs on its windshield.

In a voice that hadn't sounded good humored even when Papa had pulled her over, Sherilyn said, "Well, I'm awake now. Where are we?"

"Last sign said Shamrock."

"An hour from my house. Maybe I should take it from here."

* * *

After I stepped out of her coupe, Sherilyn turned south on State Highway 6. From my typewriter case, I dug out the map Buick Guy had advised me to keep; Oklahoma City was 112 miles straight east. The Hell's Angels had rejected that one. The next ride took me to Weatherford, the next to Yukon. I-40 met U.S. 81 at El Reno. I turned south for home. I woke after an hour's nap.

"Been away for a while?" I couldn't see the driver's lips move because of his beard. Not an unkempt hilly-billy beard, but a short Christmasy one like Edmund Gwinn in *Miracle on 34th Street.*

"Months."

He smiled. "Well, welcome home."

The lights of Hell Creek smirked, as if to remind me why I'd left in the spring.

"Where can I take you?"

"Just drop me off here at the high school."

"I sure don't mind takin' y'all over to your house."

"No. Thanks. Really. Here's just fine."

The school year had started, and I wanted to see Hell Creek High. Just a few cars were here on a Wednesday evening. But there was Stanley Jones. By himself. "Stan. Hey."

He grinned his welcome. "Hiuuuh."

"What are you doing here? Where's your mom?"

Slobber escaped his smile. He pointed to cars parked in the shade of the gym, which stayed open late for the public. I waved at his mother. "You okay today?"

He nodded. "Yeahuuuh."

I reached around for his handkerchief, wiped his chin, and opened her car door for him.

"Thank you," his mother said. "You're the only student I know of who talks to him."

I walked down Pine to the highway and stopped at the exact point where the sergeant had picked me up. *Pepper Lane, by now I hope you've realized what a swell wife you have. O'Murphy's not for an old doggie like you.*

I stepped on Hell Creek Bridge, looked west beyond my thumb and said aloud: "The entire world is behind me now." Mother's house— my home–was a mile from here. *Should I turn around? No. Time to start your new life.* Hell Creek held little for me: a one-screen movie theater, a public library and a high school library with a few thousand volumes. My hometown was an island of impoverishment. But I'd leave for college–my sea of enlightenment–in a few years. I'd live in Dallas or Washington or maybe Oklahoma City, and then I'd never see Hell Creek again. It wouldn't be easy to divorce a brother, even if the ordeal of our relationship continued to damage me.

I walked into Nabours Grocery. "I need to use the restroom."

"In the back room. On the left," said a clerk I'd never seen. Where was Miss Somebody 1920? I walked through the back room and into the gated yard, and there was my Schwinn. The tires were flat, but for some reason, no one had taken it.

CHAPTER 54

DADDY'S NOT COMING HOME

Instead of walking into the kitchen door, I knocked at the front. So many voices were inside, I had to pound louder.

Marsha called from the living room into the kitchen: "Aint Sister. Somebody's at the front door." Zandy had called her Sister; Zandy's kids added "aunt" to complete the Eudora Welty nickname. A pause, and Marsha opened the door. "Well, I'll swan." She reached with one hand, pulled me in, hugged my neck, and spun me around.

"Aint Sister!" Marsha said in a voice that commanded attention. "Cutie's back!"

Mother rushed into the room. Her cheeks and eyes were already red and clenched, so tears must have flowed before she got there. "I missed you."

"I missed you more." I'm four inches taller, so I bowed my head under her chin. Mother grabbed my entire skull and headlocked me into her chest. For years, I'd always pulled away first; this time, I waited until she ended the hug that absolved her wayward son.

"Did you find your answers?"

"No. But I found Daddy."

"He didn't want you, did he?" Biggy's I-knew-it voice rang from the kitchen doorway. He wanted everyone to realize how smart he was.

"He told me to go back home," I confirmed to Mother. "To you."

Guilt changed Mother's face. "You wouldn't have believed me if I had told you he was thataway. Some things in this world, kids have to figure out for themselves. What did he say?"

"Not much, actually. But I don't think he's ever coming home."

Mother and Biggy looked at each other. This was the elixir they'd waited to receive, even if it wasn't what they'd wanted.

I guess we'll never get over Daddy. I was exhausted and thirsty, and I'd needed to pee for hours. I slipped through the kitchen to the bathroom.

"So," Biggy slapped the back of my head as I passed, "you came crying home to Mama?"

I'd found Daddy, I'd made back from California, and now I was the center of attention. Maybe Biggy felt diminished. Maybe he wished he'd had the courage. Maybe he was taking out his insecurities on me.

So now I have to stick up for myself, don't I, Brother Love? "Stop picking on me."

"What are you going do?" Biggy clenched his fists.

"I'm not going to fight you . . . "

Biggy smiled his self-satisfaction.

" . . . but I am going to stand up to you. You're a coward, Billy. So every time you hit me, I'm going to stand up. From now on."

"And I'll knock your ass down. From now on."

"You'll have to." I said the words with enough determination that everyone in the room believed. I could see the effect on the faces of Nan and Zandy and Marsha and her girls.

Biggy looked into my eyes.

My posture and my expression informed that my defiance was already costing him. "I understand why you pick on me. You're unhappy, so you want to ruin my happiness."

Heads around me nodded.

Biggy's face darkened.

Okay. Here it comes. "And I understand why you hate Daddy. You think he left you."

Biggy's eyes reddened. "Why didn't you miss him like I did? I cried a river over Daddy."

"I did miss him. It was wrong for him to abandon us. Maybe he's not a good person. I don't know, maybe I got him wrong, I only saw him for a minute." *Less than that.* "But I've decided. I'm not going to hate him."

"No one should hate him. And it wasn't you boys." Mother moved behind Biggy. "He never liked being there for anybody. He came and went every day, and when he got back, I–we–could either be there or not, for all he cared."

Was that it? He didn't want me to need him? He didn't want to be my Daddy?

"It was different for you." Biggy's expression asked me to feel sorry for him. "You weren't his favorite."

"After we left, I think he decided to hide out."

"But why?" Biggy asked.

Mother moved in to hug him, and Biggy's fists unclenched.

"Look, if you want me to love you when we're old men, you have to love me today. We'll still be brothers, but brotherly love only goes so far."

Biggy put on a pretend face to show he didn't care.

"If you act hateful to me–real or pretend–you're going to lose me. If that happens–if I lose affection for you–it may be impossible for us to be friends. Don't be surprised if I have no use for you. Is being mean to me worth that? Because that's the price."

"What are you going to do now?" Mother asked.

"Tomorrow's Wednesday?"

She nodded.

"First thing in the morning, I'm going to ask Mr. Boone if he'll let me back in school. And I'll ask Mr. Presley if he needs me to deliver papers."

CHAPTER 55

WHAT WE HAVE BECOME

Mr. Boone proved kinder than I'd anticipated. He enrolled me as a junior in gym, human sciences, sociology and first-semester junior English. I'd have to retake the spring semester of sophomore English, but I could dual-enroll in Mrs. Lane's class in the coming spring semester.

I checked my watch: seven forty-five A.M. In fifteen minutes, Hell Creek High students would report to their home rooms. I didn't know why, but I saw seniors and juniors point out me–the most invisible kid in high school–to sophomores and freshmen.

Mrs. Macintosh's junior math class was my home room. I took the same chair as last year, directly in front of MBe. Hail, hail, the gang was all here: Scooter, Pickle, MBe and O'Murphy.

"Today is O'Murphy's birthday, but she doesn't look happy," I whispered to Sammie.

"Something in her has changed." Sammie punched my arm. "Great to see you back."

I smiled. "It's great to be here. I've missed you."

Like last year, Scooter stared maliciously at me.

You think O'Murphy still likes me? I haven't talked to her in months.

* * *

When the final bell rang, I realized, *so this is what kids without jobs do after school.* I biked to the Oklahoman's district office and apologized for leaving Mr. Presley in the lurch. He forgave and promised the next open route would go to me.

I paused my bike and watched as the frogs in the swales in front of the houses puffed their vocal sacs enormously to warn other males from their territory. Females don't croak much, Mr. Bettz had told his science class today. "But they think male croakers sound tuff and macho."

No cars in O'Murphy's driveway, no neighbors around. I spotted her hair first. Her face had been down on Spit's hot rod, arms spread to either side on the hood. Pickle stood behind Scooter. Had Spit been on top of her? In broad daylight? Right in front of her house?

I should've come back weeks ago. "O'Murphy!" I shouted. "Get inside your house."

All three brothers looked at me. O'Murphy bolted, and Spit missed a grab for her hand.

Time slowed. Events blurred into one.

"O'Murphy!" Scooter's shout sounded like an order. He caught up in three steps, grabbed her wrist, and yanked like an angry parent disciplining a child.

"I can't believe this," I shouted to him. "Why aren't you protecting your girlfriend?"

Scooter twirled O'Murphy like a square dancer and slapped her face. Spit smiled; Pickle looked aghast.

Red faced, holding up her scarlet pep-club skirt by a belt loop, O'Murphy broke free and skittered on all fours like an insect. She looked as thin as an inch of water.

Scoot grabbed her hair just as her right hand reached for the doorknob.

"Leggo. Please!" Her head bowed back as she pleaded.

"Face me!" I screamed at Scooter. "Me!"

"Go away." The sun glinted in O'Murphy's tears. "You can't protect me."

"And yet, here I am." My voice softened for her, but molten lava flowed into my eyes. I stared down the three Andersens. "Behold. Thy damnation cometh."

Pickle's gherkin shape turned. Spit's simian teeth grinned broadly, unrestrained, with his mouth open as he muttered to Scooter.

"I will strike–with vengeance and righteous anger–anyone who harms this girl." *Wow. Can't sound much stupider than that. But I think I have their attention.* "O'Murphy, lock the doors and call the cops."

"Mind your own shit," Scooter warned.

I dropped my bike in the street. If a car had to stop, so much the better. "I can't do that. I can't watch brutality. I can't witness evil and not help."

"We're just givin' her what she wants." Spit's expression looked defensive.

"What if your mother were standing here, Scooter? Would you stop this?"

"Don't you ever talk about our mother." Scooter's face flashed a brilliant scarlet.

"He's a coward," Spit shouted to Scooter and Pickle. "He ain't going to do nothin'. Go ahead, Dill Pickle. Finish what you started last semester. Kick his assss."

"You know, Spit, I've thought for months about this business of cowardice. And it's true. I am afraid to fight. But I will protect O'Murphy. Besides, you're the real cowards. If you pick on someone knowing you can't lose, isn't that cowardice too? None of you has ever lost a fight. When you do, I think your lack of bravery might reveal itself. So don't pick on a ninety-pound girl. Choose me."

Scooter's eyes morphed from arrogance to overconfidence.

I'd intended to step between Scooter and O'Murphy, but I was too angry. I charged.

Pickle hooked my arm.

I twisted out and just kept going. As if it had a mind of its own, my right fist whammed Scooter's nose. *Like you said, Gil.* I saw disbelief on his face.

"Hey!" Scooter's words welled up as if they came from a hole.

Make them promise, Gil whispered in my mind. I stared at Pickle and Spit. "I want your word you'll stay out of this." Pickle nodded instantly and dropped his fists, but Spit looked at Scooter. I challenged Spit. "Hey. Pillsbury! Swear." Spit's eyes checked with Pickle, then shrugged as if Scooter couldn't possibly lose anyway.

"Scooter? Just me and you?"

Scoot turned to assure Spit, but I didn't wait. I attacked his nose a second time. Wham. *Remember what Sammy Davis Jr. said. I'm faster than Pickle.*

On reflex, Scooter raised his hands to protect his nose.

Blind his eyes.

Got it, Gil. My right arm rested a moment to improve my aim and my timing. Wham. Wham. I punched in combination. Whamwhamwham.

Scooter's mouth opened several times, but I had no idea what he blubbered. I counted under my breath. "One, two, three. One two three." Blood spurted from Scooter's nostrils. "I broke his nose!" I shouted out loud.

I have a bigger heart than Scooter's. "Do you know what you smell?" I whispered to Scooter. "It's copper. You have less than an ounce of copper in your body, but you can smell it."

"You're hurting him! Stop it." Astonishingly, O'Murphy still hadn't locked the door. She rushed from the porch, took off her white terrycloth hairband, and wiped the blood from Scooter's nose. She looked at me with new respect, but she protected her abuser.

"MBe's right, O'Murphy. You have your mouth set for the wrong kind of boy." *Just like my mother, she thinks she can change her man. Can I change my girl, Brother Love?*

Pickle just stood there, smiling, but Spit violated his promise, pulled me off Scooter, and pinioned my arms.

"Hit him," Spit commanded Pickle.

I couldn't move. "Dillon, your brothers are mean. They hate everyone weaker than them. But you're not like that."

Go for Spit's nose.

I can't, Gil. All I can move is my . . . Oh. Got it. I leaned so far forward, Spit had to bend with me. Then I snapped backward like a rubber band. My skull crunched against something soft.

"My nose!" Spit screamed.

I stuck two fingers in Spit's eyes, Three Stooges style. "That's for MBe. And when your soul perishes from this earth, I hope you go straight to hell. Do not pass Go, do not collect two hundred dollars." *Hell Creek High, if you could see me now.*

"If I wasss you," Spit's bloody snot vibrated with the sibilants, "I'd run before we kick your assss."

"Sssufferin' sssuccotash!" I said in my best Looney Tunes voice. "If I were you, Ssspit, I'd be mad at God for making me talk like Sssylvester Puddytat."

A car screeched to a stop to avoid hitting my bicycle. The driver looked at the six of us. A witness, something the Andersens didn't want. Scooter motioned to Pickle. With one hand, Pickle restrained Spit by the shirt collar and rotated his oldest brother toward the hot rod.

"What for? I'm going to wax his butt," Spit said.

"You deserve it, Amos." Pickle admonished his older brother. "You hit a woman."

"Goddam, Pick, he hit me first." Spit blew out, trying to clear blood from his nostrils.

Pickle snickered. O'Murphy laughed out loud.

"Dylan," Spit pleaded. "Since when do we let anyone beat up our brothers?" He slammed his right fist into the hot rod's passenger door. "Aaaagh!" He grabbed his right hand.

"Now your hand is broken," I said. "Loser."

All three brothers piled into Spit's car.

Is this the first time two Andersens have been bloodied in one fight?

CHAPTER 56

ALL WHO WANDER
ARE NOT LOST

"So, you didn't give up lurking around my house." O'Murphy teased.

I wanted to thank her every time she smiled at me. "Yeah, I may have a Boo Radley thing going on." I smiled when a hint of lilac perfume lolled past my nose. *What a perfect scent.*

"Nice smile," O'Murphy looked at me. *"Qui errant non pereunt."*

Errat means wander, I deciphered. *Or maybe it means error.* "Did you take Latin?"

Her lips widened graciously and inclusively. "Two years ago, in Norman. They called it Classic Languages. Now, where have you been?" Her accusing tone sounded half serious.

"California."

"You've been in California for the last four or five months?"

"A boy's gotta eat."

"What else did you find?"

"The Summer of Love. And myself. And a lot of good people who helped me."

"You know, you're a legend now."

"Legend?" I felt my mouth drop open. "All I did was run away from home."

"And you fought Dillon Andersen to a standstill. And you fought for me. And you got kicked out of school. And you left this jerkwater town, and you hitchhiked to California. You're Hell Creek's own Jack Kerouac. Did you smoke dope and join the hippies too?"

"Modesty forbids mentioning that I lived in a commune." *Time to ask what you've always wanted to know.* "Why do you stay with Scooter?"

"I've never been sure. I guess I don't I know any better."

"But you do deserve better."

She sighed. "I think about you. When we were in science class, last semester, Mr. Bettz told us about meteors. They're like angels, always up there. It's only when they become shooting stars that we notice them. So thank you for being my angel. Have you been writing?"

I was unaccountably pleased. "Journaling. But I've got a swell idea for a novel."

"What are you going to call it?"

I paused. "*Bittersweet Chocolate Love.*"

"So it was you! I *kneeew* it just had to be you. Are you going to read it to me sometime?"

I restrained myself from blurting exactly how much I'd wanted to do that. "Why did you tell Sammie it was Tommy?"

"So I could get you to admit it was you." More tears brimmed over as she laughed. "Why did you stop Scooter? Just now."

I faked my best aw-shucks smile. "You know I can't beat Scooter in a fair fight. I can't beat anybody. I just caught him by surprise."

She took my hand. "You know, I always thought nice guys were boring. But you could change my mind. Nice is–nice. Sometimes."

I looked down to hide a triumphant smile.

"But you're even better than nice. You're decent. You're the decentest guy I ever met. Except for my Daddy."

Sometimes the hand does something the eyes and the arm and the brain don't plan. My hand slid down her forearm again, the way it had a few months after I'd met O'Murphy.

When she sat down, her skirt rose up and exposed white scars above her knee.

I put my finger on the lowest scar. "How many of these do you have?"

She looked irritated. "Is that what you really want to talk about?"

"I like you. That's why I can't let anyone–even you–hurt you. But why do you do it?"

"I wish I knew. I get this weird kind of rush. Sometimes, it's like I'm watching myself."

"Bottom line."

"Bottom line is that I hate my life."

I don't know why I'm surprised to hear that. "Ditto. But I'm just a geek; you're a pretty girl. You're destroying something perf..."

"Don't say perfect. Please, like me for who I am, not how pretty I am. I've never done a thing to deserve being pretty. I'm smart, I'm good at things, and I'm fit for more than just being admired for how pretty I am."

I nodded. "I was born intelligent, but I want you to like me for who I've become. You know, I think that'll change in a few years. College won't just be a high school with ashtrays. I won't mix cherry limeades and throw newspapers, and you won't lead cheers and be high-school perfect. People will like us for more important reasons."

She dropped her eyes and sighed a wish. "You really think it'll be like that?"

"I hope so. You sound depressed."

"Yeah. Did my so-called friend tell you I'm manic?"

"MBe? I've never heard her use that word."

"Well, I am. Officially diagnosed." O'Murphy rolled up her left sleeve. Skin from wrist to elbow was pocked with halo-shaped scars. "Cigarette burns. That's why I quit smoking."

"You are so unusual. You're a butterfly, but you see yourself as a wormy caterpillar. What do you cut yourself with?"

"At first, anything I picked-up on the street. Broken glass, gravel, pop-tops from soda cans. But one cut got infected, so I went sanitary. Now, just razors. How long have you known?"

"I saw the scars in class when I picked up your pencil, the very first day we met."

"When I first started cutting, I thought I was the only one. But I met another girl–we were friends in detention for a week or two. She was too too weird. Now I know a dozen girls."

"Seriously? A dozen?"

"They don't all cut. One girl plucks out hair. She eats it. One sticks her boobs with pins. One punches herself. I see the bruises and cuts on their arms and their legs in gym class. I can hear them in the bathrooms."

"So why do you do it? Does it have something to do with your dad?"

She seemed shocked that I knew. "Yes. But Cutie . . ."

"Please, call me Curtis."

"Curtis. What do you see when you look at me?"

"What do you want me to see?"

"I'm a whore, you know. I have the soul of a whore. There ain't nothing I ain't done."

"That's not what I see. I see a sweet person. You actually talk to me. And I like listening to you. Do you know how special that is?"

O'Murphy looked like a wounded bird. "The pain flows out when I cut. I feel relieved."

Relieved? Is that the right word? "You feel penitent?"

She nodded. "How did you know?"

"I told you. I'm no hero. I swallowed three dozen aspirin a few days before I left."

She winced. "Listen, I feel better now that I've told you. Just don't–don't tell me to stop. I don't like it when people try to make me do something." Then she smiled. "But I think I'll quit."

"When?"

"Today."

Now I felt relieved. It was as if O'Murphy had given me a place to stand on the earth. "I'd better get home."

"Curtis," she pulled on my arm and looked exasperated, "are you going to kiss me or not?"

My lips couldn't fight a smile. "Kissing you is the stuff of my dreams."

"Just don't get stuck on me. I can't start with a new boyfriend now. I think I'm pregnant."

I was stunned. "I want to help."

"You'd do that?"

"I told you, I've always liked you. And I know your secret fear."

"No you don't."

I reached for O'Murphy's left hand and paused. She said nothing, but I sensed her volatility. "You think you've already passed up Mr. Right, because he wasn't a bad boy like Scooter, or because he wasn't a sexy jerk like Richie Rich."

O'Murphy's eyes locked on mine and confessed that I was correct. Then her look changed, and I could see she'd made a decision. "Wait." She went inside and brought out the heart-shaped crimson box of Bittersweet Chocolate Love. The candies were so old, they had blotchy beige spots. She bit into one and raised the other half to my mouth.

"Mmm," I said. "Still sweet. Tell me, do you ever fall for the least mature guy you meet?"

"So it seems." She giggled and nudged her knee into my thigh.

I backed away.

Her knee made contact again.

I looked up. *Sometimes you can be incredibly thick*. But maybe girls know instinctively what to do when a boy's eyes meet hers, because she continued to make eye contact. I was still deciding when she moved, inch by inch, until our noses touched. She kissed my lips, then she kissed the little triangle over my ear. I heard my blood pressure thump. Her breathing became volcanic, and she leaned back onto the porch.

I didn't lean with her.

She returned to a sitting position. "Are you going to kiss me back?"

I did. I kissed her fully, moving my tongue to taste her lower lip. I opened my eyes, but hers were still closed.

Ask if she liked that, Cath whispered in her ear.

"Was that good?"

"Mmm."

My hand moved to her side, then slightly forward. For the second time in my life, I touched a girl's breast. O'Murphy wasn't wearing a bra.

Go for it, Cath whispered again. *This is the free-love generation.*

I know, and thank you, Cath. But my hand stopped.

O'Murphy looked as if she was evaluating me. "What are you doing tonight? I'd like you to meet my mom and my stepfather."

CHAPTER 57

THE LIFETIME OF LILLIES

Daddy died in, oh, maybe 1995. He never called, never wrote after we met, so I hadn't thought about him much in the last fifty years.

I found out when his widow called, decades ago. She knew he'd been born in Oklahoma City, and she called Information to find Pyes in the area. When I answered the phone, Beverley introduced herself and asked if I was related to Jonathan Robert Pye, or J. Bob Pyne. The few facts he'd told her about his life didn't jibe, so she got curious.

Beverley sounded stunned when I said he was my father, but that I hadn't seen or heard from him since 1967. "He told me he didn't have a family. I don't understand why he would say that. He was such a good father to my two kids."

Yeah, Sandy said he'd been a good father to her, too.

She asked if I had brothers or sisters. When I said yes, she was unable to reconcile what Daddy had told her with my information.

She said Daddy had undergone a quadruple bypass, that a patch had blown out. That was the term Beverley used. Blown out. His chest cavity filled with blood, and he died almost instantly. She seemed so mournful, it was clear she must have loved Daddy.

I was unable to reconcile my emotionless Daddy with Beverley's loving husband.

Maybe Walt really did give you a good talking to, Daddy. Maybe you thought about your life. Maybe you realized that you might pass in the lifetime of lilies. Maybe you realized that if you didn't change, nobody would be there to say goodbye. Not Mother, certainly not Biggy, and not me.

We all die twice: when we draw our last breath, and when the last person stops thinking about us. Your fate, Daddy, would have been to die only once.

Or maybe you listened to Nat King Cole's song. The greatest thing is just to love, and be loved in return.

THE END